CAST AWAY STONES

By

Richard Schinnow

Shell Rock River Press
Rock Falls, Iowa

Published by: Shell Rock River Press
                8 East Mill St.
                Rock Falls, IA 50467

ISBN 13: 978-0615601991
Library of Congress Control Number: 2012903653
Copyright © 2012 Richard Schinnow

This is a work of fiction. All characters, names and events, as well as places, organizations and dialogue are products of the author's imagination, or are used fictitiously.

First Printing November 2012

Cover art by Tom Christopher
Cover design by Jean Tennant

A time to cast away stones,
A time to gather stones together

Ecclesiastes

CAST AWAY STONES

ONE

At almost the exact moment Frederick Heinold began to feel that maybe things weren't quite so bad, that he might actually get through this harvest, wife or no wife, his brand new hired man drove his combine through the fence.

Frederick had been on his way back to the field of ripened soybeans to see how the guy was doing. He was beyond tired from the long days that stretched behind him, but hopeful now that he finally had some help. The shorn fields on either side of the road reminded him that his neighbors had almost finished their work while he still had a long way to go.

As he approached the field, he could see the big green machine churning steadily through the waist-high plants, a wake of dust and shredded chaff moiling behind it. Only a few weeks before Frederick had paid thirty-five thousand dollars for it, the most he'd ever paid for any piece of equipment. He was pretty sure his house wasn't worth thirty-five thousand dollars.

Only in desperation would he have let an inexperienced man into the cab of such a valuable piece of equipment, but that's exactly where JoAnn had left him—desperate. His wife was supposed to be helping him get this crop in, but she wouldn't— couldn't, was her version—and after more than a week of going it alone, he'd finally given in and called the labor office in Lime City. They'd sent him the little man with the pudgy fingers.

As Frederick pulled into the field, he could see that the combine's hopper was almost filled with soybeans. The gauge in the cab would be telling the man that, too, so he would know to stop at the end of the field and wait for Frederick to pull up with the wagon he was towing. That's what Frederick was thinking when the machine went through the fence.

Of all the problems and mishaps he might have been able to imagine, and there was a good supply of those, this was not on the list, and so he sat stunned for a moment and stared in disbelief at the cloud of dust that had followed the combine into the adjacent field.

"Jesus Christ!" he finally managed. "Jesus Christ!" He gunned the truck and it and the wagon bucked off across the narrow furrows. "Jesus Christ! Jesus Christ!" Words really were failing him.

By the time he pulled up to the ragged hole, the big machine had stopped a hundred feet beyond and was nesting into the settling dust. It looked like a mechanical brontosaurus squatted down for a nap. The driver had already descended the steel ladder from the cab and was slowly circling, cap in one hand, rumpled hair in the other, as if he had come upon the calamity instead of having just created it.

Maybe, Frederick thought, he thinks that if he just walks around it enough times the son-of-a-bitch will start up again. He got out of the truck and walked through the hole. There was harvester scat all over: wood chips and shiny bits of traumatized wire.

What was hardest was that he couldn't even blame the guy because he'd known from the instant he arrived that he shouldn't let him stay. After the first look, he should have told him, "Nice to meet you, now go back to wherever it is you came from." There had been the flaccid handshake, for starters, the pale, soft fingers as apologetically unassertive as the meekly grinning face which seemed to implore: "I am a total fuck-up. Please don't hate me for it."

The man mumbled toward him, but Frederick passed by without a word. It was better this way. He did not want an explanation. An explanation would surely disassemble his stressed composure because there was no explanation. Not for this. Not at four o'clock in the afternoon in the broad, glaring light of day. Maybe at four in the morning after a relentless fifteen hours in the cab with eyes locked on the brain-numbing flow of crop as the machine sucked it out of the darkness. But not now. Not now!

2

After he had hired him, Frederick had made sure to keep the man away from the obvious dangers of augers and power take-offs, had given him the safest job he could think of which was to run the harvester back and forth across the field where he only had to watch the gauges and keep it on course and, of course, turn the son-of-a-bitch around when he came to the end of a row. So much for planning and prudence which, the stilled machine assured him, were quite possibly illusions anyway.

He climbed the metal ladder and stepped into the cab. The guy hadn't shut the switch off. Why do that? The thing had stopped itself, hadn't it? There was a thick smell of oil and roasted metal—of disaster.

His foot bumped against something and he bent and picked up the empty pint bottle. He almost felt better. At least the guy had drunk himself through the fence. Frederick could understand that. As he came back down the ladder, he could see the perpetrator far off on the road, shuffling toward his next ineptitude.

The cutting blades on the front platform had hacked chunks of wood from the fence posts and chewed them into chips and splinters. The wire had been mangled into indigestible, shiny gobbets and some had passed—God, he hoped not fatally—into the threshing innards. Everything depended on this machine. There were no options, no plan B, no one to come to the rescue. He went back to the truck to get a toolbox.

II

For the next few hours Frederick pulled, cut, and cursed wire and, as had become his habit during this harvest, argued with his wife who was twenty miles away in Lime City selling real estate when she should have been helping him so he wouldn't have to hire the goddamned help that ended up costing more than no help at all.

Over the past days he had peevishly reminded her that she had promised to help him out, especially with this harvest which included more acres than he had ever farmed before. And why had he rented the extra three hundred acres of work and worry when he had been perfectly content to farm the two hundred and forty that he owned? Because she had nagged him to do so, he reminded her in absentia.

Yes, JoAnn, you did. Maybe not in so many words, but all those comments about being stuck in my old ways and avoiding progress and how I needed to get up to date and get ahead like everybody else amounted to the same thing, and now, goddamn it, you won't even help me get this crop in the bin.

It didn't work in person, either. She came back at him with that tone of annoyance she always used when they argued, the only tone he'd heard for quite some time.

"How many times do I have to tell you, Frederick? It's foolish for me to spend time farming with you when you can hire someone for a fraction of what I can make selling real estate." There was a crisp enunciation to her displeasure as she lined the words up like soldiers and marched them at him.

Besides condescension, she layered other implications into her declaration, implications that she now made more money than he did, implications that his lot would not improve unless he acquired larger ambitions and the risks that came with them.

JoAnn's ambitions for her husband were exemplified by the presence of Eldon Mathews, the largest and most successful farmer in the township, who lived just across the road. Frederick had practically grown up with Eldon and considered him the biggest asshole he knew, but JoAnn focused only on Eldon's success and ignored his character flaws. For a while she had even invoked his name in their disagreements, but Frederick had grown disagreeably silent when she did, so she had stopped.

But since Frederick could not depart his driveway without confronting the tableau of Eldon's success—sprawling ranch house, enormous storage bins, huge tractors and, worst of all, two of the latest and most expensive combines on the market—it wasn't necessary, anyway.

Over time, the tensions between husband and wife had grown and abided. The circumstances of their marriage had changed and so had JoAnn, and he didn't know what to do about it. She sure as hell wasn't going to do something just because he wanted her to, that much was established. For the first time in his life he felt inadequate, and he didn't like it. And that's why he'd rented all that extra land at a price above which the competition would pay—which was too damned much.

In a belated effort to reassert himself, he had put his foot down and refused to buy any more equipment, even though it was clear that he should have.

"I'm not going into the hole any further and that's that," he told her when she questioned this strategy.

"Well, don't come crying to me if you get into trouble."

So the expansion hadn't resolved anything. They didn't get along any better, and he was stuck with the headaches of farming all that additional ground. Frederick realized he was obviously involved in some kind of running dispute with his wife that went beyond the issues at hand, but he was damned if he knew what it was about. It didn't feel like he was holding his own.

III

"This is what you get with cheap help!" he cried aloud into the machine. "You can't hire a farmer out of the goddamned labor office." The sun had heated the metal and Frederick sweated as he worked his way into the combine's guts. Sometimes a piece of wire came free with a hard pull of his pliers, but too often he had to loosen a roller or belt to get at it, and that took time—precious time. All the while, he argued with JoAnn.

Now more than ever, time, or lack of it, was oppressing him, aggravating even small delays into a persistent anxiety. Heavy August rains had lingered into September, delaying the beginning of the harvest, so early on there was a worry about getting these crops collected before winter set in. It could come early to northern Iowa, even in November, piling snow in the fields and making harvest difficult, sometimes impossible. Like his neighbors, Frederick was nervously eager to get this crop in.

Fortunately, October had broken crisp and dry, and they finally went to work. Once the harvest had been an ancient rite of sustenance, but American farmers had transformed it into an ordeal of screaming engines, diesel smoke, and stress. While their city brethren raked leaves into rustic bonfires, Frederick and his neighbors lived in the frenzy of harvesting their crops.

He was thirty-five and had never known any other life. Despite heat and hail, drought and deluge—and undependable hired men—and despite the modest living the farm gave back for the expensive investment of time and money it exacted, farming was the only thing he had ever wanted to do. The only true dissatisfaction of his life was the steady withdrawal of JoAnn since she had gotten her real estate license eighteen months before.

They had married five years ago; before then she had lived in town and known nothing about a farm. Even so, Frederick had hoped she'd come to love life in the country the way he did.

She'd tried—at least that's what she told him—but he thought that even her initial attempts at enthusiasm were tempered by hesitancy. He had assumed that his friends would become her friends, but it was soon apparent that her social interactions with them were obligatory and superficial. Their lives were consumed by family and farming, and JoAnn's would never be.

Almost from the beginning she found reasons to make the half-hour trip to Lime City. At first it was to visit her mother and friends, but before long she took a part-time job in a clothing store. This was far from the life Frederick had envisioned, but he wanted her to be happy, so he tempered the few complaints he actually voiced.

"I kind of thought you'd be around more," he told her one morning as she got dressed to go into town.

"Doing what? There's nothing to do?"

"I don't know. What the other wives do."

"You mean like cook dinner?"

"Well, that's one thing. That would be nice."

"You knew when you married me that I don't cook."

"I guess. But I thought maybe you'd pick it up."

"No, Frederick, I'm not going to pick it up—ever. There's more to life than cooking dinner. A lot more." She slipped on her high heels, primped briefly in the mirror, and left.

Frederick tried to make the best of it. During that harvest she was around at least some of the time to drive for him or go to town to pick up a part. But after she'd passed the real estate test and gone to work selling houses in Lime City, her absences became prolonged.

The next time they talked about it he had come in from the field to find her in the kitchen, putting canned goods in the cupboard. She was still dressed for work.

"Why are you so late?" he asked.

"We had a meeting."

"You told me last night you'd be home early."

"I meant to. Hanna called a meeting. I had to go."

"I thought you were going to help out."

"I thought I could, but I've been too busy at the office."

"I need you, JoAnn."

"Frederick, hire someone."

"I don't want to hire someone. I want you to help me. Why can't you take some time off?"

"Frederick, I told you. I'm busy."

"What do you think I am?"

The silence that grew in the space between them was often enough to signal the end of a talk, but this time Frederick didn't leave. When JoAnn closed the cupboard and turned around, she seemed surprised to find him still there. She was also annoyed at his persistence. She went straight to the point.

"Frederick, I can make good money in this business. A lot more than I am now."

"I'm not asking you for a lot of time. Just a few weeks in the spring and fall, that's all." Already he was uncomfortable with their disagreement, and his voice softened. "You know I wouldn't ask if I didn't need you."

She was close to anger. They'd already had this discussion too many times before, and she was tempted to dismiss it. But she also sensed that this might be an important negotiation. They might be working out an agreement that she would have to live with.

If it were completely up to her, JoAnn wouldn't have given up anything. For the first time in her life she was making money and meeting people who made things happen, and she loved it. She was embarking on a new life, a life more interesting and vital than the new one she had begun with Frederick five years before. Maybe he was happy with farming but it was static and uneventful to her, and it would always be. For God's sake, the weather was a main topic of conversation with these people, and if it wasn't that, it was how the kids were doing in school. How could anyone expect her to embrace that?

"I need more than just the farm," she said quietly. "And this job gives me more. It's helping me develop as a person. It's..." The thought trailed off. How could she explain how much this meant to her without telling him how much the farm didn't? She resented this. She was trying to find a way for both of them to be happy, but his insistence was putting her in a place she didn't want to be. Okay, if that was the way it was going to be, she'd try another tack.

"You want me to be happy, don't you?" It was a plaintive question and it surprised him, just as she thought it would.

"Of course I do, sweetheart, you know I do." He pulled her to him, and she could see that he was relieved to see a way out of this. She also sensed that he might never have the resolve to effectively oppose her. She put her arms around his neck and drew him close. She looked into his eyes.

"You can't blame me for wanting to get ahead," she said.

"Of course not," he said. "That's one of the things I love about you. It's just that—" But the argument was over, and he knew it. It was time to let it go—and he did.

Over the next year, JoAnn became more successful than either of them could have imagined. The more money she made, the less he saw of her, for success demanded long hours, often in the evenings and on weekends. Sometimes, when she worked late, she stayed in town with her mother so Frederick woke to an empty bed. And she spent less time helping him than even she would have thought. It continued to be a sore spot with him but he managed—until he rented the extra land.

TWO

While Frederick Heinold struggled to revive his stricken combine, his wife was being kissed by the handsomest man she'd ever known. The idea that Miles Richards might kiss her and that she might want him to had occurred to her several times during the lunches they had shared through the previous week and certainly during the one they had earlier in the day. That one had included a bottle of champagne.

It had taken champagne to dissolve the last of her resistance to this feverish embrace, for JoAnn Heinold was a woman who not only possessed, but voiced, stringent opinions about the importance of social rectitude. But from the beginning she had been overmatched. Miles Richards' charm and devastating looks had bedded numerous women before her, married and otherwise.

Miles was from Florida and had shown up in Lime City a few weeks before, and JoAnn had met him at the Tailfeathers Restaurant and Lounge where she occasionally stopped for an after work drink with people from her office. He was an antique dealer, of all things, from Fort Lauderdale, in Iowa looking for furniture to sell back in Florida. According to Miles, there were undiscovered bargains in Iowa.

One afternoon he had joined her group at a table and proven an instant conversationalist, delivering witty one-liners on a variety of subjects—almost any subject, it seemed. From the first moment his ease and confidence contrasted in the most damaging way with Frederick's limited social graces.

And there were the clothes, elegant silk shirts and Gucci

loafers, which most people in Lime City had never seen before. A heavy gold chain spilled carelessly from his unbuttoned collar, accentuating the tanned face and the sumptuous dark hair that framed it. Miles was beautiful, an exotic, tropical creature that attracted her as she had never been attracted before.

He was too much for the strained circumstances of her marriage. It did not help that he was knowledgeable about real estate and could go on for hours about the lavish canal-side homes of Fort Lauderdale—or that he had singled her out for attention.

They began to have lunches together, always to talk about real estate, of course, and the lunches had led them, inevitably, to the gleaming oak library of the expensive house he had asked her to show him. It was an older home, designed by an associate of Frank Lloyd Wright. JoAnn had seen it before, but its architectural importance had eluded her. If anything, she found it outdated and in need of fresh decorating, but once inside Miles had conducted the showing with a caressing reverence that sent voltage along her spine.

"This is a house built for people to live in," he effused. "A house built for good books and paintings—Persian rugs—fine brandies—all the good things." He seemed overcome with his own hyperbole as he guided her away from the windows and took her in his arms. The kiss went on for a long time, and she kissed him back with the urgency of a moth fluttering against a light.

II

Frederick sprawled under the combine, his hands probing for pieces of wire and wood he could not see. In the warm quiet he could hear the whine of diesel engines in distant fields, and it reminded him of how much he had yet to do. It was at times like this that he really missed the old man even though his father had been dead for ten years.

The two of them had farmed the place together after his mother's death ten years before that. Emmett had never felt the need to farm more land than he was comfortable with, and he had still kept his rows clean with a cultivator rather than spraying to keep the weeds down. It was more work that way, but he liked the work. It was farming, after all, and there was always work to farming.

"They don't want to work," he'd say of the big farmers like Eldon. "They're always talking about how hard they work, but they're not working. They're driving and driving is a lot easier than working." The old man could live with the occasional weed, and he didn't mind that his fence lines were bushy with grasses and wild roses. "They were here when we got here," he'd explain.

Because of his age, Emmett's neighbors had tolerated these eccentricities, but after he died they refused to extend that forbearance to Frederick. He sensed their skeptical appraisals of him, but he'd grown accustomed to being the odd man and was usually able to accept it.

Except for the disruptive meander of the Lime Rock River, which bordered the farm to the west, the land was as flat and symmetrical as a checkerboard. It had been laid out that way by government survey when Iowa was still a territory. In other parts of the country distances were measured between landmarks, a big rock, say, or a tree or a hill, and the tracts they delineated were often odd-shaped. But here the surveys were based on the lines of longitude and latitude, all neatly divided into townships and those into sections, each a square mile containing 640 acres.

Constrained by this invisible order, roads, fences, farms, and tree lines had been laid out in rigid East-West or North-South running lines that rendered the landscape into a relentless symmetry, perfect for tillers of the land.

The early settlers had included the usual dreamers and adventurers, but over time it was the acquisitive Norwegians and Swedes and Dutch and especially the Germans who had succeeded and remained. They thrived on the symmetry and accentuated it with an obsessive drive to order their fields into precise rows of immaculate crops. Over time, the bob-wire farmers lost their land or sold out, leaving only headstones in the country cemeteries to mark that they had ever been there.

Frederick did not intentionally antagonize his neighbors, but the old man had taught him that farming was enjoyable and satisfying when a man had a reasonable amount of time to do the work that had to be done. When he was a kid, the countryside had still been dotted with farms of eighty or a hundred twenty acres, and none of them had yet specialized. Besides corn and soybeans, everyone raised oats and hay and every farm had cows and hogs and chickens. Emmet had milked thirty Holsteins by hand until he bought his first mechanical milker in 1947.

Through the forties and fifties, land prices had not ventured above two hundred dollars an acre. But during the sixties, farming began a transformation into a business, and farmers turned increasingly to specialization. Most of them grew row crops—corn and soybeans—while others specialized in milking cows or raising hogs or cattle for meat. No one kept poultry anymore. Instead, they bought their eggs and chicken at the supermarket in town, just like everyone else.

The price of land began to climb, and when it soared past a thousand dollars an acre in the early seventies, speculators—farmers and investors alike—jumped into the market and quickly pushed it higher. As farms were bought up and consolidated, their occupants moved off the land, and many of the vacated houses, barns, sheds, silos, windbreaks, and orchards were bulldozed into huge piles and set afire. The following year a field of corn or soybeans was planted over the buried remains of a farmstead that had stood for a hundred years.

During the five years of his marriage, the value of Frederick's land had risen to almost three thousand dollars an acre, a figure too exaggerated to contemplate. It was a lot of money and JoAnn had wondered aloud about the wisdom of continuing to farm it for the modest income it produced.

"If you sold it for cash, you'd only have to pay capital gains on forty percent, and if you sold it on contract you could live on it forever." Her new career was coming in handy.

He didn't try to hide his disdain for the idea. "Sell it? What the hell would I do then?"

"Frederick, you wouldn't have to do anything if you didn't want to."

"I'd go crazy doing nothing."

"I didn't really mean do nothing. It just wouldn't have to be farming. You could finish college like you've talked about. You could go into real estate."

He had no words for this, only an expression of disbelieving disgust which JoAnn found more annoying than chiding. It didn't help that he was wearing the usual oil-stained overalls and hadn't bothered to shave that morning. His thinning, blonde hair badly needed a trim, and unruly ends sprouted from beneath the seed corn cap he wore everywhere but bed. Her husband was not a vision of success.

Like so many of their discussions, this one had died without resolution, and JoAnn turned back to the stove and stirred the can of soup she was heating. Why even try? It was useless to talk to him about trying anything new, let alone selling the place. He was stuck on this farm, happy with this life, but she couldn't imagine why. It was so confining, so limiting, the same little bit of the world, day after day, the same people, when you did see them. He didn't care if he never went to town. He was content to stay here and would have been delighted if she had, too.

III

Even when there were no emergencies, Frederick spent too much time working on the combine. Despite its ungainly appearance, the machine was a sophisticated, portable factory that cut the crop where it stood in the field, separated the grain from the plant—even kernels from an ear of corn—channeled it into a hopper, then chopped the leftover stalks into a wake of masticated mulch, ready to be plowed under. On level ground, it could ingest four rows of corn or beans at a steady two or three miles an hour, and the new models could do a lot more than that.

But the machine's complexity and the dusty, uneven environment it worked in made it vulnerable to breakdown. To minimize this, most of his neighbors upgraded theirs every few years, and went into debt to do so. Debt had become a way of life for them, and most of the reason for that debt was buying equipment. Bigger and newer equipment allowed them to farm more acres with less down time for repairs. It was a way of life that many of them no longer even questioned, but Frederick was reluctant to adopt it.

The biggest practitioner of this new-is-better-philosophy was Eldon Mathews, who owned or rented close to five thousand acres. He had bought all of the land around Frederick's farm and he longed to own it, too, so that he might obliterate—once and for all—the effrontery of Heinold's unkempt presence, which he was obliged to witness every time he drove in or out of his own driveway.

"Goddamn it!" he would announce to his wife as he barged

noisily into her well-used kitchen. "Them fuckin' dandelions of his are blowing across the road, again! Hasn't that sonofabitch ever heard of a sprayer?" Then, just as abruptly, he was gone, off in his pickup, on the radio to one of his crews, his day ruined again by his neighbor's screwy ways.

One day Eldon couldn't take it anymore and decided to take matters into his own hands. He took some herbicide and began to spray Frederick's fence line across the road from his house. Frederick happened down the road and caught him in the act. He stopped the pickup in the middle of the road and got out.

"What are you doing, Eldon?"

"What the hell does it look like? I'm sprayin' weeds." He was more angry than embarrassed.

"You're spraying on my land."

"That's because they're your weeds! If you'd spray the goddamn things, I wouldn't have to. When the hell are you gonna start farmin' in the twentieth century? And while you're at it, why don't you pull this worthless fence out so you can work this ground?"

"I like that fence. The old man built it."

"Yeah, forty years ago to hold cattle, but we don't raise cows in pastures now, in case you ain't noticed. Do you know how many bushels you're throwin' away on those weed patches, not to mention the goddamn cockleburs and dandelions that blow over onto my place?"

"Maybe you need to kill off the wind, Eldon, to stop all this blowing around. Maybe you think you can afford that."

"Don't go evadin' the goddamned issue. We're not talkin' about the fuckin' wind here, we're talking about this fuckin' weed ranch of yours that keeps pollutin' my fields with dandelions and cockleburs!" For emphasis, Eldon stepped into that ill-defined but sacrosanct space that men customarily keep between them, a tactic he employed quite deliberately to intimidate the person he was talking to.

Frederick was familiar with this intrusion, for throughout the childhood they had shared, Eldon was forever bullying whomever he thought might be bullied, making lives miserable with his ceaseless aggressiveness. Several times during those years Frederick had been forced to fight him in clumsy wrestling matches that resulted in torn clothing but little else. Although he had held his own, it did nothing to curb Eldon's need to push him and everybody else around.

If possible, he would have had nothing to do with the man, but they were neighbors and there was the occasional need to communicate. He hated going over to Eldon's imposing farmstead with its sprawling, modern brick home and numerous metal sheds filled with the latest equipment, which rumor said he bought in million dollar orders. More large storage bins stood about than you'd find at a country elevator.

Since Eldon kept busy running up and down the roads in his pickup, it was usually his wife that came to the door. Sherry was invariably sullen and preoccupied, but not enough to distract Frederick's attention from the jeans she filled so well. She would lead him to the office Eldon had built onto the back of the house where she would call him on the radio while Frederick lingered near the door.

With all this you'd think you'd be happy, he thought to himself as he looked around, but he had a pretty good idea why she wasn't.

Eldon had started out modestly enough with just his parent's farm, which was smaller than Frederick's, but he'd had the good sense to marry Sherry Olson whose family owned twice that. Those two farms had formed the basis for Eldon's expansion and his rise to prominence as one of the biggest farmers in the county.

Crabgrass and pigweed and corn borers had always been problems, but now he had new chemicals to rid his fields of these plagues, once and for all. But he would never completely achieve that mission until Frederick Heinold came to Jesus or left. Eldon would have preferred the latter.

Eldon fancied himself a general, like his hero, George Patton, who would accept nothing but absolute victory. He loved to send his huge equipment down the narrow gravel roads, immense roaring tractors pulling plows or disks or planters or cultivators so wide that they had to fold up to squeeze over the bridges.

He had ripped out all of the old fences that had once defined each field, so that his equipment could work huge expanses without the inconvenience of having to turn around every quarter mile. Two of his fields each covered an entire square mile, six hundred and forty acres of featureless land that had once supported four families.

One spring morning Eldon had decided to have a little fun with his neighbor by giving him a dose of all that horsepower. Just before daybreak he sent every piece of equipment he had, to work up and plant an eighty acre field that lay only a couple of hundred yards from Heinold's house. He doubted that any piece of ground had ever been worked with such noisy ferocity before.

As much as he wanted to observe the event, he thought it better if he stayed in the office and at least tried to look like he was working. It also assured that he'd be there when Frederick came over to bitch about all the noise.

"Eldon, what are you doing?" Sherry asked when she saw what was going on.

"I'm giving that sonofabitch a wakeup call," he crowed. He started laughing, just thinking about it. Naturally, the old lady, as he preferred to call her, saw nothing funny in this and left him to gloat on his own.

Just as Eldon had predicted, Frederick was barely out of bed when the racket started. At first he was royally annoyed, just as Eldon had hoped, and his first impulse was to drive over and raise hell about it. But then he realized that all that equipment in one field was not a coincidence. Eldon was sending him an unsubtle message. It was all just a big, stupid joke—and he was the brunt of it.

Instead of getting on the phone and raising hell, he made a pot of coffee, then got the morning paper out of the mailbox and took it and a mug of coffee and a lawn chair out to the grassed area which abutted Eldon's field. Ignoring entirely the frenzied activity and noise just a few feet away, he sat in the chair in an old bathrobe, reading the paper and drinking coffee as if he were sitting in his living room.

Eldon's crew had, of course, been in on the original plot, but now Frederick had given them something equally unique and— better yet—sure to blow Eldon's top. Clyde Hancher was Eldon's foreman, although the title actually paid more grief than money. Goddamn, Clyde thought to himself. You shouldn't ought to be missin' this, Eldon. He picked up his radio. "Eldon, this is Clyde. Come on."

Eldon had been waiting near the radio in his office with his feet up on the desk when the call came in. He sure as hell knew what this was about. He started chuckling as he picked up the mike.

"Yeah, Clyde. How's it going?" He could hear the engine noise roaring in the background. "Not having any trouble, are you?" It was all he could do not to laugh out loud.

"No I wouldn't call it trouble."

Eldon would have appreciated a little chuckle from the other end, but that was Clyde: all business.

"The owner ain't been out to complain, has he?"

"As a matter of fact he did come out," Clyde told him.

"Oh yeah? Well, what did he have to say?"

"Well, nothing, exactly."

"Nothin?"

"Not exactly."

"Clyde, did he come out or didn't he?"

"Yeah, he came out, alright. He's still here."

"Well, what the fuck is he doing?"

"He's sitting?"

"Sittin?"

"Yup. In a chair."

"A chair?"

"Yeah, it's a lawn chair of some kind."

Usually Eldon appreciated Clyde's taciturnity, but there were times like this when he would have appreciated a little more information without having to pry it out.

"So, that's all he's doin'? Sittin'?"

"Well, he's drinking coffee and readin' the paper, too."

It was the first time that Clyde could recall a silence from his boss's end of a conversation. Finally, Eldon collected himself.

"I guess we gave that sonofabitch a little lesson on how we do things," he said.

"I guess so," Clyde said, but he didn't sound convinced.

IV

The whole backfired incident only increased Eldon's desire to own Frederick Heinold's farm. Its soils were of excellent quality and the location was perfect, but those reasons were secondary to his contempt for its owner. Not only that, but Frederick had outbid him on the rent for two hundred acres that Eldon had assumed was his. It was owned by a family trust in Des Moines, and Eldon tried to low-ball them, just for openers, but goddamn if they didn't rent it to Frederick. Frederick Heinold renting more land. Jesus Christ! Eldon couldn't believe it. Shit, the man couldn't take care of what he owned!

Eldon fantasized about just showing up one day in Frederick's kitchen with a suit case full of money, maybe six or seven hundred thousand in small bills—for maximum effect. Whatever it took. Just pour it out on the table and tell him, "Okay, you son-of-a-bitch. Take the money and your goddamned lawn chair and git!"

And he'd do it just like that without any of the goddamned negotiating that ended up costin' more for somethin' than it was worth. How many guys would turn down that much cash piled right there in front of them? Not many. But the Oddball would probably be the one.

Now, JoAnn would be a different story. JoAnn would take it in a heartbeat, no question. She might not be much of a farmer's wife, but she knew what a buck was worth and how to spend it. But the Oddball was too dumb to sell it, which is why Eldon didn't try out his idea—at least for now.

The only thing he could do was keep the sonofabitch on his toes and let him know that Eldon had his eye on him. His day would come, he was certain. He just had to wait—and be ready.

THREE

JoAnn lay on the king-sized bed in room 43 of the Holiday Inn and watched the ceiling shift unsteadily overhead. She was very drunk and waiting for Miles to finish whatever it was he was doing in the bathroom. She'd kept telling him that she needed to go to her mother's to spend the night and he kept telling her that he'd drop her off there, but instead he had brought her to his room.

"Just for a little while," he'd told her, "until you sober up."

It sounded reasonable and she was so drunk that she hadn't even argued.

"Miles—?" The word stuck to her tongue and didn't sound anything like it should have.

"Just another minute."

What was he doing in there? She knew she should be more forceful and tell him that they needed to go, right now. She shouldn't even be in this room. She shouldn't have spent the night drinking with him. She shouldn't—she shouldn't—she shouldn't—

"Miles."

"I'm here." He kissed her throat.

"Where have you been?"

"Preparing a little something. Here."

JoAnn rolled onto her side so she could see. There was a little table next to the bed and a small mirror on the table. He was kneeling beside it and carefully rolling a fifty-dollar bill into a little tube. Miles had more fifty-dollar bills than anyone she had ever known. When he was finished, he held one end to his nose and bent close to the mirror. That's when she noticed the little trail of white powder on the mirror. Using the rolled bill like a straw, he expertly vacuumed half of the little trail into his left nostril.

"Miles, what are you doing?"

"I have something special that I want you to try. Here." He carefully placed the tube between her fingers then held the mirror close to her face. She could see the powder more clearly, now. It looked like flour—very white flour.

"Miles?"

"Trust me. Just inhale it through the tube."

"It won't hurt me?"

"It won't hurt you. It will make you feel good."

"You're sure it's okay?"

"Of course, it's okay. I did it, didn't I?"

He brought the mirror close to her face and guided the tube and she drew the cocaine into her nose. A soothing coolness surged into her brain. She lay back on the bed. He was right. It didn't hurt. He took the tube from her and finished the powder still left on the mirror.

"What is it, Miles?"

"Nose candy," he smiled.

"It won't hurt me?"

"No. It won't hurt you."

"I'm trusting you, Miles."

"I know."

"I'm trusting you with everything."

The ceiling had steadied and she began to feel calmer, but oh so very far from her life. All that was somewhere else, too far to think about or even imagine. Miles knelt beside her and began to undo the buttons on her dress. She closed her eyes, and he undressed her with slow, practiced assurance, drawing her out of her clothing as languidly as he had drawn the powder into his nose.

"—with everything, Miles. With everything."

II

It was almost dark when Frederick finished working on the combine. As far as he could tell, the most serious damage was a belt that had broken when pieces of the fence had jammed the mechanism on the cutting platform. He'd have to go into Lime City in the morning and hope that the dealer had a spare, but the machine was dead for now and there was nothing to do but go to the house.

When he got there, his cows were milling around the feed bunkers, bawling to be fed. After a quick check of the gas-fired dryer he used to reduce the moisture content of his corn, he spent almost an hour feeding them. He wasn't surprised to see that that JoAnn wasn't home. She had probably worked late or had too many drinks and decided to stay at her mother's.

By the time he finished it was dark and the heat of the afternoon had been replaced by a chill that reminded him again of how close winter might be. His breath smoked away on a faint breeze, and a swarm of bright stars lit the sky above. Normally, he would have been delighted to be out on such a night and doing work that he loved, but tonight the delight was surpassed by weariness and regret and anger at JoAnn's absence.

He went into the house and made a sandwich and sat on the couch to eat it, reading a three-day old newspaper and largely ignoring the TV he'd turned on. When he woke at three, he was still on the couch, still wearing his work clothes. JoAnn would have been furious, but of course she wasn't there.

He knew that he should go upstairs and take a shower and go to bed, but he was restless and, strangely, didn't feel as tired as he should have. He put on a jacket and went out to check the dryer. The corn inside it was dry enough, so he augered it out and replaced it with wet corn from one of his wagons. Because of the rainy fall, the moisture content of the corn was still high, which reduced the price the elevator would pay for it, so he—like his neighbors—dried it down to an acceptable level. It meant more work and, of course, more expense.

When he had finished, he went back into the house and went to bed.

III

JoAnn woke to the unsettling realization of lying naked next to a man she hardly knew in a strange room bathed in garish red light that seeped through the heavy curtains. She lay still, listening to the unfamiliar rhythm of Miles breathing, trying to sort things out. Her mouth was dry and her head hurt, and she was in trouble. She had to be in trouble. What had she done? She drew the watch on her arm close enough to read in the dim light.

Oh god, it was after eight. She was certain that Frederick had worked late, but afterwards he might have tried to call her at her mother's, but JoAnn knew she had gone to Dubuque for a few days to visit a sister. Still, he would wonder why JoAnn hadn't been there. Why hadn't she? Oh God, why hadn't she? But maybe he hadn't called her there? But even if he hadn't, he would probably try to reach her at her office. She had to get there before it opened.

She couldn't believe she'd blundered into this mess. Somehow the night had gotten out of hand. They'd had dinner and she'd drunk more than she should have, and then they went dancing, which she loved and Frederick never cared for. They kept drinking and drinking champagne, which she'd never cared for before, but which tasted better and better as the night went on until the bar ran out of champagne and they began to order other things.

Through it all, Miles remained self-assured and in control. He never seemed to get drunk and sleepy like Frederick did, and he paid for everything from the roll of bills he carried in his pocket.

And somehow they had ended up in his room—this room— and she'd stayed—oh, God, she'd stayed. She'd begged him to take her to her mother's but Miles had other ideas. The white powder, for one thing. My god! And she'd taken some! And she knew what it was. He didn't have to tell her. She didn't live in a vacuum. So, besides sleeping with another man she'd broken the law, too, and used an illegal drug. Cocaine, for God's sake! But regret was useless. She had to get out of there.

She looked for her clothes, which she remembered Miles taking off as if he were unwrapping a gift. She rarely let Frederick undress her, but she'd let this guy do whatever he wanted. They were scattered on the floor and she gathered them up and took them into the bathroom.

When she switched on the light, the image in the mirror made her wince. Could I look any worse, she asked herself. She felt sour and used, and she desperately needed a shower, but there wasn't time. She put the stale clothes back on.

When she peeked through the curtains at the parking lot, she could only see Miles' El Dorado. She must have left her car somewhere. It took some shaking to wake him.

"Miles, where did I leave my car?"

"I can't remember," he mumbled. "Take mine." He didn't even open his eyes. She went through his pockets until she found the keys.

IV

When she pulled into the office parking lot, JoAnn was relieved to see that Frederick's truck was not there. She felt even better when the secretary told her he hadn't called. Maybe she was okay. Maybe he wasn't looking for her—yet.

May as well find out, she thought as she dialed the number for the farm. Nothing. He was probably already in the field. At that moment Frederick walked into her office wearing a familiar sour face. She hoped he wouldn't notice she was wearing the same clothes that she had on yesterday.

"Have you had breakfast?" he asked.

"I—no," she said.

"Come on." Without waiting for her, he walked out the door.

At the restaurant he ordered the full breakfast and ate quickly, like he always did when he was preoccupied. Sometimes it annoyed her, but not this morning when it meant that he had something on his mind other than where she'd spent the night. She drank coffee and dabbed at her eggs.

"What's wrong?" he asked. "Are you alright?"

It startled her. "Yes. Why?"

"I don't know. You're not eating your breakfast, for one thing. I thought maybe you might be under the weather."

"I'm alright. I'm just tired."

"Tell me about it."

It wasn't a sincere reply, but she decided to let it go. She didn't want to say anything that could lead the conversation back to last night. Frederick pushed his empty plate away and looked at her.

"Why do you think I'm in town?" he asked. JoAnn felt a jolt

in the pit of her stomach. She studied her cold eggs without looking at him.

"I don't know, Frederick. Why?"

"You know how you're always telling me to hire someone to help me finish this harvest?"

"Yes."

"Well, I did. Do you want to know how it worked out?"

She looked at him and the old self-pitying look on his face. He was adding some smugness, too.

"You're going to tell me whether I want to or not, so just tell me."

"I will tell you, JoAnn, not that you give a good goddamn. He got drunk and ran my combine through a fence, and I'm in town to get a part so I can fix it!" He seemed to swell with indignation as he said it.

"He what?"

"He almost wrecked my combine!"

"I'm sorry," she said calmly, "but it's not my fault."

"I keep telling you that I can't just have anybody out there, but you never listen. It could have been worse than it was!"

She realized that he wanted some kind of reaction from her that was commensurate with his, but she couldn't muster it.

"Do you understand what I'm saying, JoAnn? You act like you're in a haze or something."

"I'm not in a haze, but what can I do? I'm sorry you had a bad experience, but it's not my fault and you keep acting like it is. You'd think I'd driven it through the fence."

He looked away from her and scanned the restaurant. There were other couples there, some of whom seemed to actually be enjoying each other. He'd thought that maybe this would convince her, but nothing had changed.

"I stopped by your mother's." he said.

JoAnn felt the jolt in her stomach, again.

"This morning?" she asked. She focused on the trace of milk on his upper lip.

"Yeah, an hour ago. There was no one there."

"Mother's in Dubuque, visiting Bessie."

"You stayed there alone?"

"What makes you think I stayed there?"

"Didn't you?"

"Yes." There. She'd done it. A lie.

"I thought you hated to stay by yourself."

"I do."

"Why didn't you come home?"

"I showed houses to almost eleven o'clock. It's the new plant manager. He works all day so he has to look at night."

"You could have come home then."

"I was tired—and hungry." She looked away, again.

"You know, we live on that farm together."

"We've been over all this. You may love it out there, but I don't. I'm just trying to find a way to make it work."

"Yeah, sure." He hated that it was true, and it was even harder when she was so straightforward. But he appreciated her honesty. If they could stay honest with each other they could get through a lot of things. He reached across the table and took her hand. "I just want to see more of you." They were the first words he'd spoken without anger or resentment.

"I know. I'm—I'm trying, Frederick. I'm trying."

Her face seemed drawn and tired to him, vulnerable even, and it softened him even more. He wished there was a way that he could just hold her, but everything was moving. He had a crop to get in. There wasn't time. He stood up.

"I've got to go," he said.

"Okay," she said, and got up to follow him out. Somehow she had escaped. She was saved.

FOUR

Frederick dropped JoAnn at her office and headed back to the farm. Now that the apprehension of his sudden appearance had worn off, she was overcome with a profound weariness. She sat at her desk and tried to work, but it was hard to stay focused. Her throat was dry and her temples throbbed, and she couldn't stop thinking about the night before.

Miles Richards had come into her life like no one before. She was dazed and confused, but mixed with those feelings was a flutter of anticipation, a current of excitement. It was a dangerous excitement, to be sure. And it wasn't just the cocaine or the champagne—it was Miles.

She still had his car. Was he going to call or just show up? At ten o'clock she gave up trying to work and asked one of the other agents for a lift to the Tailfeathers to retrieve her car. The woman had been one of the group the previous night.

"You were smart not to drive home," she offered pleasantly on the way over.

"I thought I'd had a little too much," JoAnn said.

"Champagne will do that."

"I guess—and I don't even particularly like it. I don't know what got into me."

"Well, that Miles is pretty persuasive."

"Miles? Yes. He certainly enjoys a good time, doesn't he?"

"He seemed to have his eye on you."

"Oh, not really. He's that way with everyone, isn't he?"

"Oh, not everyone." Her reply was conspiratorial—and worrisome. She'd noticed that? Who else had? JoAnn was glad

27

when they got to the car.

To distract herself she decided to do a little shopping. It sounded more appealing than trying to work and there was something else. Last night Miles had actually laughed at her modest panties as he'd pulled them off and held them up. She'd tried to grab them but he tossed them aside.

Frederick was always trying to get her to buy the skimpiest things, too, but she preferred the full size because they covered the stretch marks on her stomach. But it was Miles she wanted to please. She picked out a tiny pair. Only a man would like these, she thought as she paid for them. With that finished, she decided to go back to the office.

It was almost two before Miles called. "Where's my taxi service?" He sounded a lot more rested than she felt.

"I don't think I should come over there in the middle of the day, Miles."

He laughed. "Did you think you were invisible last night?"

"A little less conspicuous, don't you think?" He laughed again.

"If you say so. But you could just park in back and come up the stairs.

She tried to be assertive. "Miles. I don't feel comfortable with this. Couldn't you grab a cab?"

"JoAnn?"

"Yes?"

"Did I turn into a pumpkin overnight?"

"Of course not. It's just that I really need to make some calls. I'm a working girl, you know."

"Of course you are, but you've got to eat. Come and get me and I'll take you to lunch."

"I think lunch is what happened to yesterday."

"What was wrong with yesterday?"

"Nothing was wrong with it. It just got a little out of control, that's all."

"Look, I promise. I'm only talking about lunch. And then I'll send you right back to work." She felt too tired to argue—not that she wanted to, anyway.

"Promise?"

"I promise."

"Okay, but just lunch."

"Ten minutes," he said, and hung up.

She still felt uneasy about going over there. It was a small city and a lot of people knew her. That was one of the mixed blessings about real estate. You wanted people to know who you were, but sometimes you didn't want them to know. The funny thing was that she had actually picked up clients from out-of-town right in the lobby of this same motel and never thought a thing about it. Of course, she hadn't slept with them the night before.

The new plant was bringing in a lot of new people, some of them managers and engineers who flew in for just a day or two to shop for houses. A friend of hers who was a loan officer at one of the banks had gotten her a list of the people transferring in, and she had already made four good sales to them. She just had to hope that everyone who saw her with Miles would assume that he was just another client.

And he really was—kind of, although she knew much less about him than she did her clients. He had asked her to show him the Prairie School house, but was he really interested in buying it—and could he afford to? She didn't know. Did he have a house in Florida? He'd never really said. He spent money faster than anyone she'd ever known, but she had no idea how much money he had. He was driving a Cadillac convertible, but it was five or six years old and actually a little on the tacky side.

Despite these questions, her heart beat faster as she drove to the motel—and it wasn't all from nervousness. Miles excited her, no question about it. He was beautiful and fascinating and so different than Frederick.

"JoAnn. JoAnn," she chided herself aloud, but JoAnn wasn't listening.

By the time she knocked on his door, her knees were shaking.

"Yes, who is it?"

"It's the cleaning lady," she said, going along with the joke.

When he opened the door she almost leaped into the room. Then, they were kissing hard, and she was glad that she'd come.

"Do all of the taxis in this town provide this kind of service?" he asked.

"I don't think so." She felt feverish from the kiss and sat down on the bed.

"Are you okay?"

"It's been a long morning."

"Did something happen?"

"My husband was looking for me."

"Oh. And what did you tell him?"

"That I stayed at my mother's."

"Your mother's? She lives here?"

"Yes. I stay with her sometimes when I work late."

"And Mr. JoAnn goes along with that?"

"Yes."

"Wow! That's perfect!"

"What do you mean?"

"I mean that you're lucky you have such an understanding husband."

His smile seemed to mock her. He had no idea how much anxiety this was causing—or the risk she was taking. And did he even care for her? Those thoughts sobered her and the doubts flooded in. What was she doing?

He put his arm around her.

"JoAnn."

"What?"

"What's wrong?"

She looked at him. He seemed to really want to know.

"I've never done anything like this before."

Over the years Miles had heard this from at least a dozen women, and it had lost its intended effect long ago. If so many women were untruthful to their husbands, how could he trust any of them? He had decided some time ago that he couldn't. This rationale erased any misgivings he might have had to begin with.

He sat on the bed and put his arm around her. "Once in a while everyone needs a little adventure," he explained. "You've been working like a dog and your husband is too busy to give you any credit. You're just enjoying a little reward. In a few days I'll be heading back to Florida and all of this will be just a memory—and our little secret."

She frowned.

"An adventure? I never thought of myself as having adventures."

"Why make it hard on yourself? Enjoy it like I do. It's not hurting anyone. I won't be sticking around to complicate your life. I promise. My business is in Florida, and I've got to go back soon." He could see that his pep talk wasn't cheering her. Like so many women he'd known, she was looking for significance where there wasn't any.

"I don't know, Miles," she said. "This is confusing to me."

"Come on," he urged. "Let's have some fun. Let's go to lunch."

II

While Miles drove and chatted, JoAnn slumped in the seat and tried to sort things out. One of the things she had found in her marriage was predictability. Frederick was dependable and she knew that she could trust him. She had been betrayed once, painfully, and she was determined that it never happen again. That's why even during the difficulties of the past few months she had never considered leaving him. Such thinking would have betrayed her idea of herself, a loyal, sensible woman who would never leave her husband simply because she'd tired of him.

A single night had tossed her life upside down. She was behaving in a way she couldn't understand and risking everything that only yesterday had seemed important to her. Why couldn't Frederick be more flexible? Why couldn't he possess even a few of the graces that Miles wore so effortlessly? But that was never going to be. Frederick was always going to be exactly who he was.

Not even Miles' promise to leave, to end these complications, brought any sense of relief. Instead, she felt more and more remote from her life and from the person she had thought herself to be.

FIVE

It was a thirty minute drive back to the farm, and Frederick spent it thinking about the dismal state of his marriage. He remembered their first couple of harvests together, before the novelty of the farm had worn off for JoAnn. She had actually enjoyed pulling wagons behind the pickup, and he'd taught her how to run the dryer and she'd done well. She always ran to town for a part, when he needed one, and often brought food out to the field. A few times she even cooked a full meal, always a major event for her.

And there had been other good memories of that time, the quickies on the seat of the pickup and once on a tarp right out in the field. To combat the numbing boredom of the hours in the harvester, he concocted preposterous sexual fantasies and—despite her steadfast modesty—even talked her into trying a couple. Now, he had only memories of her bare legs stretched across the seat, shirt unbuttoned, bra pushed up above the dark nipples, the kinetic flash of dark hair between her thighs.

Usually, it was up to him to initiate sex and sometimes, even in the early days of their relationship, Frederick would have to persist if they were going to make love. He'd learned early on that her modesty was susceptible to a few drinks, and there had been a number of occasions after they'd been out and he was driving them home when she undid his belt and zipper and fondled him until he found a place to pull over.

At those times it was clear that she enjoyed the power that sex granted her even if she would never admit it. Usually, they made love in the darkness of their bedroom, and too often it felt like an accommodation on her part. For him it had never become a comfortable part of their life. In the banter of friends he heard the complaints about their sex lives, too, and that helped to accept his own circumstances.

Above all, Frederick loved his wife. At times he would have been hard-pressed to explain why, but he did and that love influenced every thought he had of her and every action. It tempered his frustration and his anger, and nourished an optimism for the future that reality didn't always justify. What is more, he trusted her and admired her drive, which he felt he lacked—even if couldn't admit it to her.

Although it seldom showed on the surface, he wasn't completely comfortable with the differences that set him off from his neighbors. If so many people he'd known most of his life were doing things differently, then maybe there was something to these changes. Maybe it was time for him to make some himself. That's what JoAnn was pushing him to do, but he was resisting. And why? The inertia of his life had carried over from his father but was that a reason to cling to it?

Frederick's mother had died when he was only nine and left Emmett with little idea of how to finish raising him. The two of them occupied the big house together, fixing or not fixing meals as they pleased, doing the laundry only when there was nothing left to wear. The farm was their world, and they had little need for town except as a source of food and parts.

Frederick rode the bus to the school in the nearby town of Rock Falls, which consisted of nothing but a small grocery store, a tavern, and a gas station. He never developed an interest in social activities or sports. Instead, he roamed the farm and the shores and shallows of the Lime Rock River, fishing for bass in the summer and hunting rabbits and squirrels and pheasants in the fall.

Emmett was a strong, quiet man, content to let his son develop to the tune of his natural talents. Even as a small child, Frederick enjoyed taking things apart, although he didn't always manage to get them back together. Emmett would come into the shop and find the lawnmower scattered across the floor, his son sitting happily in the midst of its parts. The old man never chewed him out, though, for he recognized the boy's curiosity as a natural aptitude for mechanics, a valuable thing on a farm. By the time he was twelve, Frederick was well on his way to becoming a capable mechanic.

He was almost thirty before he realized that his father was the most knowledgeable man he had ever known. It was true that most of what Emmett knew applied to farming, in one way or another, but farming encompassed many disciplines and the old man had mastered many of them—and with such subtly that it took his death for Frederick to realize it.

Before the whites came to northern Iowa, the land from which the farm had been measured was sparsely timbered wetland, almost bog. Ten thousand years before that, the last glacier had ground the underlying limestone into dust and then retreated. The dust became the early soils on which grasses and forest eventually grew. From these developed a rich, water holding loam, which grew fine crops in dry years but poor when it rained too much.

To drain away excess water, farmers dug shallow trenches and lay lines of clay tile into them and covered them over. These led water away to ditches and creeks, which then carried it to the Lime Rock River. Over a period of forty years, Emmett laid thousands of feet of tile and transformed the farm into one which produced excellent crops almost every year.

Some of this subterranean web of trickling water had been drawn on maps, but much of it was mapped only in his mind. He could walk across a field and tell Frederick that a wet spot was caused by a clogged line that Frederick did not know existed. Once, after the two of them had walked wordlessly out into the center of a forty acre field, the old man had slowly turned and taken his bearings from a constellation of obscure marks: the weed covered stump of an oak, a granite boulder, the intersection of two roads and, for all Frederick knew, the position of the sun itself.

"Try it here," the old man had told him and when Frederick dug, the tile was there, four feet below his boots.

After Emmett died, a neighbor told him that his father had been the best man with a team of horses that he'd ever known, but Frederick had never seen his father drive a team of horses. Another told him that the old man had once been in demand for his ability to splice a hay rope with such cleverness that the splice was no thicker than the rope itself, which allowed it to pass smoothly through the pulleys as hay was lifted into the mows.

All of these were talents of an age in which change had occurred slowly, an age which no longer existed.

II

Troubles or no troubles, he had to get back to work. Whenever he left the farm—for whatever reason—the work stopped and waited for his return. There was no one else to do it. His cows had to be fed and watered every day, seven days a week. Planting and harvest were the most intense activities on the farm with long stretches of work broken only by short naps and hurried meals.

Once he had established a rhythm, he could go on for days, not taking time to shave or bathe until JoAnn complained. Although he tried to get at least some sleep every night, he knew neighbors who worked forty-eight hour binges followed by a half day of sleep and another half day of grogginess. It was all an effort to get through the ordeal as quickly as possible. The bucolic pace of the old days had been replaced by frenetic activity.

When he drove into the yard, his dog Molly came stretching from her sunning place on the front porch. She was a mixed collie, a smart hunter who could still sniff out and chase down her dinner if she had to, although her best days were behind her. She liked to ride in the pickup with him, examining the world with alert intensity as it passed by. He opened the door and she hopped in the truck for the ride out to the combine.

It took Frederick two hours to replace the belt. When he had finished, he topped off the fuel tank with diesel from the drum in the bed of the pickup and savored a final, quiet moment as he relieved himself against a tire. Then, he climbed up into the cab and went to work.

SIX

It was barely one o'clock in the afternoon and the champagne had once again dissolved JoAnn's resolve. Miles had driven them over to a small restaurant at a nearby lake and immediately asked to see the wine list. She had promised herself that she would not get started again, but she felt too enervated by her mood to put up much resistance to his cheerful insistence that she share a glass with him. Only a glass, of course, again.

Up to then, the day had seemed impossibly long and discouraging but now the wine lightened her pessimism. She had a second glass and then Miles ordered another bottle. Might as well, she told herself. She didn't want to go back to work and she didn't want to go home.

If Miles felt any ill effects from the night before, he wasn't showing them. He seemed as amiable and relaxed as always. And, of course, he was as carelessly handsome. Did he, she wondered, find her attractive or just a convenience? He undoubtedly had other women, many women, she surmised, probably beautiful and exotic women, the kind that lived in Florida. Did she measure up to them? She wanted very much to. When he went back to Florida, she wanted him to miss her.

She sipped her wine and tried to recall the night before, but much of it was dissolving in a pleasant haze. He leaned toward her and smiled and talked in that way he had. It was wonderful to have him so expertly attentive.

As the wine warmed her emotions, she suddenly wanted to return that specialness to him even though it would mean more risks to her marriage. But it would all end in a few days. She might as well enjoy them.

It was a clear, bright day and they sat at the window and looked out on the empty lake. She couldn't remember the last time she and Frederick had spent a carefree afternoon together. Farming even dominated his leisure. If he wasn't struggling through planting or harvest, he was working on his equipment or fooling with his dumb cows. She couldn't see where he'd made a nickel on them over the past three years, but he argued that he had the pens and sheds and corn to feed them with. Besides, he added, the farm had raised cattle for as long as Heinolds had owned it. She couldn't convince him that it wasn't an excuse for losing money.

When they first married, he had still kept a few chickens and a heifer for milk, of all things. The refrigerator had been crowded with huge jars of skim milk and heavy cream—and dozens of brown eggs. After a few months of putting up with the clutter, she had put her foot down. The animals had to go and all milk and eggs would henceforth come from the supermarket in Lime City. Anxious to please his new bride, Frederick had not argued and gone along with her wishes.

There were other things she had to change. Even though Emmett had been dead five years, the house was still full of the life he and Frederick had shared. A large, round oak table still sat in the center of the kitchen, and in the mornings Frederick would sit at it, drinking coffee and listening to the market reports on the radio. Square, yellowed cupboards lined one wall and overhung a narrow countertop covered with the same faded linoleum that covered the floor. The stove and refrigerator were almost antiques.

Off the kitchen was a small pantry with shelves half-filled with dusty jars of canned vegetables and fruits. Since they could not tell when they had been put up, JoAnn threw them all away. The kitchen led into a dining room furnished with an even larger table, chairs, and a walnut sideboard. On the walls, faded photographs of long-departed relatives hung in frames not dusted since Frederick's mother had died.

Beyond the dining room was the living room, crowded with furniture last fashionable in the 1950s. Two huge, sliding oak doors separated it from the drawing room. Since his father's death, Frederick had used it as a bedroom and went upstairs only to use the house's sole bathroom.

The house was nearly a hundred years old when they were married, and it had been a sturdy, impressive structure in its time, probably one of the finest houses in the area. However, the electric wiring—which had been added in the 1940s—and the indoor plumbing—which had followed soon after—were installed with a clumsy obviousness that reflected more concern for function than appearance. As a result, wires and pipes ran over the surfaces of walls and ceilings rather than within them. They seemed an eyesore to JoAnn although Frederick seemed not to notice. He loved the great, quiet rooms with their ten-foot ceilings and would never have changed them on his own.

JoAnn, however, was eager to refresh the house and make it reflect the new life that they had begun. Eager for her to like her new home, he agreed immediately to the changes she wanted, which began with the remodeling of the kitchen. During several weeks of noisy and expensive renovation, it was rewired and replumbed and the ceiling lowered two feet. The old cupboards were torn out and replaced by new ones, the linoleum was covered with carpet, and new appliances were selected and installed. She did all of the painting and picked out the material for the curtains herself. After the kitchen was finished, she converted one of the upstairs bedrooms into an office for him and replaced the cigar boxes he had used for storing papers with an actual file cabinet. When she had finished, Frederick had to admit that it looked pretty good.

The project absorbed her and left him to run the farm without having to worry about her growing bored or lonely. It was wonderful to have her in the house when he came in, and he did not mind doing much of the cooking, an activity which had not been discussed in detail during their courtship.

Most of their socializing with other farmers took place at the infrequent wedding dances, sometimes held in farm sheds, sometimes in the old grange building in Rock Falls. Their marriage had been more or less endorsed by the neighbors who, although they had never met JoAnn, assumed that a woman's presence in Frederick's life would surely have a sensible effect on it.

When the newlyweds did not start a family within the first two years, their assumptions began to wobble and were further weakened by JoAnn's reluctance to join in the social functions of the other wives. She always seemed to have an excuse for not helping out at the church or going to activities at the school; even worse, Frederick appeared to be the same man he was before he married.

During the second year of their marriage, a Farmer's Chamber of Commerce had been organized. JoAnn thought that the group sounded like just what the countryside needed to make it more progressive, and she urged Frederick to join.

"I've never joined anything," he told her. "Not even the Farm Bureau, and everyone joins it."

"But this will be different," she argued without really having an idea about how it might be. "You can get together with other farmers and talk about how to improve things."

"What things?"

"The same things they improve in the city. You know, community activities." He still didn't understand, but he relented. She really seemed to want him to.

As it turned out, the chief beneficiaries of the new organization were the wives for whom it provided opportunity to exchange gossip in person as well as over the phone. While the men sat in one room and droned over such arcane matters as who should be the group's president, the women sat in another and enthusiastically drew up lists of get-togethers. The men failed to see that just being farmers doomed their efforts at even the simplest collective action. They loved farming because they didn't want to work with other people. They liked doing things their own way.

It took the men hours to nominate and elect officers—even though they could have pretty much named them from the start—and further hours to agree on and begin to plan their first and last, as it turned out, civic project—the restoration of an old schoolhouse in a nearby county park.

After a half-dozen meetings, their initial enthusiasm ran down like a clock that no one knew how to wind, and the organization withered. Even the lingering enthusiasm of the wives could not sustain it. After barely a year, the only reminder of the group's existence was the doorless, half-painted shell of the schoolhouse.

By the time the Farmer's Chamber of Commerce succumbed

to lack of interest, JoAnn did not mourn its passing any more than Frederick. The K-Mart dresses, acrylic hairdos, and incessant gossip gave her claustrophobia. Halfway through the first meeting she realized that she did not and would never belong with these people, and she was happy to realize that Frederick did not, either. He might be a farmer, but at least he was an interesting farmer.

Shed of her social burdens, JoAnn turned again to remodeling, turning the largest of the bedrooms into their room and another into a study. The closets were small, so she commandeered the one in their bedroom for herself and put Frederick's things in another. Frederick thought that maybe she was going a little overboard. Why couldn't they use the downstairs parlor for a bedroom during the winter, like he had? That way they'd save on the heat bills.

"Because it's not a bedroom," she had firmly told him.

During their second year together, he won a trip to the Virgin Islands in a seed corn contest, and it turned out to be such a glorious break in the long winter that she asked him why he didn't sell his cows so they could go somewhere warm every year. It was after this question that Frederick first demonstrated a peculiar display of disgust: a sour expression, part wince and part scowl, finished off with a brooding silence.

She found this disproportionate reaction to what she considered a perfectly reasonable question, stupid. Later, after she had experienced it a few more times, it came to epitomize his frustrating inability to intelligently discuss problems. She learned to retaliate with unexplained silences of her own, often for trivial or even non-existent transgressions, which left him satisfyingly perplexed.

As she ran out of rooms to remodel, boredom set in and she began to find ways to spend more time in Lime City. The hamlet of Rock Falls lay only three miles away, but she never went there. Instead, she drove the twenty miles to Lime City, which, with forty thousand people, provided more variety.

Her mother still lived there, and occasionally JoAnn spent a night with her, but Loretta clung to old antagonisms which could render her critical and hard to get along with—especially if she had been drinking, which her daughter thought she did too much. Other than her mother, JoAnn had several women friends who she saw from time to time, but their conversations were never more than casual and superficial. The person closest to her was Frederick.

Influenced by her mother's skeptical take on the human race—and men in particular—JoAnn had developed her own distrust as she grew up. It had been reinforced by a college sweetheart who intimated a shared life together, got her pregnant, then caddishly reneged on fatherhood and marriage. He had offered to pay for an abortion, but she turned him away with a glaring silence and sunk into lonely depression.

His family owned a string of restaurants in Des Moines, and he was always well dressed with plenty of money to spend. He seemed substantial and she had trusted him more than she had ever trusted a man before. His abandonment of her only reinforced the sense of betrayal her mother had cautioned against for years.

It had happened during the spring semester of her junior year at the University of Northern Iowa where she was majoring in education. After JoAnn stopped going to classes and the failing marks were sent home, Loretta took the bus to Cedar Falls to find out what was happening. JoAnn hated her arrival and would not at first tell her what had happened, but her pregnancy was becoming obvious and there was little to do but admit it.

Rather than be angry, as JoAnn had expected, Loretta was surprisingly supportive, and she took her daughter home with her to await the birth. Early in her eighth month, she almost miscarried and the doctor ordered her to bed. She spent several weeks there, worrying about the huge responsibility that she was soon to deliver. Then, only days before her due date, the child forced its way into the world and never took a breath. It had been a son.

Except where the skin had stretched on her breasts and stomach, there were no physical reminders of the worse days of her life. Emotionally, she felt a mixture of loss and relief. In a way, her life had been given back to her and she was determined to make the best of it.

The next semester she went back to finish her education classes. Not until her student practicum during her very last semester did she discover that she hated teaching, and so she graduated from college as unprepared to make a living as she had begun.

She returned to Lime City and for lack of anything better took a job as a secretary at a real estate and insurance agency. The money was poor, but she stayed with her mother and managed to make ends meet.

Frederick had his insurance there and stopped in several times to resolve some damage he'd suffered from a hailstorm. Her first impressions of him were the same as everyone else's: a balding, tall, slightly stooped man in his late twenties who seemed indifferent to how he dressed or impressed people. Late one morning after he had just come out of his agent's office, he stopped unexpectedly at her desk.

"What are you doing for lunch?" he asked.

"I don't know."

"How about having it with me?"

She hesitated. He had caught her completely by surprise. She knew that the girls expected her to go with them, just as she did every other day, so she had a ready excuse. But there was something about his earnestness and patience as he stood waiting for her reply that made up her mind for her.

"Okay."

She was twenty-four when they met, and he almost twenty-eight, but JoAnn had always felt older than her peers, anyway. The few young men that she'd met since moving back seemed emotionally stranded between the sweet irresponsibility of college and the sobering realities of life. Two of them had already been married and divorced. There was a disquieting restlessness about them that made Frederick seem settled and secure. She found it comforting that he knew exactly who he was.

Like her, he seemed in no rush to get married. For that matter, he seemed in no rush to do anything. The other girls in the office kidded her about landing a rich farmer, but nothing about him looked rich, and on a farm was the last place she planned to live.

He began seeing her in May, and they enjoyed the humid Iowa summer, frequently driving to the lake for dinner, sometimes lingering in the late afternoons at a bar. In August she had a week's vacation and they saw each other every day. By then she had gotten to know him better and what she learned was reassuring. Frederick Heinold was exactly what he appeared to be. That is, until mid-September when he disappeared.

He had told her that harvest was approaching and that he would be very busy after it began, but that did not explain his precipitous drop from her life. During the first week, he did call once, but he seemed distracted and had little to say. It was not reassuring. Without the prospect of his phone calls or their evenings together, her life became dull and routine, again. And, too, there was an office status attached to a woman with a man, and that disappeared when Frederick did. Worse was the embarrassment of trying to explain his absence.

"He's just busy," her mother told her, "he's a farmer. He'll be back when the work is finished." Loretta actually approved of Frederick. Few people she knew were steadier or more dependable than farmers. There wasn't an ounce of falseness to him, and that inclined her to trust him. "He might not be flashy like some of these guys, but I think you can count on him. He owns two hundred and forty acres, you know."

"As if that means something," JoAnn replied.

"It means that he's not just a fly-by-night. There's some substance there."

"I don't care," she said with some bitterness. "I don't have any interest in a man who abandons me for corn."

"He'll be back. Just hold your horses." But weeks went by and she did not hear from him.

As bad as she felt, she couldn't bear to spend every night on the couch with her tipsy mother and the blaring TV set. She became an alternate on the office bowling team. She didn't do much bowling, but it entitled her to spend the evening with the team—which meant drinking with the team. Invariably, the subject of the evening would shift from bowling to men.

"They're all creeps," the receptionist declared with some forcefulness. "You bust your ass for them and they leave you cold."

JoAnn had never busted her ass for a man, but she nodded sympathetically anyway.

"Here I am holding down a job and raising two kids, and the son-of-a-bitch is shacking up with an eighteen year old kid," another woman volunteered. "That's how old I was when he knocked me up the first time."

"I didn't know you were married," JoAnn replied.

"Christ, yes. Nobody can find the bastard long enough to serve him the divorce papers." The aggrieved took a long pull from her beer, and the brief camaraderie collapsed into wounded brooding.

It left JoAnn feeling even more lonely and depressed, and she almost called Frederick when she got home, but in the morning she was glad she hadn't. He was obviously getting along without her.

One day a few weeks later, one of the insurance agents asked her to go to a movie with him. His name was Harold Senneff and he was nice-looking and personable, and JoAnn might ordinarily have said yes. But there were extenuating circumstances. Harold's wife had walked out on him, leaving him devastated. Even worse, she had abandoned him for their mailman who was, by all accounts, skinny, bearded, and homely. Although Harold was indifferent about whom she had run off with—being generally totaled by the event itself—his fellow employees viewed the mailman with barely restrained hilarity, and the fiasco suffused the office like an in-house soap opera that did little for productivity.

Having been warned that Harold did nothing on his dates but lament his departed wife, JoAnn begged off, but the pathetic state of Harold's life further convinced her of love's predictable unpredictability. Faced with the imminence of another long, lonely winter, her spirits sank.

II

One October morning while JoAnn sat at her desk, working through a pile of claims, she looked up to see Frederick standing before her. He was smiling.

"Hello," he said, seemingly unaware that he'd been absent for five weeks.

"Hello." She hated the soft eagerness of her reply.

"How about dinner tonight?"

"I don't know. I think—"

"I've been missing you," he said, and she said yes.

He had been busy with his harvest just as her mother had said. Even though he had been honest with her, she still didn't find his explanation a legitimate reason for neglecting her.

"There is such a thing as a telephone," she reminded him.

"I know that it's hard to understand, but once I begin I just want to stay at it until I'm finished."

"It doesn't sound like a very normal life to me."

"No, I guess it doesn't, but there are an awful lot of good things about farming, too."

"Like what?"

"Sometimes it's just the land itself, the sun breaking across a field at first light. And then at the end of the day, when it goes down again, and everything gets still and quiet. In the springtime the new calves come and they're just beautiful. Clean, stiff-legged little things running around, trying out their legs." His face had grown serious as he talked, but now he smiled at her. "You don't know anything about farming, do you?"

"No."

"It's nice to be your own boss, too. Oh, there's time when I've got so much to do that I wish I was just punching somebody's time clock, but most of the time I like being responsible for my own life—for what I do."

"Isn't it kind of lonely?"

"Not really. There's so much to do that time passes fast."

"Maybe for a man, but how about a woman?"

"There's plenty for a woman to do."

"Like what?"

He had to think for a minute. What did women do? What had his mother done?

"They cook, take care of the house—help out in the field if they have to." JoAnn looked away.

"I don't think I'd like that," she said.

Frederick thought about women he sometimes passed on the roads, driving tractors or pickups with a grain wagon behind. They didn't always look like they liked it either, now that he thought about it. They seemed a little odd in their borrowed men's coats, often topped off with a scarf tied under the chin to protect a precious hairdo.

"Who wants to be a hired hand?" she asked rhetorically, and the conversation dwindled away.

III

His talk with JoAnn raised questions that Frederick had never thought of. He'd always considered farming something anyone would like, but now he saw that it might not be everyone's cup of tea. Finding a woman to share his life—and he'd always assumed that one day he would—might be more difficult than he thought.

Like many young men he had relegated marriage to some subsequent period of his life when he would have lived out his singleness and grown ready to share his life. With the arrival of his twenty-eighth birthday he began to wonder if that time had come. Twenty-eight, with thirty closing fast. And then what? Forty—fifty—sixty! Suddenly, he could feel life rushing on.

He'd had a few girlfriends, one of them for a couple of years, but each time they'd drifted apart with more or less the same lack of intensity with which they'd drifted together. He liked women and they seemed to like him well enough, but nothing serious ever happened. He'd always assumed there would be another and there always had been.

After his talk with JoAnn, Frederick began to pay more attention to the single women he encountered and almost immediately he noticed there were fewer of them. Some of those he'd dated had since married and begun families. The pool of prospects had clearly shrunk. Was life passing him by? He began to regard JoAnn as he had never regarded another woman—as someone he might spend the rest of his life with.

IV

The months passed and life became a routine for them with TV or a movie on Friday nights and dinner out on Saturdays, but for JoAnn it was enough—at least for the present. The following summer she planned to visit a college friend in Georgia to check out the job possibilities. That might help her to make the changes in her life she needed to make. There was no doubt that her job in Lime City was a dead end, and there was no doubt that there were few available men.

If she were to get on with life, she had to move somewhere else, somewhere vibrant and growing like Atlanta. But that could wait until summer. Frederick might not be the man that dreams were made of, but he made the long, winter days and nights bearable. When one of the girls in the office offered to line her up with a friend, she said no.

It was early March and they had just finished dinner in a favorite steak house when he set the ring on the table. Their talk about the farm months before had seemingly closed the door on any possibility of marriage, and now—suddenly—there was a ring.

"Frederick, I don't know what to say." She stared at the diamond as if it had dropped from the sky.

"I want you to marry me, JoAnn. I think that we can be happy together. I know that the farm would be a big change for you, but I think you'd get to like it. We've both had a little time to experience life. It's not like we're two teenagers."

He was looking for some sign of encouragement from her, but he could fathom nothing but silent shock. The ring lay, untouched. When she looked up at him her face was flushed, but she said nothing.

"Farming is a good life," he pressed on. "It's quiet and healthy—" He began to struggle. "I just paid the place off and we can weather a lot if we have to—I—"

Her silence was quickly eroding the confidence he'd mustered for this. It looked like she was going to tell him no. JoAnn would have loved to say something, but she couldn't connect her voice to any of the thoughts that fluttered through her mind. Her silence pushed him forward.

"If you're worried about living out in the country, you know we're not that far from town. Look how often I come in." He had not rehearsed that, but now he was desperate to make his case.

"Could I work in town?" she asked. "I mean, if I had to?"

Hope resurged in him.

"Yes," he said. "If that's what makes you happy. I want you to be happy."

JoAnn took a deep breath and picked the ring up. She had been caught completely unaware, but when she looked at him she could see that he had thought about this for some time. That would be Frederick. He wouldn't be impetuous, she was sure of it. She could depend on him. She turned the ring slowly between her fingers and the stone glinted in the candlelight. Then she slid it on.

"Okay," she said. "I will."

SEVEN

As JoAnn and Miles walked out through the door of the restaurant, the afternoon sun blinded them and she clung to him as he led her to the car. It was almost three and she was tipsy.

"I don't think I'm in any shape to work," she told him. "Besides, the day is almost gone."

"Let's go for a ride," he said.

If Miles was feeling the effects of the wine, he didn't show the slightest sign of it. He drove north into the country on a gravel road that rose and fell over gently rolling hills. The fields and roads were deserted except for a lone harvester that pulled over to let them pass.

"Farmers," Miles sniffed and shook his head at the big machine as they passed it. "Nothing but farmers and miles and miles of nothing."

"Miles and Miles," she repeated and they laughed.

"If I had to live here, I'd live on the lake," he said. "To get away from all this boredom."

"Would you ever live here?" she asked seriously.

"Not if I could help it. I've got to be near the water."

"Is there a lot of water where you live?" She wanted him to talk about Fort Lauderdale.

"There's a little something called the Atlantic Ocean."

"And lots of canals?"

"Yes, canals everywhere."

"With beautiful houses all along them."

"Yes."

"Do you have a house?"

"I'm between houses right now."

"You move a lot, don't you?"

"I like to buy low and sell high." He smiled at her. "You know how that goes."

"But you travel a lot, don't you."

"I used to travel a lot more when I was in the import business."

"Import business? What did you import?"

"Mexican goods. Pottery, furniture, Indian paintings, rugs, stuff like that."

"You never mentioned anything about it."

"I guess not."

"Are there other things you haven't told me?"

"Of course."

She glanced to see if he was going to elaborate, but he wasn't.

"The mysterious stranger," she said. "A nice stranger, but a mysterious one."

Miles thought about the things she didn't know and smiled. He had slipped back into his old attentive self, which he could do as easily as putting on a different shirt, but he was bored with this place and with JoAnn.

He had been driving slowly and as they rounded a hill he pulled over and stopped. They could see a long way. A small creek wound far below and disappeared into a copse of trees. The sun was low and the shadow of the car stretched beyond the ditch. The sun gently warmed the car. JoAnn slid across the seat and nestled beside him. The wine had dissolved her inhibitions and she wanted to be close to him. She wanted him to touch her.

"I love spending time with you," she told him and she raised her head so he could kiss her, which he did. "I love the way you do that, too." He smiled and fished a joint out of the pocket of his jacket. "One of those funny cigarettes," she said.

"That's right." He lit it with his lighter, drew deeply and held the smoke in his lungs, then offered it to her.

Here I am again, she thought without distress. Her life was so far away that she couldn't even see it. She was taking it off and putting it back on. Did it even fit anymore? She pinched the joint between two fingers and tried to inhale the way he did, but it still felt harsh on her throat. He laughed when she coughed, so she didn't want to. She held the smoke in her lungs for a few moments, then the smoke spurted from her mouth and she did cough, but Miles seemed not to notice.

She had never tried marijuana before meeting him, and she'd always thought that cocaine was something that only addicts living in slums used. And now she had tried them both. She smiled dreamily.

"What's so funny?" he asked, already knowing.

"I like the other stuff better," she giggled. Most people do, he thought.

"I should have brought some," he said. Actually, he had some stashed in the trunk but he was saving it for something else. When he leaned against the door on his side, he noticed the bag lying on the back seat. He reached to pick it up. "What's this?"

She'd forgotten all about it. "Oh, I bought some things this morning."

"What things?" He pulled the panties from the bag. "What have we here?"

She giggled and grabbed for them, but he held them away. "Miles! Give me those!" She sought to find the tone of impatient annoyance that always worked with Frederick.

"I want to see them," he said.

"Some time, maybe, if you behave yourself."

"You are funny," he said.

"Miles, I am not funny." She did sound funny.

"Put them on."

"What?"

"I want you to put them on."

"I will not! I told you, maybe some other time—if you're nice."

Indignation—petulance—Miles knew these tactics, but he'd never cared for them.

"Is that so much to ask—for you to model them for me?"

"The answer is yes—and no, I'm not going to."

He looked out at the empty country, the empty road.

"JoAnn. I told you that I want to see them." His voice had shifted into something that she wasn't sure she'd heard before.

"That's too bad, because I'm not going to change clothes in this car." She slid away from him to emphasize the point.

"I don't mean in the car."

She looked at him. He was still smiling. "What? What do you mean?" she asked.

"I mean not in the car."

She looked at him for some reassurance that he was only kidding, but she could find none in the smile that wasn't really a smile. Her heart sank. She wanted the old Miles back. She wouldn't beg, though. She suddenly felt the need to set things straight.

"You can forget about that completely!" She pulled her arms across her chest and looked out through the windshield. She wanted him to know that the subject was closed. Miles took a leisurely pull from the joint and offered the stub to her, but she refused to look at him.

"JoAnn. Are you familiar with the expression 'fuck or walk'?" He had never used that word around her and it sounded crude and harsh. If they'd been someplace else she might have gotten out right there.

"I certainly have not." She looked sharply at him. "It doesn't sound very nice."

"Oh, it's just kind of a game we used to play when we were kids. You and I are playing a variation. We'll call it put on the panties or walk."

"I don't care what you call it, it doesn't sound nice and I'm not playing."

"The rules are simple: you get out of the car and put these on—" He lifted the panties for emphasis. "—or I leave you here and you walk."

"Miles! For God's sake, don't even say such a thing! Tell me that you're kidding." There was nothing in the smile to tell her that he was. She was no longer with the man who had been so nice to her, who she had decided to go to bed with because she trusted him so much. He was gone and she was beginning to fear whoever had replaced him. "I don't want to play anymore. I want to go home."

Her bluster was gone and she felt small and alone. He had not moved toward her. The panties dangled from his hand like a taunt. She put her hand on the handle of the door.

"Don't be foolish, JoAnn. Just put them on and we can go." His voice was even and pleasant.

"I don't like this. I don't like you like this."

"Just do as I say and I'll be nice."

"I'm not taking my clothes off and that's final!" She opened the door.

"If that's the way you want it."

She got out and slammed the door.

She stood in the sudden chill and looked at the empty road. My God, what had she gotten herself into? And she'd left her coat in the car. But she wasn't going to open that door for anything. She'd freeze first. She'd show him.

Suddenly the power window lowered. So he was sorry. He'd come to his senses and wanted to tell her that he was sorry and to get back in the car. But he merely gazed at her with that horrible smile and did not speak. The only sound was the wind worrying the weeds in the ditch.

She wasn't going to give in. She wasn't going to give him his way. He had no right to treat her like this. She had never been treated like this.

When he started the engine it was hard not to look. And then the car moved slowly forward, the gravel crunching under the tires, and she could hear the window rise, again.

She crossed her arms against the cold and kicked at the gravel. The heels she was wearing looked too fragile to be walking down this road in. In the periphery of her vision, the car moved steadily down the hill and then began to climb the next swale, all at the same unhurried pace, climbing until it crested the hilltop and disappeared. A lone, scudding cloud drove its shadow across the hill. The emptiness of the road and the countryside was forlorn and lonely. The remains of her anger drained away. She felt like crying.

She couldn't remember the last farmhouse they had passed. How far was it? The wind gusted urgently against her. Her hands and feet were already cold. Why hadn't she grabbed her coat? What a wasted, foolish day. She stared at the hilltop over which the car had disappeared, but she didn't really think he would come back.

There was no point in waiting for someone to come along. She started walking away from where he had gone, but it was into the wind and very cold, so she stopped and started back, retracing her steps. It didn't seem to matter which way she went, anyway. She had no idea where she might find a house.

The gravel on the road scooted treacherously from under the pumps, so she had to watch where she stepped. The last thing she needed was to turn an ankle.

The car was almost beside her before she heard it, the window already down.

"JoAnn," he said, but she didn't even look up. She stopped and faced him.

"I'd like to be taken home, please." Her voice trembled with cold and emotion.

"I'd be happy to," he said reasonably. "Just do what I want you to do."

"And I told you, I'm never going to do that!" She turned and started walking again, reenergized by anger.

He drove alongside her for perhaps a hundred feet before he spoke, again. "Have it your way."

And then the car moved away with the same nonchalance as before.

She started walking again, and a sharp stone caught in her shoe and she stopped to take it out. She was shaking with cold and her hands were stiff and red—and she had gone nowhere. Nowhere! She looked off, again, in both directions. The sun was lower, the shadows longer. The wind had risen and was flailing the weeds in the ditch. Tears started down through her mascara as she started off, again.

This time she saw him coming, and she stopped and waited. "Why are you treating me like this?"

"Why are you being so stubborn?"

She began to cry from frustration and hopelessness, but he smiled as if she were a willful child, a smile she now knew could mean anything. Clouds were crowding the sky and it was colder under their shadows.

"You're being mean."

"You're being stubborn."

"Because I don't want to strip?"

"It's not about undressing," he told her. "It's about which of us is stronger. You're used to getting your way, but you're not going to get it with me. One of us has to give and that one is you. It doesn't really matter what the issue is."

"It matters to me and I'm not going to do it!"

"Have it your way, then, but this is the last time I'm asking.

I'm not coming back." The car began to move.

"No! You can't!" The words came from her chest, like a spasm. She didn't mean them. She hated that she'd said them and hated him for making her say them, but she was too cold and miserable to go on.

"Then put on this lovely thing that you bought to wear for me." He offered it across the space between them so she could almost touch it.

"No—I can't!" Surely he would understand and stop this.

"Okay. If that's the way it's going to be." There was no hope in his voice and she knew that he was going to leave. He turned from her and put the car in gear.

"Wait!" she shouted. "Give it to me."

"When you're ready."

"What?" But then she knew what he meant and without taking her eyes from him she began to fumble and pull at the zipper at the back of the dress until she had gotten it loose and then she pulled the dress down over her shoulders and hips and let it fall around her feet. The slip came next and then the panty hose, her feet stepping on them as they fell about her.

Through all of the gym classes of her school days and all of the doctors' offices she had ever visited, and even in the most intimate moments of her marriage, she had turned away to remove her underwear. But here in the taunting wind, in an act of humiliation and acquiescence, she faced her tormentor as she stripped off her bra and panties.

When she was naked, she stooped and gathered the clothes and held them for a moment like a kind of offering—and then she pushed them through the window.

As they drove, Miles turned up the heater and rubbed her numbed feet. Moments before she had felt helpless anger and humiliation, but now those feelings had collapsed into the deepest weariness. She was empty. There seemed to be little left of JoAnn Heinold.

EIGHT

Late in the afternoon the weather turned cold and cloudy as a front moved through, and Frederick listened closely to the weather reports on the radio. With so much corn still standing in the field an early snowstorm would be disastrous. But the wind remained in the northwest and kept the moisture to the south.

There was little he could do but worry. Every time he filled his grain wagon he had to stop everything, haul it in to his bins, unload it, then go back to the waiting combine and start anew.

In the evening he fed his cattle. Though they could be stupidly contrary, he had always liked cows, and he enjoyed the break that feeding them gave him. He clearly remembered the years his father had milked Holsteins and how they had stood bawling in the yard with their swollen udders until Emmett let them into the barn to be milked.

Each would walk stolidly to its own stall and begin to eat the grain placed there while his father cleaned the pink, mottled teats and attached the pneumatic cylinders of the milking machine. It sucked the milk from the udder in little peristaltic shudders while the cows contentedly ground the grain between their massive jaws.

Each animal had a name by which his father coaxed and soothed it. "Move over a little, Bell. That's a good girl." He emphasized his instructions with the reassuring pressure of his hands and body. Even as a small child, Frederick would come out to the barn when his father milked, and he loved the smell of the solemn bodies, so huge yet gentle.

On winter nights, when the temperature dropped to zero or below, the cows exhaled yeasty clouds of breath while the barn cats stroked and purred against his father's legs until he milked a pan of milk for them. JoAnn was right about his cows not making money, but she didn't have the memories he did. She held her nose against the smells that he found evocative and even pleasant.

Despite their morning fight, he missed her and hoped she would come home early so they could share a meal. At noon he had taken some steaks out of the freezer to thaw, but by seven she had not appeared and his hopes slid into the old self-pitying anger. He didn't care how busy she was. She knew what he was going through—how much he needed her. And goddamn it, it was her fault that he'd gotten in this to begin with. But he knew better.

"Never stake your life on one crop," the old man had often told him and he'd forgotten it.

But the old man had never been troubled by doubts like Frederick's. He'd lived in his world for so long that he had no interest in adjusting to a new one—and he didn't have to. But Frederick straddled the world his father had lived in and a new one filled with bewildering change: much as he might have wanted to, he could no longer belong to the old and he was struggling to accommodate the new one.

Even before JoAnn had come into his life, he'd worried about where he fitted in. Farming—his whole life, for that matter—had always come so easy that it seemed to lack significance. How could there be any meaning in something that didn't have any challenge or risk? The rapid changes going on around him only amplified his uneasiness. He questioned what a lot of people were doing—buying more land and equipment and going into debt to do so—but if so many were doing it, how wrong could it be?

JoAnn's success in what she liked to call the real world was the convincing event. After just a year, she was making more money selling houses than he was on a farm that had been in his family almost a hundred years. Even though he argued against many of her ideas, a part of him knew that she was right. He was stuck in the past, and he needed to take more chances.

The obvious thing had been to expand by renting more land.

He bid on a couple of smaller parcels during the previous winter, but his bids were too low and Eldon got both of them. By the time that the three hundred came up, he felt a little desperate. It was now or never, or at least now or wait until the next year and he didn't want to do that.

He bid too high, of course, but that's why he got it. He had to borrow most of it, but that was laughably easy. The bank had his farm for collateral, so they weren't worried. They almost threw thirty thousand dollars at him.

Once he got home and began to think about what he'd done, the doubts settled in. Owing that much money scared him, and that's why he wasn't going to borrow to buy more equipment. He'd just have to get by on what he had, at least for this year, and hope for the best. Of course, part of that hope had been that JoAnn would help him.

III

It had been dark several hours when he saw the lights of her car turn into the driveway. When he came into the house, she was sitting in the kitchen, sipping a glass of wine. Her coat was thrown over a chair.

"Are you staying?" he asked with a look at the coat.

"Yes. I'm just too tired to hang it up." She said it with convincing weariness.

"I'd hoped you'd come home earlier." The words sounded harder than he meant them to, but she didn't react.

"So did I," she said without looking at him. "It was a long day." She slumped in the chair and looked utterly beaten. He wanted to put his arms around her.

"Are you okay?"

"I'm alright. I just need a good night's sleep."

"Are you hungry? I got some steaks out."

"No. I'm just going to finish this and go to bed." Frederick was hungry to talk to her, but it didn't look promising. He got out a steak and began to fry it.

"Are you sure you don't want to eat?" he asked her again.

"Yes. I'm too tired." She finished the wine and set the glass on the table. "I'm going to bed," she said and went upstairs.

When the steak was done, he put it and some toast on a plate and took it up to her. She was undressing when he walked in the bedroom, and he saw the panties right away.

"When did you get those?"

JoAnn looked at them as if she had just discovered them herself. "Uh—today. You've been after me to get some and I was in Younkers and I saw these—."

"You wore them home?" He was still fixed in the doorway, the plate in one hand.

She felt her face going red.

"Of course I did. What does it look like?"

"I mean, from the store? You wore them right out of the store?"

"I don't know why you're so surprised. You've been after me to buy them."

"Sure, I know I have—but women don't wear underwear out of a store. Do they?"

"I don't know what women do, Frederick. I only know what I do, which, I can see by this interrogation, seems to have been a mistake."

"No, it's not. It just took me by surprise, that's all."

"Well, was it worth it—buying them? Do you approve?"

"Yes," he said.

She took a couple of steps toward him. "So, you like them?"

"Yeah, I like them a lot."

She put her arms around his neck. "Show me how much."

NINE

At about the same time that JoAnn Heinold was diverting her husband's interest from her new underwear, Miles Richards sat in a dark corner of Antonio's Lounge, discussing business with Roland Higgins, a dark, heavy-set man who knew nothing about antiques. They had met several nights before at a party thrown by a local rock band, and it was there that they discovered a mutual appreciation of Lime City's newest and most prestigious drug.

The band had provided most of the cocaine for the party, but Miles had generously contributed from his own dwindling supply—free samples of what he had come to Iowa to turn into a growth industry. Since he was a stranger, Roland had been wary of him, but he'd agreed to meet Miles at Antonio's where he felt less vulnerable.

"I'm accustomed to getting a little something up front," Miles was telling him.

Roland laughed. "Not around here, you ain't. Where was that?"

"Houston, mostly, and Miami."

"I don't know about fuckin' Houston, but I've done a little business in Florida and it was always cash at time of delivery."

"Well," Miles said smoothly, "it depends on who's doing the business—and, of course, the volume."

"Well, I'm doing the business, and I'll take all that you can get me—but it's cash on delivery." The words came out black and strong, just like the coffee he was drinking.

Miles leaned closer. "With an advance I could get more

product."

Roland could have laughed again, but instead his eyes scoured the room—a habit he had developed after serving two short terms for possession. "You're talking to the wrong guy," he said. The nervous thrum of his fingers on the table filled the silence between them.

Miles hesitated. He hadn't considered this response. Cocaine was hot in the Midwest and he thought these locals would be eager for it. Of course, he'd also assumed that they'd lack the sophistication of the big cities where he'd lived. He'd counted on a down payment that he could leverage into a substantial buy, and he wasn't getting anywhere.

"I'm sorry to hear that. Do you know anyone else who might be interested?"

"In giving you money before you deliver the goods? No way. We might be a bunch of hicks, but we ain't brain dead."

"There's always some risk with a product of this nature," Miles went on, "but the return improves with a certain volume."

Roland wasn't surprised by Miles' persistence. He was familiar with the curious impracticality of druggies, their preference for speculation over hard reality. He prided himself on not sharing it. "Why don't we just start with a trial-size order," he said. "If everything goes alright, we can go on to bigger things."

"It doesn't seem like much," Miles said. His disappointment was obvious.

"Eight thousand bucks seems like a lot to me, man."

II

Two hours later, Miles had his second business meeting of the night, this one with a young farmer who had also been drawn to the entrepreneurial possibilities of dealing drugs and to whom, Miles now knew, he had made an ill-considered delivery of a large quantity of amphetamines—on credit.

Miles had ignored the possibility that one of these farmers might actually try to rip him off and given Billy Meyers two large plastic bags, each containing five thousand pharmaceutical quality tablets. Billy was supposed to deliver the drugs to a dealer he knew in Minnesota and return with the money—Miles' money—the next day. But that day passed and then another and it became a week.

When Miles finally found him one night at Antonio's, the kid had nothing for him but an excuse.

"It's comin' man. I expect her back any time now. I been meanin' to call you."

"Her? Who is her?"

"The girl who made the delivery. I told you I had to lay it off. The pill business is down around here with all this interest in coke. You got any coke?"

"You're three days late."

"Hey, what can I do? I'm doin' the best that I can. Maybe she had car trouble." He talked loudly enough for others to hear. It was another reason for Miles to scowl.

"Car trouble?" he said, pushing his voice down to where he hoped the kid would take the hint. "For a week?" The kid looked away, bored with the hassle. Miles scanned the room, but no one was paying attention to them. "Where I come from this would be considered a serious breach of etiquette." He tried to make it sound as serious as he felt it was, but Billy didn't look worried.

"I ain't rippin' you off," the kid said. "It's just a little delay."

Miles took a hard look at Billy Meyers and did not like what he saw: a small, blonde, pimply kid whose foot danced restlessly under the table and who was much too skinny for this corn fed country.

"When?"

"Soon, man, I told you."

"When?"

"Day after tomorrow for sure." He still hadn't looked at Miles.

"That's too long."

"You wanted it for sure." He made it sound like it was Miles' fault.

Miles wanted to take him out to the car and stick the gun up his nose. "Okay. Day after tomorrow."

"I promise, man."

Miles hated that word.

III

After Billy left, Miles stayed at the lounge to have another

63

drink and think about how sick he was of this corn country. He was there because a friend in Lauderdale had told him how the small cities of the Midwest were just discovering coke and what a great market it was going to be. There was already an established network of dealers dealing grass and acid and pills, and he just had to plug into that. By buying the stuff right off the boat, he could bypass a lot of pockets and keep the mark-up for himself. He had made this trip to explore the possibilities and put together an investment package for a major buy.

The possibilities didn't disappoint him. The small city possessed a substantial community of young professionals—doctors, lawyers, business people—many of whom had used marijuana since their college days and were now eager to indulge in a drug whose notoriety and social status had already been established by the trendy patrons of Beverly Hills and Aspen.

Isolated by the sprawling distances of the country and bored by the claustrophobic winters, they were the most self-conscious and status-seeking group of people he had ever encountered outside of a gathering of black pimps. The exorbitant price and cerebral high of cocaine validated their use of it, and they quickly adopted the rituals of mirrors and locked bathroom doors into their over-dressed social gatherings while the police distracted the community with politically soothing busts of penny-ante marijuana dealers.

Miles had never been to Iowa before and he didn't like it when he got there, but he was willing to put up with the inconvenience if his business there allowed him to spend most of his time in Florida. The drug trade around Miami and Fort Lauderdale was prolific but also risky, especially for a man working alone. Iowa was the sticks, but it was safer than the labyrinthine treachery of South Florida where he had to worry about other people in the business as well as agents of the DEA who seemed to be planted everywhere. To cover his activities, he established himself as an antique dealer and had already purchased several pieces that he would take back to Florida in a U-Haul.

So far, he had failed to find anyone willing to invest in a large buy. The town had plenty of small dealers some of whom occasionally gathered on a cluster of barstools at Antonio's—intense, watchful birds who took turns flapping off to the bathroom or a car, then returned, wiping their noses and exuding an air of elevation.

Most of them were the peculiar graduates of the late 1960's or early '70s, kids from middle-class families who had gone off to college and become enmeshed in the shaggy ambience of the antiwar movement. The two principal myths of that period had been: one, everything about the war and the people that supported it were bad, and, two, everything about drugs, regardless of their possible harm or the questionable nature of their sources, was good.

They had remained at Kansas or Wisconsin or Iowa until their parents quit paying the tuition or they were no longer vulnerable to the draft. Afterwards, some of them had returned to Lime City with the only real skills they had acquired—using and selling drugs. Here they remained, psychically and socially arrested by the drugs and the paranoia that went with the business. Like adherents of an aging monastic order, they had taken unspoken vows to the communion of the high and the shabby, suspicious camaraderie with which they shared it.

Miles, himself, had grown up into this milieu in the northern suburbs of Chicago, and might have been swallowed by it if he hadn't been drafted into the army. There were plenty of drugs in the army, but there was also structure and order, which were generally antidotal to the zonked self-absorption of the chronic user—except, of course, in Vietnam, which he had been lucky enough to miss. But after he was discharged, he went back to the only business he had ever known.

He mustered out in Texas and spent some time in Houston before moving to Florida. Despite the abundance of drug smuggling and dealing that went on there, Miles' lack of contacts limited his activities to small, peripheral transactions. These provided an uncertain livelihood, which constrained him to a succession of mildewed apartments, most of which he shared with women who paid the rent.

Because of his good looks, women were always the cheapest and most available commodity in his life. When he needed a place to stay, he found a woman. If he needed clothes or a little seed money, he found a woman. He had bought the Cadillac on contract from a middle-aged Fort Lauderdale woman to whom he had never made a single payment.

As cocaine spread throughout the country, its importation into Florida from the Caribbean and beyond became a thriving industry. It was reported in the newspapers that it was impossible to find currency of any denomination in the Miami banking system that didn't bear traces of the drug.

Despite the money dealing could produce, Miles' career languished. Finally, in an attempt to ingratiate himself with a group of Cuban smugglers, he lied his way into a job driving a fast boat out to a freighter anchored off Ft. Lauderdale. Having never been in those waters, even in daylight, he became confused by the miasmic lights and wandered about, uncertain of which ship to approach, until he ran low on fuel and had to give it up.

The next day, appropriately frightened, he contacted the man who had hired him.

"You fucked up, man. We was countin' on that boat and when you didn't show up, we had to load more stuff on the other boats. It's a good thing we didn't lose nothin' or you'd be dead now, you dig?"

Miles nodded emphatically.

"And don't be tellin' people you can do somethin' that you can't—not these people, anyway."

Miles kept nodding, in relief as much as anything, as he moved toward the door. And then he was through it and almost running toward his car.

After that, he kept to himself, living in a succession of cheap apartments with a succession of women, dreaming of the big score that would put him on a canal in Lauderdale with the Bertram tied up in back.

IV

JoAnn slept fitfully until almost eight o'clock, when Frederick came in and woke her.

"God, I'm late," she said when she looked at the clock. Frederick sat on the bed and ran his hand over the sheet that covered her hips. He was happy with their lovemaking of the night before and hoped for an encouraging sign of more.

"You seemed so tired that I let you sleep in."

"I wish you hadn't," she said irritably. "Would you hand me my robe, please?"

"No," he teased.

"Frederick, I'm late."

"I'll call in and tell them you're sick. You can just hang around all day and take it easy."

"By myself, I suppose."

"I'll be around if you need me." There was conspiracy in his voice—and hope.

She longed to burrow back into the bed, but she knew all too well the expectations that last night had inspired in him. She felt used and worn out by sex. It was too painful to even think about the way Miles had treated her. And then she'd had to deflect Frederick's surprise at the underwear. She had planned to soak in the tub and then go quietly to bed, but she had carelessly worn the damned panties home and then there was nothing to do but satisfy him—if that were ever possible. And now he was hanging around like a homeless puppy when all she wanted was to be left alone.

"Frederick, I'd like to, but I've got to go in even if I am late. Would you call the office and tell them I'll be in around twelve? I'm going to take a bath."

"Sure," he said.

When he leaned to kiss her, she could smell the familiar odor of diesel fuel on his clothes.

"You smell like a tractor—and you need a shave," she told him.

"I'll change clothes and shave if you stay home."

"Go," she said and pointed at the door. He went into the bathroom and began to fill the tub. When JoAnn lowered her body into the water, she found that he had gotten the temperature just right and the bubbles rose luxuriously to her chin.

Frederick had gone downstairs to clean up the small batch of dishes that had accumulated and make a fresh pot of coffee. When he had finished, he made some toast and carried it and a mug of coffee up the stairs. The bathroom door was ajar, but he knocked anyway.

"Yes?" Her reply was tinged with annoyance.

He took the tray in and sat it on the edge of the tub. JoAnn's eyes were closed in pleasure and her body relaxed and open as he had not seen it for a long time. The heat of the water had dissipated most of the bubbles and revealed her long body, now turning pink from the warmth of the water. Her breasts were modest, each sloping gracefully to a purplish nipple. Below those were the pale striations of her stretch marks and below those the assertive darkness of her pubic hair. All of these—even the stretch marks—were desirable to him. No other woman interested him in the least.

She slowly opened her eyes and saw the tray. "Thanks," she said in genuine appreciation. She saw how he was looking at her and she reached and took his hand and pulled him to her for a kiss. "I'll try to get home early," she said.

TEN

Eldon Mathews stood in the bed of his pickup, topping off the two big fuel tanks he carried there and wishing that his wife wasn't such a goddamned sour puss. A few minutes before he had gone into the house to fill his thermos and found her in the kitchen in her bathrobe. Busy as he was finishing up his field work, he had seen little of her the past two days. Not that it really mattered much. They had been married over twenty years and the sex had run out so long ago that Eldon couldn't remember when it had ever amounted to anything.

But, he'd been working steady for days with only his crew for company and finding her unexpectedly like that had got him excited. She had her hair pulled up like she always did when she took a bath, and he could smell whatever it was that she put in the bath water. He had come up behind and put his arms around her and ground his two-day beard against her neck.

"Eldon."

"What, Honey?" He had not called her Honey since the last time he'd tried this, three weeks before.

"I just had my bath." There was a chilled remoteness to her words that she did not have to practice.

"I know you did. I can smell it on you." To emphasize its effect on him, Eldon moved his groin slowly against her hips. His massive forearms trapped her against him but she did not struggle. Instead, she executed what appeared to be the slightest contraction of every molecule in her body, a kinetic shrinkage that compacted, closed, and sent without utterance of a single word an unmistakable message: leave me alone.

Eldon had heard it before—many times—enough to know that further entreaties would be fruitless. He released her and turned away, then turned again.

"Goddamn it! I work like a dog and what do I get for it? Nothin'! You act like I had scours or somethin'." Without the slightest interest in his presence, she began to rinse the coffee maker at the sink. "Sherry?"

"I'm not in the mood, Eldon."

"What the fuck is new?" he offered and walked out.

From the first days of their marriage Sherry had learned to fear and then hate Eldon's preference for pawing her over all other forms of communication. Because of his size and abrasive personality, intimidation came easily to him, and he used it to the exclusion of other social skills. Like his two hundred and fifty pound body, his talk was overbearing and excessive. What Eldon said wasn't important to him—only that he was talking and others were listening.

They had married in 1959 after a short, prophetic courtship, during which she barely held him off in the front seat of his father's Chevrolet. According to the chatter of the other girls in school, most, if not all, boys acted like Eldon did. It may have explained his behavior, but it didn't reduce the desperation she felt when locked in his grasp.

He was the son of a farmer and her father was a farmer, so the basic eligibility requirements were covered. The other boys might occasionally talk about something else, like sports, but not Eldon. The only thing he was interested in was farming and her father liked that. Sherry had few ideas herself about how to choose a mate, and her father's approval of her suitor seemed to be all the excuse she needed to say yes when he asked her to marry him.

On their wedding night in a Minneapolis hotel room, Eldon drank too much while she could not seem to drink enough, and he tore off the veneer of civility he had managed through their engagement like a piece of tissue paper. Panicked by the realization that the beast was loose and there was no one to save her, she curled reflexively into a clenched, fetal conformation that he pried open like an oyster.

From that night on their connubial relations deteriorated into a series of sporadic sexual raids which produced two children and a thousand psychic scars. After his initial puzzlement, Eldon dismissed his wife's reluctance as a peculiar female oddness, which somehow confused pain and unpleasantness with one of life's great—if short-lived—pleasures.

Fortunately, as a husband he had his rights and he claimed them often in the earlier years. If getting his needs met required a little physical parrying and conquest, then that was all right, too. Lying beneath his grunting bulk, her wrists trapped in his massive hands, Sherry tried to distract herself with fantasies of emasculating murder.

Eventually, she learned that her resistance only aroused him, and when she stopped trying to push him away and ceded nothing but cold indifference, his ardor shrank away. Disgusted, he would roll off her body and lie there, complaining about her remoteness, but also wondering to himself why he could no longer sustain what had once come so easily.

Was Sherry responsible for this loss of manhood or was it departing on its own? Naturally he blamed her, but the doubts hung around, a dilemma he almost explored one night with a prostitute on a Kansas City street corner. But just as he was concluding negotiations, he thought better of it. What if it was him and not Sherry? Did he want to know?

II

When he finished filling the tanks, Eldon headed the truck toward a field near the river that Otto VerHelst was plowing for him. Otto was a tough old bird who could spend an entire day driving the big Steiger tractor and never complain—unlike some of the other whiners who worked for Eldon. The old man had owned his own hundred and twenty acres for as long as Eldon could remember, somehow holding onto it despite the prodigious drunks which had overcome him over the years and for which he was chiefly known.

Otto had grown up on the same farm that he now owned, a mild Lutheran boy who forswore drink and, as far as anybody knew, the other temptations of the flesh. When the Great Depression set in, his father, like many others, found he had too many mouths to feed and set Otto, only fifteen, off on the road to fend for himself. He wandered to the Dakotas and Montana to work the wheat harvests and even tried ranching, but eventually found himself in Seattle, where he enlisted in the United States Navy.

The Navy took him to Hawaii and the Philippines and eventually to China, where he served on a gunboat on the Yangtze River in the years just before World War II. Once in the Navy, he did begin to drink and smoke although his stringent upbringing restrained him for a time from the debaucheries of his shipmates—until he arrived in China where his long delay from the pleasures of the flesh amplified his discovery of them. He exploded amongst the brothels, fighting and fornicating and, most of all, drinking his way across a landscape of oriental dissolution.

Not until 1945 did he escape the long war in which he had been trapped and come home to take over his father's farm. Others were returning from the war, too, and there were fetes and ceremonies to celebrate their homecoming, but Otto wanted only to be left alone. He was sick of war and sick of the Navy and the land began to heal him.

He had missed out on that part of his life, when men usually find and marry their mates, but family and old friends began to suggest women that he might meet and possibly wed, for there was an unchallenged belief—among men as well as women—that a wife improved a man and made his life happier. He might even have believed it himself, for less than two years after he mustered out he wed Leona Fritz, a woman from much the same background as his. Leona was not pretty, but she knew every bit of farming and they worked the land and raised livestock and began a family together.

In the ten years that followed, Otto tilled his fields and raised his children in an unbroken routine of reasonableness and responsibility. And then, one afternoon, without apparent provocation, after he had hauled a load of corn into the Rock Falls elevator, he did not come home—for four days. His bender took him across four counties, one of them in Minnesota. As far as anyone knew, he did nothing but drink, sleeping only when he couldn't go on, sometimes in his car, sometimes with his head on a bar. He quit only after he had run out of money.

No one, including Leona, had ever seen this particular Otto VerHelst. People who had known him for decades were disbelieving at first, but he convinced them the next time he went off and the time after that. None were more distressed about this incarnation than his wife. She had married one man, but now occasionally had to share her life with another—and one that she did not like.

Over the years, the unpredictability and severity of these occurrences increasingly disturbed her until Leona was eventually rendered permanently and nervously suspicious—and vengeful.

By the time Otto was in his sixties, she had taken to pursuing him wherever the drinking led, eventually capturing him, then hauling him to the alcoholic treatment center in Forest City. There, in what Leona considered just punishment, he was enrolled in group therapy sessions where younger patients babbled on about the impossible complexities of the present while Otto dreamed of the slippery Asian bodies of his past. Many people considered his excursions regrettable but harmless and felt that Leona's measures were excessive. But for her, they were never enough.

When he wasn't drinking, Otto was still considered one of the steadiest, hard-working men that could be found, which is why every year Eldon hired him to help out during the planting and harvest seasons.

"That old man can work," he'd tell any of his men in earshot, although they never seemed to take the hint. Not once did Otto take a drink or let him down, a claim that couldn't be made by many of the men that Eldon had hired over the years. Some of them had quit after only a day or two, preferring to hang out in the tavern rather than suffer the abuse he carelessly spilled about him.

The field where Otto was plowing bordered the Lime Rock River just north of Frederick Heinold's pasture. Until now it had been forty acres of pasture, scattered with mature oak and maple trees. But now that there was almost no tillable land left to buy, Eldon—like others—began to look at pasture that could be converted to cropland. When the price of an acre of tillable dirt reached twenty-five hundred dollars, he decided to take action.

He hired a D-7 Caterpillar tractor to bulldoze the trees and shrubs into huge piles of slaughtered wood, and put his men to work burning them. Because the wood was green, they were forced to spread used tires on it, along with hundreds of gallons of diesel fuel. Even then it burned reluctantly. In the warm summer evenings the pitchy amber flames guttered under the thick smoke, and the mingled stink of sour wood and burning rubber hung in the air so that Frederick Heinold could smell it in his sleep. In a month of brutal work the whole forty was cleared, and now Otto was ripping the topsoil, preparing it to be planted the following spring.

Eldon pulled into the field and stopped, puzzled that he couldn't see the tractor. The plowing wasn't finished, and he hadn't passed the old man on the road, so where was he? Otto seemed to have disappeared along with a ninety thousand dollar tractor. Eldon reached for the roll of antacids in the glove compartment.

This just wasn't like the old man. He put the truck in four-wheel drive and started slowly across the plowed ground. When he got to the last freshly turned furrow, he turned and followed it down toward the fence that separated the field from Frederick's land. Long before he got there, he could see the hole.

He stopped near the fence and shut off the truck's engine and listened. Somewhere distant in the obscuring woods he could hear the tractor laboring in low gear. He got out and began to walk toward the sound, stumbling on the torn roots and pieces of rock embedded in the newly plowed earth. Jesus, he thought, as he picked up the pace, where are you old man? It looked like it could be headed toward the river. He was suddenly afraid and breathing hard.

He had followed the plowed trail some seventy yards into pasture when he came upon the big tractor, its nose jammed against the trunk of a huge, unyielding oak. The transmission was locked in low gear and all four of the huge rubber tires humped and smoked against the underlying rock they had excavated.

Carefully, Eldon stepped between the dangerous wheels and climbed the metal ladder to the cab. Through the window he could see Otto slumped over the steering wheel. He opened the door and reached across the old man and switched off the ignition, then he eased him back into the seat. Otto slumped there, his head back a little, his eyes staring at nothing.

Eldon had never been alone with someone who might be

dead, as he suspected Otto was, and he wasn't quite sure what to do. He felt like he shouldn't just leave him until help arrived. What if he was just a little bit dead, waiting for someone to revive him and bring him back to life? The only person available was Eldon.

"Goddamn it, Otto!" he said aloud. "Why couldn't you do this somewhere else?"

As carefully as he could, he got the old man under the arms and pulled him out of the cab and down the ladder. He stretched him out on the ground on his back, then knelt and tried to find a pulse. His hand was shaking pretty badly, so he couldn't tell if he felt something or not. Otto's mouth was open and Eldon put his ear next to it and listened. He could hear labored breathing but he thought maybe it was his own.

The year before he'd had to take a Red Cross course in order to get his certification to apply herbicides, and now it reminded him that Otto might require a combination of mouth-to-mouth breathing and chest massage. The trouble was, he couldn't recall anything about the routine—except that doing it wrong could damage the person you were doing it to. Now, he regretted having to take the goddamned course which only burdened a man in a situation like this to do something long after he'd forgotten what.

As he knelt beside the old man, he became increasingly certain that Otto was irretrievably dead and probably had been before he even got there. Maybe it would be better if he didn't do anything. Somewhere he'd read that it wasn't good to revive people who had been dead too long. They ended up in a coma that could go on for years with tubes sticking out of their arms. But what if people asked him why he didn't do something? He looked at the old man's eyes, which wasn't easy. There wasn't any message there.

The corners of Otto's mouth were stained with tobacco juice, which pretty much ruled out the mouth-to-mouth part. That left massage. Now, how did that go? He swung one leg over the body so that he was straddling it, his shoulders over Otto's chest. The body beneath him suddenly seemed terribly small and frail.

Suppose they did an autopsy afterwards and found that the cause of death was crushed ribs and maybe a collapsed heart, all inflicted by the clumsy interference of the man who had tried to save him? He'd read where even doctors wouldn't help people at accidents for fear of getting sued, so what the hell was he doin'?

As he looked down at the sinking face, he knew that if he didn't do something right now, there wasn't any sense in doing anything at all—which didn't sound like a bad idea. Aw, fuck it, he thought. Leona ain't gonna sue me even if I do kill the old bastard.

He placed the palms of his hands on Otto's chest where he thought he was supposed to and pushed. There was a soft almost mushy give that didn't feel right. There was supposed to be a firm tympanic resistance, like the bottom of an empty can being pushed in. He moved his hands a little higher and gave a sharper thrust which produced the unmistakable sound of cracking bone.

"That's enough of that," he said getting to his feet. "The old fucker can die on his own without any help from me." He walked back to the pickup and got on the radio. "This is Top Dog calling Base. Come in Base."

He waited a few seconds, but Sherry did not reply. Probably yakkin' on the phone or watchin' a soap opera, he thought. Sometimes he thought she ignored his calls even when she wasn't busy. She'd be sorry when she found out that poor old Otto was lying out here, needing help.

"Base to Top Dog—over." It was Sherry.

"I didn't interrupt your nap, did I?"

"I was out checking the dryers."

Sure, he thought, and I was changin' my tampon. "You need to call an ambulance. I think Otto's had a heart attack or somethin'."

"Heart attack? Who?"

"Otto. Otto VerHelst."

"Oh, Otto. Is he okay?"

Now, why in hell did she ask him that? Others were undoubtedly listening in on this channel like they usually did, so he didn't want to come right out and say he thought Otto was dead.

"Ah—no, he ain't so good."

"Where is he?"

"At that field I'm clearin' by the river. You know how to tell the ambulance to get here?"

"I think so."

"Just tell them to come straight west from the house and take a right at the T. You got that?"

"A right at the T. Okay." She clicked off.

Eldon dug a pouch of Beech-Nut out of the glove box and scooped himself a chew. Here he sat with his finger up his ass while his men did who knew what. Clyde might even run out of fuel and it would be Eldon's goddamned fault because he was messin' around with this.

And it was hard to tell how long it might take an ambulance to get there. Lime City was twenty miles away and the dumb bastards had a way of getting lost on the country roads and wandering around while some poor unfortunate expired.

He had often told Sherry, "If I get hurt, goddamn it, load me in the pickup and drive me to the hospital. Don't wait for those dumb asses to show up." Goddamn it, he thought, maybe that's what I should do. Throw Otto in the back and haul ass for the hospital. But he decided to wait for the ambulance.

As it turned out, several people—including Eldon's hired man, Clyde—had monitored his brief conversation with Sherry. Clyde thought about running over there, as much as for a break in the routine as anything, but he figured the boss would just chew his butt, so he stayed where he was.

The transmission had also been heard by others who lived beyond the radio's effective range so it had been garbled to one degree or another. A farmer who lived almost ten miles to the south came in for lunch and told his wife that he'd just heard that Eldon Mathews had a heart attack. A month later, in a Lime City hardware store, another man walked up to Eldon and told him, "I thought you was dead."

It was close to an hour later when he heard the siren keening urgently. He got out of the truck and waited expectantly until it suddenly appeared, siren screaming, lights flashing, flying down the road. But rather than pull into the field, it rushed past and down the road and—just like that—disappeared from sight.

"What the hell?" he said in disbelief. "Well, I'll be dipped in shit." He picked up the radio, again. "This is Top Dog to anybody. Come in."

"Eldon, this is Jerry Weaver. What's up?"

"Jerry, I'm sittin' here in that forty acres I just cleared over by the river with a—a—sick man, waitin' for a goddamned ambulance that's runnin' up and down the roads like a chicken with its head cut off."

"Who's sick?"

"Otto VerHelst."

"Is he drinking?"

"Not today, Jerry."

"Well thank God for that. Do you want me to come over?"

"Naw. I just want you to keep an eye out for—" Suddenly the ambulance reappeared, roaring along in the opposite direction. "Never mind, Jerry! I got to run this idiot down."

Eldon tore off across the field and down the road after it. The big wake of dust the ambulance threw up made it easy to spot but how the hell was he going to stop it? He couldn't see shit through all that dust, and it was dangerous to pass.

Eldon followed along behind for a while, until he realized that the driver was never going to see him through the cloud. "Fuck this," he said and bore grimly through the blinding grit until he drew alongside the surprised driver. Even then it took some high speed arm waving to get him to pull over.

When they got back to the field, one of the attendants listened through his stethoscope for a heartbeat. "It's too late," he said standing up. "From the look of him I'd say he's been gone for a while."

"Yeah. That's what I thought, too," Eldon said. "Poor old guy." Just before the ambulance attendant covered him up, Eldon could see that Otto's eyes were still open, but they looked dead, now, clearly dead. Why didn't he see that before? The old man seemed so much smaller than he could ever remember him. He felt like he should say something. "He was a hell of a worker," he said.

III

JoAnn had gotten to her office just after noon and spent an unenthusiastic hour trying to find a new listing to show her biggest prospect. She had already shown him half dozen houses, but the more he looked, the more uncertain he seemed to become. Unfortunately, real estate wasn't the problem that preoccupied her, though. That problem was someone called Miles Richards. She hoped that he would call so she could tell him off, but he hadn't bothered.

Earlier, while she had soaked in the tub and Frederick had waited on her, her mind kept returning to Miles. He had made such an elaborate effort to attract her—and then to treat her like that. Why? She thought about what she would say to him, if she got the chance, especially the last line—get lost. But he had to call before she could get her revenge.

When she got dressed for work, she fished her dowdiest bra and panties out of a drawer and put them on, not that he was going to see them anyway. She was just declaring, if only to herself, that she wouldn't allow anyone to treat her that way.

Once back in the office, she struggled to get her mind on work. As she had spent more afternoons with Miles, her desire to sell houses had dwindled. And then, suddenly, he was gone, probably forever, leaving her restless and unsatisfied. All of the unspoken promises, the newness, even the taboos she had broken with him, had brought a whole new unimagined life that she didn't even realize she'd miss—until he took them away.

But she needed to ignore those feelings and concentrate on work. She needed to get her old life back.

IV

Miles was making a rent payment to the young cocktail waitress in whose apartment he had spent the night. He had drunk the night away at Antonio's, running his Fort Lauderdale line on anyone who would listen, which pretty much winnowed down to the waitress. When she got off at one, they went to her place and did some coke. They finished off the night in bed together.

When he woke around one in the afternoon, his mouth and mood were both sour. He had drunk too much, something he usually tried to avoid. The only thing he wanted to do was go back to sleep for a few hours, but his benefactor had other ideas. She fondled him into an erection and had her way.

Miles preferred to sleep ten or twelve hour stretches without even the breathing of another person to disturb him, and he would have checked back into the motel were his funds not so low.

That kid had better come through with the money, he

thought bitterly. If he didn't, Miles was going to have to show him that he meant business, that he was screwing with the wrong guy. It was all unnecessary and stupid, and he was beginning to really dislike Billy Meyers.

V

Frederick had been hard at work on his corn when he heard Eldon's call for the ambulance. Otto VerHelst had been an unvarying feature of his life, a presence immune to illness, maybe even exempt from death. It was impossible to think of him lying in a field, unable to get up.

Most of the old-timers like Otto had sold their farms or left them to sons, and moved into houses in town or one of the numerous nursing homes that had been built to receive them. For decades, they had been standard fixtures of the Rock Falls Tavern where they went to socialize.

With thumbs latched into the chest pockets of their Osh Kosh overalls, they had lounged sagely in the scuffed oak chairs that lined one wall, rolling their own from cans of Prince Albert or spitting dollops of chewed Copenhagen into the stained cuspidors.

These men were walking testaments to a big chunk of the twentieth century, and it had been wonderful to listen to their stories, which they loved to recite to one another. It was like a loosely organized quilting bee, except that the panels were anecdotes and stories instead of cloth. But now, the old men and the chairs were gone, and all that remained were memories and the indomitable Otto—and now he was down.

When he went in to eat lunch, he called Eldon on the phone. Sherry answered. "He was dead by the time Eldon found him," she told him. "He's over fixing your fence right now."

"My fence?"

"Yes. After he passed away, he somehow managed to put Eldon's tractor down into your woods."

Although he knew that Eldon would take care of things, Frederick drove over anyway. When he got there, Eldon and Clyde had just finished stretching new wire across the hole.

"Well, Freddy. The old man finally give out on us," Eldon said.

"Sherry just told me."

"I tried pumpin' his heart to git it restarted but it was too late. The ambulance driver thought maybe he was gone even before he went through the fence." Frederick looked over into the pasture where the ripped furrows disappeared into the trees. "She hung up on a big tree down there or she woulda gone into the river."

Frederick walked over to the silent tractor. "It looks okay," he said.

"Just that little dent in the front, and ten or twelve hours wore off the tires. I'm lucky she didn't catch fire."

"Was it a heart attack?"

"That's what the ambulance driver thought. It took him quick. He had his eyes wide open and this look on his face like he was trying to catch his breath." There was an odd, monotonic quality to Eldon's voice that caused Frederick to turn from the tractor and look at him. "He didn't manage to get her shut down, but I'll bet he was tryin'. He always went like a son-of-a-bitch, you know, and I used to kid him about it. The bigger the tractor, the better he liked it. After fartin' around behind a team of horses all those years, he liked to just eat a field up with a big tractor, so I made sure he always got the biggest one. I guess I'm lucky he didn't really wreck it good, although you know how that goes. Maybe the engine or tranny's got damage I can't see, and it won't show up until the warranty won't cover it. Goddamn it, I hope not," he said, turning from the fence to confront the tractor with this new threat. "I got ninety-three thousand in the son-of-a-bitch!"

Frederick started toward his truck. "Looks like you got things under control," he said. "I probably better get back to work."

"Yeah, okay Frederick. We almost got her patched up. I didn't think you had any cows down here but I thought I'd better get her fixed right away since it was my man and all, even though—"

"I appreciate it, Eldon. See ya." Frederick got in the truck and drove back across the field.

"What an oddball," Eldon said. "He didn't seem to care about the old man at all."

ELEVEN

JoAnn did her best to distract herself by browsing through a couple of women's clothing shops, but it didn't help. The clothes, especially the lingerie, only made her think thoughts she shouldn't be thinking. When she got back to the office, there were no calls and her mood drifted even lower. She had expected Frederick to at least call as he usually did after they had reestablished connubial rapport, but apparently he was too busy for her, too.

She sat behind the desk and scanned the furnishings which she had so carefully collected and arranged over her short career: the requisite framed recognitions and certificates, several photos of her which had appeared in the newspaper, two overstuffed chairs, two reproduced paintings in the European style. On the desk were various knick-knacks and a small, framed photo of Frederick looking unnatural in an improbable coat and tie.

She had spent almost two years assembling the ambience of success, and now she could not draw a particle of emotional sustenance from it. At this moment, nothing in her life had any significance: not her work nor her success, certainly not her marriage. She longed for the phone to ring to break this spell of desperate introspection, but it would not, and its silence only magnified the hollowness that filled her. After a while, there was nothing to do but get up and leave.

II

When JoAnn got to the farm, Frederick was not there. His

old truck sat near the bins, so overloaded with corn that it appeared to be sinking into the ground. It symbolized the enormous load that he was carrying through this harvest, and a part of her suddenly felt for him. Still, it was his stubbornness that had gotten him into this predicament. As far as she was concerned, if he'd just bought the right equipment and hired some help, he'd be finished by now and happy that he'd taken on the extra acres. If she had helped him more, she'd just be giving in to his stubbornness.

Of course the man he'd hired had turned out to be trouble. It was ridiculous to hire someone with no experience just to save a few dollars. He had probably put him to work without giving him enough instructions. She remembered how he had done just that with her during their first harvest together, and how he'd made those nasty faces when she didn't do something fast enough or when she killed the engine on the tractor—as if everyone was born with an ability to instantly understand a machine they had never operated before. That's how all these farmers were, though. They grew up working on equipment of one kind or another and assumed that everyone else had too.

The kitchen smelled of burnt coffee. As usual, Frederick had left it on the warmer and the remains had evaporated down to a quarter-inch of bituminous syrup. Washed dishes were stacked next to the sink, evidence that he was getting along without her. Even though she had overseen its remodeling and decoration, the kitchen—like everything else on the farm—belonged more to Frederick than her. And it always would.

Traditionally, the kitchen was the most important room in a farmhouse. It, not the living or dining rooms, was the gathering place, the warmest and most lived in room. It was also the undisputed domain of the wife, the place where she made and maintained her reputation.

Although the food was never fancy, it was tasty and always served in generous quantities. In the summer a farm wife planted and tended a big garden from which she harvested tomatoes, corn, squash, cabbage, potatoes, beans, beets, strawberries and more for her table. Because of her skills in these things, she was appreciated, even prized. She lived with a palpable sense of involvement and belonging. Her estrangement from all of these elements was just another reason why JoAnn didn't fit in.

These thoughts only deepened her sense of alienation. If she didn't belong here, where did she belong? She was separated and drifting from her life and anchored by nothing—certainly not by her husband who longed for her to be what she could never be. Perhaps what Miles had told her was true, that she was living a life that was bad for her because it had nothing to do with her.

"There's a real world out there, and you need to live in it," he had told her. "You're not a hick like these people. You've got style, you're ambitious. You want more out of life than this, don't you? I'll bet that you don't have one friend who's a farmer."

She had actually felt something like a thrill when he said it because it explained her restless dissatisfactions and suggested possibilities that she had never thought of. More than anyone she knew, Miles lived on the edge of life, an agile surfer cutting along the face of uncertainty, seemingly indifferent to the everyday worries that other people had. But did she want to live like that? Could she? At this moment she didn't even know where he was or if she would ever see him again.

III

Frederick had put in a bad afternoon, which had stretched into a dismal evening. He had forgotten to order fresh diesel for his big storage tank and ended up pumping fuel too near its bottom where water and other impurities collected. In the afternoon the engine began to sputter and lose power. Finally it died completely and he knew that the fuel filter was plugged. He needed to replace it with a new one, but that would have meant knocking off and driving into Lime City to buy one. Instead, he decided to flush this one with fresh fuel and hope it would get him through the rest of the day.

Now, in the darkness, with only the light from a flashlight, he had removed the filter for the third time. His clothes were soaked and slick with fuel and he felt a little sick from the penetrating fumes. And he was mad. Mad at himself, mad at the goddamned equipment, and mad at JoAnn who, it was clear, no longer gave a damn for this farm or him. Tired of the futility, he threw the filter as far as he could out into the darkness.

When he got to the house, it was only nine, but when he went upstairs, JoAnn was already asleep. Just great, he thought. He went back down to the kitchen and got the dishwashing detergent from under the sink and scrubbed off as much of the diesel as he could. He looked like hell but he didn't care. He needed something to drink and a little company. He figured he might find it in Rock Falls.

The Falls Tavern was something of a landmark, even if nobody thought of it as one. As a matter of fact, when a group of local citizens put together a history of the little town, they left it out completely. During the summer the tavern did a good business with people who came out to the country to enjoy the beauty of the Lime Rock River, which flowed through the town, and in the winter it was frequented by snowmobilers who used the frozen river as a cross-country trail. But its mainstays were farmers, like Frederick, who enjoyed being able to go there right out of the field.

When he walked in, there were only four customers—about right for a weeknight—and, of course, Betty Petrowiak, the barmaid who had worked there for years.

"Why, hello Frederick. Ain't seen you around her for a while."

"I've been pretty busy, Betty."

"Ain't everybody. Sure something about Otto, wasn't it?"

"Yeah, it sure was."

"It musta been pretty terrible to find him like that."

"I imagine it was." He was looking over the bottles arrayed on the back bar, deciding what to drink. He wanted something more than beer.

"Did you see him?"

"Yeah. I went over there."

"What'd he look like?"

"A little shook, maybe, but mostly just the same."

"No, Frederick. I meant Otto."

"Oh. No, I didn't see him. They'd taken him away by the time I got there." He could see the disappointment in her face. Besides her duties as dispenser of drink, Betty was an enthusiastic gossip, and death was a prized topic. She could talk for hours about an illness or a divorce, but a death could provide conversation for days, even weeks. Especially one with a little drama—like Otto's.

"I heard that his eyes were wide open—and his hands were on the wheel like he was still drivin'."

"Well, I didn't see him, so I couldn't say. How about a

bourbon with a little water." Betty disengaged and began to mix his drink. Maybe it wasn't a good idea to come here on the same day that Otto died, he thought. She was capable of overwhelming the place with morbidity, and morbidity wasn't what he was looking for.

"Here you go." He hadn't drunk whisky for a long time and the sharp bite felt good.

"How's JoAnn?" she asked.

"Good," he said as neutrally as he could. He raised the glass, again, hoping that she'd change the subject or go away.

"I ain't hardly seen her since she started working in Lime City."

Me neither, he thought, and set the empty glass on the bar. "That hit the spot. I think I'll have another one."

"Comin' up," she said, and he could see that for the moment the business side of her had pushed aside the gossip. Betty always poured a little extra booze in the first drink, a practice, which annoyed the frugal sensibilities of Otis Crawford, the man who owned the place.

"You're supposed to make 'em all the same," he scolded whenever he caught her doing it. "Right to the white line and no more."

"A primed pump gives more water," she replied and went on doing it her way. Betty knew it was good for business, which was more than Otis had ever been able to figure out. She knew she'd cut back on the drinks she made after that first one—and if the customer kept drinking, she'd taper off even more. It was an art with Betty, and it was the rare person who ever noticed.

Otis would grumble that he should fire her, but everyone knew that he never would. He'd come back to Rock Falls after doing his time in the military and bought the place, but he—and everyone else—quickly discovered that he wasn't cut out to own a bar. If only one customer were in the place he'd complain that business was terrible, but if there were two, he'd complain that he was too busy. For years he'd tried to sell it, but insisted on asking so much that there was no way anyone would buy it. Betty ran the place as if it were her own, which left Otis with little to do but complain and play pitch with the customers.

Tonight, the Falls Tavern was a little short on joviality, but it still had the advantage of being a short, safe drive home, always an important consideration for a man interested in drinking. Frederick hadn't decided to get drunk, but neither had he decided not to. After he finished the second bourbon, he decided not to decide on anything. It was nice just to be there away from the noisy combine, listening to talk and the thump of the old jukebox.

After an hour, somebody suggested a game of blackjack and—though Betty didn't care much for the idea—she got a worn deck of cards from behind the cash register. They played for quarters past one o'clock when Betty kicked them out and closed up. By then, Frederick glowed with whisky and didn't want to stop. He would have run the night clear into dawn, but there was no one to run with, so he headed for home.

In the western sky a half-eaten moon threw light over the empty landscape. He had always found the moon a benign, even pleasant presence in the sky. He thought about all the nights he had stood under its light, all the moments of his life it had presided over. It always touched him most when he was alone, yet it never made him feel lonely. He couldn't see a single light working in a field anywhere. Of course not. They were finished and asleep in their beds like he should have been.

But the whisky and the pleasantness of the past few hours had dissipated his worries and at this moment he truly loved his life. Sure he was having problems, but they had been created by the extra land he rented—by the challenge he'd made for himself. He had taken his own risks and even if he got beat up some it was okay, because it was what he wanted to do.

The rest of the world could punch a time clock if it wanted to, but not him. It wasn't in him and it never would be. These were beautiful crops that he was harvesting and he was going to make some money—maybe enough to get JoAnn the fur coat she was always talking about—and maybe enough to take her back to the Virgin Islands. She'd love that.

It was in this state of well-being that he climbed the stairs to their bedroom. He left his clothes lying on the bedroom floor as he stripped them off and crawled carefully into bed. JoAnn was on her side with her back to him, wearing a favorite flannel nightgown to which she would soon add a pair of socks. But it wouldn't have mattered if she'd been wearing a diving bell—he was in the mood and her body exuded an inviting warmth.

Slowly, cautiously, he ran his hand down her leg until it came to the hem of the gown. Then, just as slowly, he slid it under the fabric and back up until it rested on the inside of her thigh. He listened closely for a telltale change in her breathing, but it was steady—restful.

He knew better than to do what he was thinking of doing, and he would not have even thought about it had he not been drinking. But he had been drinking—and she was lying there, warm and smelling sweetly of the bath she'd taken.

His fingers traversed the scant inches to the thicket of hair between her thighs and began to move in small delicate strokes. After a few seconds her breath quickened as her body responded, even though she was still asleep. Then, she murmured as she did when aroused and turned onto her back.

As she did, her thighs opened, a movement which Frederick's intoxicated libido took to mean that all was well: she was not only available, but inviting him to continue. Encouraged, he gently increased the pressure of his fingers, kneading the moist softness until she began to moan. And then she turned for him and was no longer asleep.

IV

If JoAnn's mind could have established itself in that moment when she emerged from sleep into passion she would have been furious, but in fact her body had insurrected to Frederick's caresses and wanted urgently for him not to stop. Even after they were finished and she lay half asleep and listened to him begin to snore, her anger did not reassert itself over the exhausted languor that she felt. In seconds she, too, fell deeply asleep.

It was a different story in the morning when she woke to the forbidden smell of diesel fuel in her sheets. Frederick had, of course, already abandoned her for his true mistress and gone out to work. Once again she had been used and abandoned. Furious, she tore the bedding from the bed and threw it down the stairs.

V

As JoAnn was throwing her tantrum, Frederick was finishing his chores. The bourbon had left him a bit of a headache, but otherwise he felt terrific. There was no tonic quite like the one he'd enjoyed with JoAnn when he got home. He had taken a chance there, but it had paid off. Before they were finished, there was no doubt that she wasn't angry with him. On the contrary, it might have broken the ice between them. He hoped so. He was tired of the fighting. Sex had worked before and he hoped it had again.

He came in around seven-thirty and started to fry some eggs and bacon. He tried to keep the noise down so that he wouldn't wake her. He wanted her to sleep in even though he would be heading for Lime City right after he had a bite to eat. Maybe she'd still be there when he got back, he hoped.

JoAnn was not asleep, but taking another bath in an effort to rid herself of the lingering odor of fuel. Usually a bath relaxed her, but not this morning. The longer she steeped in the hot water, the angrier she became—and then she heard him moving about in the kitchen.

He was just finishing his breakfast when she came through the doorway. "What the hell was the idea of coming home in the middle of the night and—and—and raping me!"

"What?"

"You heard me, you son-of-a-bitch! You come sneaking into my bed and fuck me while I'm asleep!"

"Rape? I didn't rape you! I had a few drinks and I started fooling around! You acted like you liked it!"

"Did you bother to ask me if I was even interested?"

"Well, no. I—"

"That's right. And the reason that you didn't ask is because you knew I'd say no!"

"Hey, we're supposed to be married. I didn't know that I had to get written permission!"

"Married? Do you call this married?"

"You know, you're right, JoAnn. Any resemblance between this and an actual marriage is purely coincidental!"

"Oh, you're married alright—to this farm!"

"If you weren't so goddamned busy running around in town all day and give me a hand, I wouldn't have to be married to it!"

"My job is just as important as yours!"

"Selling houses never did and never will take twenty-four hours a day, and you know it!"

"You have no idea what I do with my time!"

"That's for goddamned sure, but you sure as hell aren't spending all that time selling houses!"

"And what's that supposed to mean?"

"It means that you could spend more time helping me out!"

"This farm is not going to be my life like it is yours! I told you that before we got married!"

"What about me, JoAnn? Am I a part of your life? Am I a part of any of it?"

"I have given plenty of my life to you—and to this farm—even when I didn't want to, but now that I've found something that I love doing, you can't stand it!"

"That's not true. I'm happy for you—but I need to see more of you! I need you."

"You don't need me, you need a driver—and someone to screw when you feel like it!" Even as she spoke, she knew she'd gone too far. That's not how he felt about her and she knew it, but it was too late.

Frederick paused as if she'd slapped him, and when he spoke it was with a coldness she hadn't heard before. "Well, what else do you have to offer? You can't cook and you don't want to—"

"Don't want to what? What? Go ahead and say it!" But he didn't. This fight had already gone too far. "Okay, then. I'll say it. I don't want to have kids, and this is the reason why. If we had one I'd be more tied to this place than I am!"

"And that would be terrible?"

"For me it would."

"Well, we can't have that, can we?"

"No."

"I guess I should be happy that you come back at all."

"I may not, some time."

"You're gone so much, now. I wonder how I'd know."

"You'll know," she said bitterly and walked out.

TWELVE

Miles had killed the last twenty-four hours with drink, drugs, sex, and sleep, and now he woke to the unpleasant realization that he had to call Billy Meyers—again. He was almost out of money, all because the little prick hadn't paid him. He was fed up with everything about this place and wanted nothing more than to get in the Cadillac and head south. But he couldn't even do that until he got his money.

He swung his legs onto the edge of the bed and sat there collecting his thoughts. Behind him in the bed his benefactor slept on, her face hidden under a swirl of hair. He took a cigarette from the pack she'd left on the nightstand and dialed the number Billy had given him.

"Hello."

Miles couldn't tell if it was the kid or not. "I'm calling for Billy Meyers." There was a pause. "This is Miles Richards," he added.

"Yeah, Miles."

"We need to get together."

"Yeah, right."

"Tonight." He tried to say it as forcefully as he could without raising his voice.

"Sure, Miles."

"What time?"

"I don't know—ten?"

"Where?"

"In the country, south of town. There's an old building site."

"Why in the country? What's wrong with town?"

"I like the country."

"I don't."

"It's safer."

"For you, maybe." Miles heard what sounded like a laugh.

"You want your money, don't you?"

Miles took a breath before he replied. "Yeah. I want it."

"Then we'll meet in the country."

"Don't screw me around, Billy."

"I ain't, but you're gonna hafta meet me out here if you want to get it."

"You'd better have it all."

"Do you want it or don't you?"

Miles had to pause again before he went on. "Yeah, Billy. I want it."

"Okay. Here's the directions."

II

Frederick drove toward home, feeling better. After he'd picked up the filter and a few groceries he'd stopped by a florist's and had a dozen roses sent to JoAnn's office. He was sick of fighting with her and by the time he got to town, he felt he had to do something to make things better. But for now, he was hesitant to talk with her, even to apologize. Things might blow up, again, and he wanted desperately for that not to happen. Flowers were the best idea. They'd worked before.

The day was sunny and warm and it raised his spirits just to be driving back to the farm. Migrating blackbirds streamed south through the pristine sky, reminding him that fall was quickly slipping away. By the time that he got home, he was anxious to get back in the field. He put the milk and eggs in the refrigerator and left the rest in bags on the counter. As he headed back over to the harvester, he passed Eldon going like a bat out of hell, as usual, one hand holding the radio dramatically to his mouth. General Patton, he thought.

After he installed the new filter and primed it, the engine coughed reassuring black smoke and clattered to life. That's better, he thought. A lot of work was still waiting, but so be it. He needed it to distract himself from his troubles. He did not know how to please her. He did not know how to fight with her or make up with her, and it all left him confused and defeated.

Machines were another matter. Sometimes he fought with them, too, but he knew how to fix them and make them run. In the greater order of things that might not seem like a lot, but today it was enough.

III

When JoAnn got to the office, there was still nothing from Miles, but it was just as well. Her marriage was threatening to fall apart, and he would only complicate things. She needed to think about what she was going to do if things got worse—although it was hard to imagine that they could. At least she wasn't completely dependent on Frederick. She'd saved over eight thousand dollars that he didn't even know about. That would keep her head above water for a while. She could even buy a house if she had to.

Her mother had always preached that she shouldn't rely completely on a man, and now she was seeing the truth of that—again. Work was the only thing in her life that was going well, and she needed to focus on it. Already she was the best salesperson in the office and she could do even better if she moved into town. Fortunately, she had a closing to get ready for the next day. A closing meant success and money—and money meant independence.

Just after lunch the grinning receptionist brought Frederick's flowers into her office. They were pink, which he had decided was her favorite color, and the note read "I love you, Frederick" in the neat script of the florist. She was not surprised. The true reason for the roses was to make him feel better so he could congratulate himself on being conciliatory and generous. He'd expect her to go all warm and mushy when she saw them, but she wasn't feeling warm and mushy. They might have been more successful if the note had read "I'm sorry" or "I was wrong," but it didn't.

The prospect of such a predictable and unsatisfactory resolution depressed her, and she let the flowers lie in their box for some time before she found a vase and put them in water. She and Frederick had been through this before, and it seemed as if they were now headed for the same unfulfilling result.

But how could they be different, if he never changed? When

things got difficult between them, he fixed them with flowers. It had worked when she had bought into it, but now she couldn't, and the roses seemed more representative of Frederick's limitations than his thoughtfulness. Unfortunately, all the women in the office thought them wonderful, so she was obliged to act delighted when they were delivered.

She was saved from these bleak ruminations by the arrival of her client, a middle-aged woman whose husband would also be working in the new plant. After some obligatory gushing over the flowers, they left in JoAnn's car. By the time that they got to the first prospective house, she had adroitly explained how her wonderful husband was always making these thoughtful gestures and no, they didn't have children, yet, but were thinking of starting a family, soon.

She didn't feel the slightest dishonesty as she dispensed this illusion of domestic tranquility. Creating a bond with a buyer—no matter how superficial it might be—was part of her professionalism, no different than studying the market she worked in or carefully learning what it was that her client wanted. JoAnn prided herself on her ability to subvert her emotions to the demands of her work. Agents who could not do that sold by their moods, a weakness she observed most contemptuously in women.

When she returned to the office, it was six-thirty and everyone had left for the day. She still hadn't decided if she was going home, and she wasn't in the mood to stop by her mother's, so she went to the Tailfeathers for a drink and a bite to eat. There had been a time when she wouldn't have gone there by herself, but she had gotten to know the bartender and some of the regular customers well enough to feel comfortable by herself. The manager, Sammy, greeted her warmly and suggested that she sit with a small group of people seated near the fireplace. She was glad and disappointed to see that Miles was not among them.

She chatted and ate and had a few drinks. After a while she stopped looking at everyone who came in. By the time she left, it was after nine and she knew that she wasn't driving out to the farm. Frederick wouldn't like it, but he needed to know how unhappy she was with him. She'd be at her mother's, so he couldn't say much. If he called, she'd talk to him but she wasn't going to share his bed tonight.

THIRTEEN

Miles had spent a long, edgy afternoon waiting for night and his meeting with Billy Meyers. He had been too nervous to sleep and had spent the time smoking cigarettes and watching game shows on the girl's tiny TV. He was feeling butterflies that he hadn't felt for a long time, and it was a feeling that he didn't like. Concluding drug deals in questionable locales was a part of the business, but he felt particular uneasiness over his impending meeting with Billy Meyer.

Everything about it was on Billy's terms, which was all wrong. Billy owed him money not the other way around. He'd come to realize that the kid had a lot of risk attached to him. To begin with he was careless. If he could have, Miles would have just walked away, but he couldn't afford to. That money was just about all he had. Dealing drugs could be risky and unpredictable. There was no getting away from it. If he was going to be in this business, he had to deal with situations like this.

The girl had crawled out of bed a little after two, and made several catatonic trips to the bathroom before she woke sufficiently to say hello. A tall blonde, she had grown up on a farm, then discovered the relative sophistication of Antonio's. Now she waited tables there, spending most of her money on clothes and make-up and using a lot of coke bought by other people.

Naturally, Miles was a hit with the women in the place, and she had taken considerable satisfaction in having caught his eye. But as gregarious as he was at night, she found him moody and reclusive during the day and had learned to leave him alone.

Today, he looked tense and had barely looked at her when she spoke to him.

A little before five, the girl went off to work and Miles showered and dressed. Time had slowed and he still had almost four hours before the meeting. He was too nervous to eat, but he craved something that might calm him. Finally, he drove to Antonio's where he nursed two vodkas as slowly as he could. He would have liked to have had a couple more and a little snow for a chaser, but he knew that he needed to keep a clear head. He could wind down later.

II

Following Billy's directions, Miles drove six miles south of the city, then turned east onto a gravel road. The sky was overcast and the only light came from farmsteads scattered distantly on the countryside. The wind had come up and was blowing random bits of weeds across the road. He didn't pass any houses.

About a mile from where he was supposed to meet Billy, he stopped the car and went back to the trunk. Behind a section of paneling he found the nine-millimeter automatic in the plastic bag where he had left it. He slid it out and checked the clip. It was full. He'd had little experience with weapons, even in the Army, and had shot this one only a couple of times. Unfortunately, guns went with the business, just like people like Billy Meyers. He'd hoped the weapon would reassure him, but it only felt cold and heavy.

He slipped it into a pocket of the jacket he was wearing, but the fabric sagged with the weight and slapped against his hip. Not only that, it fit so tightly that he doubted he could get it out if he needed it. He thought about slipping it into the waistband of his trousers like people did in the movies, but that seemed like a bad idea, too. He fingered the safety just behind the trigger, and tried to remember when it was on or off.

Finally, he just laid it on the seat beside him and drove on another mile. The dark night swallowed his headlights and he had to slow to a crawl as he looked for the turnoff. Finally, he spotted a rutted dirt track running off into the darkness. He turned in and followed it, trying to straddle the deep ruts that had been carved out by farm equipment. Weeds grew high above the car right up to the edges of the primitive road and the wind slapped them against the sides of the Caddy. His hands sweated on the steering wheel.

He drove at barely more than a crawl for perhaps a half mile, when a weathered building materialized in the head lights. When he got to within fifty feet, he stopped. It was a farm shed of some kind, long abandoned and neglected, standing amidst the swaying weeds. It fit what Billy had told him, but he couldn't see anyone around it. His mouth was dry. He had never felt so vulnerable.

He switched off the headlights, and everything disappeared until his eyes adjusted to the darkness. In the distance the lights of Lime City created a faint glow in the sky that weakly silhouetted the building, but otherwise he couldn't make out anything. He wanted to light another cigarette, but hesitated to reveal himself. His right hand found the gun and curled around the grip but it didn't reassure him. Goddamn it, where are you, you little bastard?

Then, off to the right, he thought he saw movement. Was it the wind or Billy playing with him? He was on the verge of flooring the car and just getting the hell out of there. Steady, he thought. Steady. He needed this money and he needed it now. He laid the gun back on the seat and opened the door and got out, hating the brief illumination of the dome light. He peered in the direction of where he thought he'd seen movement.

"Billy!" The wind blew his voice off into the darkness. "Billy, is that you?" Then, he saw it again. It was someone, he was sure of it. "Hey!" he yelled and came around the car. "Billy!"

"Yeah."

"What the fuck are you doing?"

"Just being careful."

Now Miles realized that the voice was coming from only a few feet away. He thought he could see the kid.

"Where is it?"

"Here."

"Well, give it to me. I'm tired of fucking around."

Suddenly, Billy was standing in front of him, handing him a package. Even that close he really couldn't see the kid's face. Miles grabbed it and went back to the car.

He counted it out under the dome light, then picked up the gun and got out. Holding it at his side, he walked back toward Billy. Anger had overcome fear and he was ready to do something.

"You're short," he said as he walked toward him.

"No I'm not."

Miles stopped, too angry to care how this played out. "Yes, you are. We set a price and this isn't it."

"I told you that I would try to get that much. They wouldn't go for it."

"Then take it out of your commission."

"Why should I? I took all the risks." The kid's voice did not sound concerned.

Miles was sure that he couldn't see the gun, so it wasn't doing any good. He took a couple of quick steps toward him, the weapon still against his thigh, but Billy moved away from him into the darkness. Miles felt an advantage.

"Kind of jumpy, aren't you?" he asked.

"Just careful." Billy's voice was farther off.

"I can see why, you little fucker. I want my money."

"You got your money."

"I want all of it."

"That's all there is."

"Okay, asshole." Miles brought the gun up as he said it.

"Eddie!" Billy yelled and instantly a powerful beam of light flashed out of the dark and lit Miles up. Blinded, he reflexively brought his arm across his eyes.

"Don't do nothin' sudden!" Billy yelled. "You got a twelve gauge pointed right at you!" Miles was frozen in the light, his hand extended, the gun pointing at nothing.

"Drop it right there, then get in your car and go."

Miles opened his hand and the gun dropped and he turned and stumbled to the car. When he turned on the headlights, Billy was not in them. He gunned the car around through the weeds and back down the track, the frame bouncing off the ruts.

The Caddy swerved back onto the road and roared off. His vision was still marred by drifting clots of gray and purple, but he knew he was lucky to be out of there. It had happened so quickly. He should never have lost his temper and taken the gun. It could have gotten him killed, and that would have been a lot worse than losing the money. Billy Meyers had ripped him off, no doubt about it, but he had held all the cards. He wouldn't last two weeks in Florida—but this wasn't Florida.

III

By the time that he got back to Lime City, Miles really needed a drink, and he went right to Antonio's. Roland was in his usual corner seat from which he could watch the room.

"Mind if I join you?" Miles asked.

"Go ahead," Roland said without really looking at him. Miles thought maybe he was Mexican with the type of heavy body that clothes never fit, even though Roland liked to think he was quite a dresser. He slouched back in his chair to accommodate his stomach, which easily filled the space between him and the table.

"You're still around?" Roland asked.

"Not for long."

"How'd you come out on your little deal with Billy?" A smirk went with the question. Miles looked at him.

"You know Billy?"

Roland laughed. "Yeah, I know him. Everyone around here knows him."

"I'm surprised he's still alive." Miles said.

"You had to meet him in the country, right? In the dark?"

"Sounds right."

"That's how he stays alive," Roland said. "He's fucked too many people. He's a speed freak, a crazy motherfucker."

"One of these days he's going to cross the wrong person."

"I take it that you weren't the wrong person." Roland said. Miles looked away, annoyed, and Roland took the hint. "So, what are you gonna do now?"

"I'm getting out of here—back to Florida. I hate this place."

"So, you're going to go away and leave that rich pussy cryin' for you."

"What are you talking about?"

"JoAnn Heinold." Now, Miles laughed. "You think I'm kiddin'?" Roland went on, "Her old man's got enough money to keep you in nose candy for years."

"JoAnn Heinold? Her husband's a farmer."

"That's right, but he's a big-time farmer."

"She doesn't have any money."

"Her husband's the one who's got it, and what's his is hers in this state."

This was news to Miles. The only thing he knew about JoAnn's husband was she wasn't very happy with him. "If he's so rich, how come she never mentioned it?" he asked.

"It's all tied up in land. I bet he's got at least four, maybe five hundred acres. At three thousand an acre, you figure it out."

Miles did. "She's a hick," he said.

"A rich hick—and she loves your ass."

"Where'd you get that idea?"

"I saw you at the Tailfeathers together, winin' and dinin'. She was eatin' it up, hangin' on every lie you were telling her. The only thing her old man wants to do is hang out on the old farm."

"Do you know him?"

"We were in a couple of classes together out at the college. He's dull. He ain't interested in nothin' but farming."

"What makes you think she'd leave him?"

"You're askin' me?"

"I'm sick of farmers," Miles said, finally. "I'm sick of this place."

"Suit yourself," Roland shrugged, "but you're talking about some real money there, and you don't have to risk your neck to get it."

"I'm sick of farmers," Miles said again and looked around for the waitress.

IV

JoAnn was a little tipsy when she got to her mother's house. She carried her overnight bag upstairs to her old bedroom, then came down and flopped on the living room couch. Her mother sat in a recliner, a mostly finished drink on the table beside her. JoAnn was not surprised to see that she didn't look happy. Over the years she had come to know that look all too well—it often meant a lecture was about to follow.

"Don't you think you're staying in town an awful lot?"

Here it comes, she thought. "Why should I stay out there? I never see him anyway, during harvest."

Loretta rolled her eyes at what she considered her daughter's blatant carelessness. "He needs you out there. He's probably getting run to a frazzle."

"I told him to hire somebody. I've got my own work to do."

"There's a lot more to farming than just driving a tractor, you know, a lot of things that you just can't hire any old somebody to do."

"I know that, Mother."

"Sometimes I'm not so sure you do."

"You're never very sure of anything I do, are you?"

"I don't know about that, but I think staying in town as much as you are is a mistake."

"I suppose that you'd like me to be more like you—an obedient little wife who's still afraid of a husband who's been dead for twenty years."

"Your father had his faults, but I always knew where I stood with him. There was none of this pussy-footing like Frederick allows you."

"Frederick doesn't allow me anything. He's not my lord and master."

"I know he's not and it's too bad. You two are going to fool around with this marriage and the next thing you know it will be over. They don't run on automatic, you know."

"If it takes a dictatorship to have a good marriage, I'd just as soon be by myself."

"You probably will be, if this keeps up, and you can take satisfaction in knowing that you did it all by yourself, without any help from anybody."

"Thanks for the vote of confidence. You could take my side once in a while, you know."

"I'm not taking anybody's side, JoAnn, but if you want this marriage to last, you're going to have to start putting in some effort."

The drinks she'd had made JoAnn's head feel thick, and she was tired of this argument, which seemed like just another version of an argument that had been going on all her life. Why should she make an effort when she felt so little for her husband or her marriage? She'd married to find some sense of belonging and rootedness, but she felt neither of these.

Her mother thought it was JoAnn's responsibility to keep the marriage together, not Frederick's. It was always on the woman.

That was how she'd been raised and nothing had changed, but for JoAnn it was different. Still, she couldn't bring herself to tell her that she and Frederick might be finished.

While Loretta went into the kitchen to fix some sandwiches, JoAnn tried to distract herself by watching TV. The talk with her mother had brought her down, and she would have preferred to just go upstairs and go to bed. Instead she waited until Loretta brought out the TV trays, and then they ate and watched one of her mother's favorite reruns until she fell asleep.

V

True to JoAnn's prediction, Frederick—believing in the efficacy of roses—had come in early, showered and shaved, and prepared a nice steak dinner for them.

When she did not come home by six, he called her office where no one answered. By seven-thirty, he had eaten his food and part of hers and was finishing the remains of a fifth of Canadian whisky, the only drink he had in the house.

He had not called JoAnn's mother. If she were there, he didn't want to know.

The prospect of this meal had buoyed his whole day, and he had gone over in his mind all the things that he was going to tell her: how much he needed her, how the farm wasn't enough to make his life complete. He was going to admit his mistakes and express his longings and hopes for their life together. He was trying to see, as she had pointed out so often, that there was much more to life than the farm. It was enough for some people but not for them, and they—he—needed to look beyond it. JoAnn had already done just that and he had resented it, but now he wanted to reach toward her.

He had intended to tell her all of this and more, but there was no one to tell it to and he fell from the great hopes of the morning into the gloomy haplessness of his own company.

He lingered at the table, sipping the whisky and brooding over the bleak symbolism of JoAnn's empty chair and unused plate and silver.

He thought about calling Loretta and he thought about driving into Lime City to find her and he thought about retreating into Rock Falls to soak away the gloom, but he did none of these things. Instead, he pushed the empty glass away and went to change into his work clothes.

FOURTEEN

JoAnn woke up early in her old bedroom. The gray light coming through the window told her that the sky was overcast, but it was no less promising than the mood that had stirred her. Frederick had not called, as she had been so sure he would. Even as she lay there, the uncertainty of her life was growing.

Her eyes drifted over the fading flowers of the wallpaper her mother had put up when she was ten. It still reminded her of the morning when her mother had come upstairs to tell her that her father had suffered a stroke on the way to work and died. Herbert Greiman had so filled their lives with his restless energy and booming voice that his leaving had seemed impossible. And yet he had left, swiftly and precipitously, and her mother had never completely recovered.

Loretta had been as shattered by the sudden unexpectedness as the death, itself, and for months after she was plagued by panic and terror over what was going to happen to them. She couldn't comfort herself, let alone her daughter, and JoAnn was left to find her own way through the wreckage. She withdrew from her schoolmates and missed the budding social functions of her adolescence. Instead of going to parties and dancing and having her first boyfriend, she stayed for hours by herself in her room.

But now, her old refuge could not comfort her. She got up and dressed before her mother got up. When Loretta did come downstairs, her face was puffy and her breath was sour. For some time, now, JoAnn had been worried about the narrow scope of her mother's life. Although her car was eleven years old, it had less than four thousand miles on it, and she'd never driven beyond the city limits. The only people she knew were older relatives or friends and they had begun to pass on. Her doctor of many years had died three years before, and she was always vague when JoAnn asked her if she had found a new one. Although she watched TV incessantly, she avoided the news programs. Her evenings were comprised of sitcoms and Canadian whisky.

In recent years JoAnn had urged her to widen her life by getting out more and making new friends. For a period of months she had called almost every day to see how she was doing and to encourage her. At first Loretta had resisted, but then she had given in and actually joined a card club, but only JoAnn's persistence kept her at it, and she lapsed as soon as the prompting stopped. The experience taught JoAnn that her mother preferred to live the way she did, and it was the last time she would try to change her.

When she got to her office, it was with a sense of relief from the claustrophobia of the house and her mother's life. She had her problems, but there was also freedom and possibility. Here, people were busy with their tasks, life was going on. The purposeful activity reassured her, and she poured herself a cup of coffee and went to work checking over her paperwork and numbers before going to the bank for her closing.

When that was over, she bought the buyers—newlyweds still in their early twenties—lunch and picked up a good lead from them. Their compliments on the job she'd done for them reminded her that she was damned good at what she did, and her old confidence surged back.

By one o'clock she was back at her desk and busy making calls. At one-fifteen, Miles walked through the door.

II

His arms were wrapped around a large bundle of what could only be flowers, and he stepped up to the desk and grandly offered it to her. "I brought you something."

"I see." She didn't move. "You have no idea how ineffective those are."

Miles didn't know what she meant, but he was suddenly struck by one of the few moments in his life when he could think of nothing to say. His reaction was exactly what she had hoped for.

"You're looking well," he told her.

JoAnn leaned back in her chair. "Am I?"

"Exceptionally, but then you always do."

"So, you're being nice today." Her voice was chilly.

"I'm trying." There was another silence. He looked at the vase of Frederick's flowers. "I see that you like roses."

"Yes, I do. But not from strangers."

"I thought maybe we'd become something more."

"Oh, I did, too...until our last time together. But that was very *strange*, don't you think?"

"Yes, it was. It was unforgiveable. That's why I brought these—to apologize."

"Apologize?"

"Yes."

"Do you really think that you can apologize for—for forcing me—to do that!" She struggled to keep her voice down, but the sudden flush of her face revealed her anger.

Miles actually found her reaction encouraging. It was clear that she was feeling more than she wanted him to see. He sensed an opening. "JoAnn, I want to try, even if you choose not to accept it. My behavior was terrible, and I wanted to tell you in person."

She studied him. This was a Miles she hadn't seen before. She let him steep for a moment in the silence as she savored the advantage she felt. "Would you close the door, please?" she asked. He turned and closed it, then came back. She leaned forward for emphasis. "I have never been treated like that in my life!"

"And I've never treated anyone like that, believe me!"

"Why should I? Why should I believe anything you say? First, you treat me as if you really care for me, and then you turn on me!"

"I know," he said. "I know."

"I thought you'd gone back to Florida and I would never see you again and I was glad! What are you doing here?"

"I started back," he said. "I was almost to St. Louis and then—

I stopped."

"Why?"

"I knew that I had to come back."

"To Iowa? The place you hate so much? Why?"

"Because of you."

"Me?"

"Yes, you. You're the reason I came back. I missed you, JoAnn. I didn't want to, but I did." It was a decisive stroke and the reaction in her face told him that he had caught her by surprise.

The only reason she'd even talked with him was to punish him. Wounded as she was, she had no intention of believing him, but he'd broken through her anger with this sudden declaration of feelings she'd never dreamed he could feel for her.

He could certainly have left it at that and been back in her good graces, but he couldn't help himself. In a kind of celebration of the way he'd played this conversation, of the way he'd led her to exactly where he wanted her to go, he needed to deliver the coup de grace, the most devastating words a man could say to a woman in those circumstances: "I'm in love with you."

"You're what?"

"I know it sounds crazy but it's true. JoAnn, I'm in love with you."

"You're in love with me?" She looked straight into his eyes and he looked back into hers, and she could not see that he did not mean it.

"Yes. I am."

She sat back in her chair, flummoxed. "You have an awfully odd way of showing it."

"I know. I'm not very good at this."

"If you really feel this way, why did you treat me like that?"

"I wanted to hurt you."

"Hurt me? Why?"

"Because you were hurting me."

"Hurting you? How?"

"Oh, it wasn't intentional. I know that."

"Miles, I don't understand."

"When we started out, we both knew that it was going to be a temporary thing with no strings, no complications, but then I could feel it becoming something more. After a while, I realized that I didn't want it to be temporary. After all, what was in it for me? You've got a life—a career, a husband and what do I have? Nothing? And then when I saw the underwear—"

"The underwear? What about them?"

"It was like you were taunting me with them, telling me 'look what I've bought for my husband to enjoy.' I got a little crazy."

"Crazy?"

"Yes, crazy. You've never seen me act like that before, have you?"

"No. That's why I was so hurt. I couldn't imagine what had come over you. You'd always been such a gentleman."

"I'm ashamed of the way I acted JoAnn, and it will never happen again. Please say that you'll forgive me."

She took her time over this, not to make up her mind, which she had already done, but to savor this sudden change in her life. Mere seconds before she'd been struggling to find something hopeful to focus on, and now, in the space of a few moments, a whole new set of possibilities had arrived. Miles Richards had declared his love for her as no man ever had. His departure was no longer a certainty. The most beautiful and interesting man she'd ever known wanted to be with her.

"I do forgive you, Miles. But if anything like it ever happens again—"

"It won't, JoAnn. I promise." As if to seal his vow, he proffered the bundle of flowers.

She took it and, as she pulled the wrapping away, a great, sheaf of red roses tumbled onto her desk. There were at least two dozen, and they were breathtaking. She gathered them up.

"My God! They're beautiful!" She leaned giddily across the table and kissed him. "I need to put these in some water." She paused for a moment, then looked at the roses Frederick had sent. Compared with the bold brightness of Miles' offering they seemed obligatory and inconsequential. "These are beginning to fade," she said, and she dropped them in her wastebasket.

III

Since the evening that JoAnn had not come home, almost twenty-four hours of work and fitful naps had passed for Frederick. When he tried to sleep, he was beset by dreams that kept waking him, dreams of frustration and futility. In one, he was confined to the cab of the harvester as he pursued JoAnn through the streets of Lime City. As he chased her, she would angrily turn and berate him, but the huge machine moved so slowly that he could never get close enough to talk.

His depression nourished his fatigue and he found himself fumbling some of the simplest and most familiar tasks. It was a bad sign. Working around farm machinery could be dangerous especially if one got careless or tired. Although the equipment had gotten much safer over the years, there were still occasional deaths. He knew several men with missing fingers and one who had lost most of his right hand when a gear had grabbed his shirtsleeve and tried to pull him through a thresher. He kept reminding himself that he needed to be careful.

When she did not come home on the second evening, he called his mother-in-law.

"Loretta, is JoAnn there?"

"No Frederick, she's not." There was a decided slur to her pronunciation. She'd been drinking. He knew better than to talk to her after she'd had a few, but he persisted.

"Did she stay there last night?"

"Yes." She said it right away and he believed her.

"Well, is she going to stay there tonight?"

"I don't know. For God's sake, haven't you talked to her?"

"No, I haven't. I've been busy, Loretta. I'm still trying to get my crop in. Did she say anything?"

"About what?"

"About tonight. What's she going to do?" It sounded pathetic, even to him.

"No, Frederick. She didn't."

"Goddamn it, Loretta, I don't know what to do!"

His mother-in-law had barely been holding her tongue, but now he had opened the floodgate. "Well, you'd better do something! This staying in town and acting like she isn't even married is ridiculous!"

"She tells me that she has to. She says she has all this work to do. Every time I ask her for a little help she gets mad!"

"Lay down the law, Frederick! Be a man! My God, you're not roommates, you know. You're married!"

"I feel the same way, but she's got a mind of her own."

"You tell that girl that you want her home after work, and then make sure that she gets there! You just can't give JoAnn all this leeway! She doesn't know how to handle it!"

"I'm sick of fighting with her! It's all we do."

"For God's sake, Frederick, take charge of your life!" She hung up.

Just great, he thought, I call her up to talk about this and she blows a gasket, too. But he knew she was right. He was too reasonable and his wife was taking advantage of it. She didn't have to stay away this much. Even her mother thought so. He picked the phone up and called her back.

"Loretta? It's me again."

"I know," she said wearily.

"If JoAnn shows up, you tell her to get home—now! Tell her I'm fed up, okay?"

"Yes, Frederick." She didn't sound convinced.

"Good. Goodnight, Loretta."

"Goodnight, Frederick."

He almost slammed the phone down for emphasis, but it wasn't the old lady he was mad at. She was on his side. She agreed with him. Maybe JoAnn would listen to her. His new sense of purpose picked him up. He felt like doing something. Maybe he should go into Lime City and find JoAnn. But if she wasn't at her mother's, where would he look? It was twenty miles over there and he might not even find her.

He washed up a bit, then wrote her a note, revising it several times to get the wording just right: "Went to Rock Falls. Be back later. Stay home. Frederick."

That ought to get the message across. He laid it on the kitchen table and left.

IV

JoAnn and Miles were having a drink together at the Tailfeathers. As usual, she had concocted a pretense for their being together, but the need for it hadn't arisen. Other than the manager, who was completely indifferent, they didn't know anyone in the place.

Miles had come to understand that this ruse was something JoAnn did as much for herself as for appearances. It reinforced, somehow, her belief that what she was doing was legitimate. She wasn't fooling around on her husband, she was having a drink with a client—the same one she'd been having drinks and lunches with for weeks. The need to rationalize her behavior so she could think well of herself was a powerful motivator, and one Miles had observed in other women. Sometimes he found it useful.

For the past hour he'd been obliged to express his contrition, again, through several variations, which he had now tired of. He was ready to change the topic.

"So. Where did the other roses come from?" he asked.

"Frederick."

"Ah, the thoughtful husband."

"Not really. It's his way of making himself feel better. And it's a lot easier than saying I'm sorry."

"Why would he need to do that?"

"Because we're not getting along."

"Things are not so good?"

"No, they're not. Last night I stayed in town at my mother's. I doubt if he even noticed. The only thing he really cares about is his farm."

"Does he farm a lot of land?"

"Yes. Too much."

"And how much is that?"

"Over five hundred acres."

Roland knows what he's talking about, he thought.

"That's part of our problem," she went on. "He thinks that I should help him out more, and I don't want to."

"Doesn't he understand that you've got your career?"

"That's what I keep telling him, but he doesn't listen. That's what this whole problem is about; that and the fact that I don't like anything about farming.

"I'm not surprised," he said. "That wouldn't be any life for you."

"I know, but he can't see that. He wants me to live his life and I can't do it. We've grown so far apart that I wonder what's going to happen to us."

"What do you want to happen?" he asked.

She looked at him. "I'm not sure."

"Am I making things worse?"

"You're not making them better," she said, "but they weren't going so good before I met you." Miles was almost disappointed. "Frederick is against my success," she went on. "I think he's afraid of it. But you're always supportive—and interested. You make me feel like I'm important and what I do is important."

"You are important," he said and for emphasis he reached across the table and took her hand.

Normally, she would have avoided this gesture in such a public place, but this time she didn't pull away. Something profound was happening, and she didn't even look around to see who might be watching.

V

When Frederick got to the Falls Tavern, several other farmers were there, standing around one end of the bar, complaining about the headaches of farming. Sooner or later, regardless of individual political preferences, they got around to blaming the government. The election of the peanut farmer in '76 had temporarily raised their hopes, but these had flickered out in all but his staunchest supporters.

Most of them didn't even vote. Their politics consisted of standing around in a bar, one foot on the rail, doggedly muttering frustrations into the face of a doggedly muttering listener. It was true that Eldon Mathews had once loaded his biggest tractor on a flatbed and hauled it fourteen hundred miles to Washington where, with hundreds of others, he circled the White House in a diesel-stinking, traffic-clogging protest against low commodity prices.

The chief result of this breach of civility was general embarrassment by everyone who knew him and a personal phone call from his senator telling him that it wasn't his brightest idea. Afterwards, Eldon was uncharacteristically quiet about the whole business.

By eleven, Frederick had his fill of drink and talk, but he hung around another half-hour just to let JoAnn experience a little more of the waiting end of the waiting game. The drinks coupled with the lack of sleep made him drowsy, and he drove slowly, wondering how she was going to react to this new marital tactic and trying to rehearse his side of the conversation that would probably take place.

When he drove into the yard, her car was not there. "Goddamn it, Frederick, you sure showed her," he said out loud and he laughed bitterly at the irony. He lingered in the truck, not wanting to go into the empty house. He thought about driving back to Rock Falls and finishing the night out there, but he was already drunk. Fuck it, he thought. Fuck it. He got out and went inside. His note lay on the table where he had left it. She hadn't been there.

"Yes sir, you sure showed her, Frederick. You sure showed her, alright." He went into the living room and sprawled on the couch, laughing and wiping his eyes.

VI

After they had finished two bottles of champagne at the Tailfeathers, JoAnn was drunk and Miles had talked her into a stall in the men's room where they inhaled a whole line of cocaine off Miles' little mirror. Afterwards, she had jokingly stripped off her panties in the car as they drove to the motel.

"You've got to promise to take me to my mother's before it gets light," she told him.

"I promise," he said.

"I need you, Miles. I need you to take care of me tonight. Everybody else is mad at me, but you aren't are you?"

"No, JoAnn, I'm not."

"Frederick is mad at me, my mother is mad at me. I need you to take care of me, Miles. I'll worry about tomorrow, tomorrow, but tonight I don't want to worry about anything.

"I'll take care of you, JoAnn. I promise."

FIFTEEN

Frederick had fallen asleep in a nest of crumpled newspapers on the couch, and it had taken some time for the ringing telephone in the kitchen to finally wake him. He was dead with weariness and the lingering effects of the whisky, and even after he woke it took a while to collect himself. And then he realized that it might be JoAnn.

"Hello."

"Frederick?" He did not recognize the voice.

"Yes. Who is this?"

"A friend. Your wife is in room two-twenty at the Northstar Inn in Lime City, and she's not alone."

"My wife? JoAnn? Is something wrong?"

"The Northstar—room two-twenty. Have you got that?"

"Yeah, I guess, but is she okay?" But the caller had hung up.

Now he was awake and trying to sort out the message. It didn't sound like an emergency, but what was it? Was the guy talking about JoAnn, or was there some kind of mix-up? But he'd called him Frederick. Who was it—and why had he called? He couldn't make sense of it.

He had to let the phone ring for some time before Loretta answered it.

"Loretta, it's Frederick. Is JoAnn there? I need to talk to her—now."

"Frederick, what's this about? What time is it?"

"Loretta, it's urgent. I've got to talk to her. Go get her, now." He could hear the phone being set down as the old lady went to wake her daughter. It seemed like a long time before she came back on.

"You can't talk to her now, Frederick."

"Why not?"

There was another pause. "Because she's not here."

"She's not? She didn't spend the night there?"

"No."

"Then where is she?" And then he knew.

II

Frederick had the window down as he drove toward Lime City so the cold air could stream against his face. His body had not yet burned off the alcohol he'd drunk, and he felt hot and thirsty. But more than that, he was scared. Never could he have imagined a trip like this, rushing through the night to confront a terrible possibility. Through all the problems he and JoAnn were having, the one scenario he'd never imagined was that she might be seeing someone else—and now he was driving toward that possibility.

He drove through the parking lot of the motel until he found her car. Until that moment, he'd held onto the hope that things weren't as they were beginning to appear, that it was all a mistake of some kind that would later leave him feeling foolish for having gone even this far. But it was her car, with her license plate. Up until this discovery, he hadn't been sure what he was going to do when he got to the Northstar, but now he had to go on. He parked and climbed the stairway to the second floor and went down the carpeted hall to the door with the dreaded number 220 on it.

As he stood staring at it, he thought of all these days he'd spent alone, his foolish hopes of finding her home when he got there. He thought of the meals he'd fixed for them that she hadn't shown up to eat. He thought of all her excuses, her anger because he wanted her to spend more time with him—her husband!

And then he thought about how she might have been betraying him all the while. And it was too much, a breaking point, and something that he'd never felt before flared in his guts and screamed for him to kick in this door and avenge his trust and his loneliness.

He trembled with the force of these wracking storms while the numbers burned before him—two two zero. Whatever he might do, she had caused to happen. Frederick had never raised his hand against another, but now he was excused to act violently for the oldest reason there was. If JoAnn was in that room with a man, Frederick could attack him, and maybe her, too. People would shake their heads in understanding and, if it came to it, the strictest judge would mitigate the consequences.

At that moment, when he had nothing left to lose, something held him back, a fragile, tenuous idea of himself that he hardly understood. Things were bad—very bad—and no matter what he decided to do, they were going to get worse. But there was something even more valuable to lose than his wife. There was himself.

III

After calling JoAnn's husband on the payphone in the lobby, Miles had gone back to the room and lay down. Although he knew her husband could not possibly get there for at least thirty minutes, his nervousness prompted him to listen. Beside him, she lay naked, sleeping as if she had been drugged, which in a way she was. Everything JoAnn had told him about her husband suggested that he was not violent, but who could predict what he might do in these circumstances?

Miles had considered other, safer, options like leaving before Frederick got there. He could have left the door unlocked so he could enter to find her naked in the disheveled bed, the sheets stained, and the ashtray filled with incrimination. It would have been less risky for Miles, but if he was going to go this far, he might as well make sure there were no doubts about JoAnn's unfaithfulness. Better that than to let things stumble along for some protracted and unpredictable length of time.

It was almost five when the footsteps came down the hall and stopped outside the door. Miles held his breath and waited, the cigarette poised bare inches from his mouth. He could almost hear the accelerating thud of his own heartbeat. At any moment the door might burst open and a man that he had never met—a very angry man—would come through it.

The tension became unbearable. How stupid he'd been! What

if the man he had invited and left the door unlocked for was at this very instant brandishing a gun—or a knife or some other weapon? He listened for the sound of a cocking hammer, any sound that might tell him what was coming. The cigarette had burned down to the filter, and he hurriedly snuffed it out in the ashtray. No sound came from the door. What the hell was going on?

Finally, Miles couldn't stand any more. He had to do something. He slid off the bed into a crouch, but there was no place to hide on the floor, either. He'd made sure of that. JoAnn slept on, oblivious. A chair stood against the wall, and he crawled to it. Better than nothing, he thought.

Then, something moved outside the door. What? He braced, but then he heard them: footsteps—going away—down the hall—disappearing. What had happened?

He couldn't believe it. Whoever was out there hadn't even tried the door. Why? Miles sat back on the bed and listened, but there was nothing but silence. All of this and nothing had happened! What the hell?

Obviously, it had been her husband. Who else could it have been? But why hadn't he done something? Anything? Was he coming back? Now, there was more uncertainty than ever.

For over an hour he sat in the chair, smoking and listening, until morning light began to creep through the window. When he lay back on the bed, he still couldn't sleep. It didn't look like his plan had worked.

IV

When JoAnn finally woke, it was past nine and she knew that she was likely trapped in the worst deceit of her life. The man who had promised to deliver her safely to her mother's house slept on, leaving her to face the consequences by herself. She was too hung over to even feel panic. There was only an oppressive throbbing in her head and stomach. She longed to roll over and go back to sleep, but if there was any chance of rescuing herself, she had to get up now. She crawled out of bed and performed enough cosmetic repair to go to work.

When she got to the office, there were no messages. It didn't mean anything, of course. She didn't know what to do. The aspirin she'd taken had barely eased the ache in her head. Only one thing would, she knew, and that was more sleep. She sat back in her chair and was about to close her eyes when Frederick walked in. His eyes were wild.

"Where were you last night?"

"Frederick!"

"And don't lie to me! I'm sick of lies! Where were you?!"

"Why are you yelling at me?!"

"Because you didn't come home and you didn't stay at your mother's, that's why!" He came around the desk and leaned down until his face was inches from hers. "Where were you last night?"

"At the Tailfeathers."

"Not until four-thirty!"

"I don't know what time I left! I had too much to drink!"

"I called your mother's at four o'clock and you weren't there, and your car was at the Northstar when I got there at four-thirty!"

"The Northstar. What were you doing there?"

"I was there because someone called and told me my wife was there with a man!"

"A man?!"

"Yes, JoAnn, a man!"

"And you believed this—a voice on the phone?" The shock of his sudden appearance was passing and she was scrambling to find a foothold in this confusion before it swept her away.

"Your car was there, JoAnn! I saw it!"

She felt as if he were standing on her chest. A livid splotch of crimson had spread from her neck up into her face. He had cornered her and begun to pummel her with outraged accusations.

She could have smashed his face, she so was sick of it hanging over her, trapping her, accusing her. She hated him and his self-pity, his blaming her for everything. She was finished with this, with him. She stood and shoved by him, but he caught her arm.

"I want an answer, JoAnn, and I want it now!"

It was as much a cry of anguish as a demand, a sure sign to her that he was faltering. She glared with all of the anger and contempt she could bring to bear against the pain and sorrow that was tearing him apart. In that terrible moment when their eyes met, neither could see the other. Frederick saw that it was hopeless, a ruin, and he let go of her arm. Their marriage was over as neither could have imagined.

V

Less than an hour after the breakup, Frederick began drinking at the Royal Roost, a working man's tavern on the south end of Lime City. There, in the subdued company of the morning alcoholics, he tried to steady his bewildered panic. The Roost sold only beer, but the shoddy bar and clientele seemed appropriate for the state of his affairs.

After noon, he moved on to first one, then another of the bars he had sometimes frequented in his single days and switched to whisky. Occasionally, he encountered someone he'd known from the old days who inevitably asked him how things were going. In reply he merely offered a damaged smile and a nod to the bartender. It would have been impossible to explain how badly things were going, and he didn't want to try.

In the middle of the afternoon he finally achieved the alcoholic haze he had sought since morning. It was a state of temporary grace which mercifully filtered his recollection of the circumstances that had brought him there. Later yet, he abandoned the city for a leisurely tour of several small town taverns.

Fortunately, he did not encounter anyone he knew. He did not feel like talking and wanted only to enjoy his anonymity among the conversations of others. Beyond the neon beer signs that adorned the windows of these establishments, the world went on, and that was fine with him, but he needed to take a little break.

SIXTEEN

When Frederick wandered into the Falls Tavern sometime after ten, there were a dozen people there, most of whom he did not know. And, of course, there was Betty.

"Frederick, you look like you been rode hard and put up wet," she told him, and he knew that he probably did.

"I have, Betty. I sure have." As soon as he spoke, she knew he'd already had too much to drink. "A little whisky, please."

"Maybe we'll wait a little while for the whisky," she said. "Why don't I make you a cheeseburger and a bowl of the chili I made today?"

Frederick smiled agreeably and sat down in a booth. A group of kids clustered around the pool table, drinking beer and challenging the winner in a series of games. He didn't know any of them. One of the girls was older than the others. She wore faded jeans and a black turtle neck sweater, and her chestnut hair was pulled into a pony tail that fell almost to her waist. And she was pretty.

Betty brought the food, and Frederick ate and watched as the girl won game after game. She had a sure, even stroke that drove the cue ball exactly where she wanted. Betty came over and picked up the empty dishes.

"How was that, Frederick?"

"Just great, Betty. That's about the best chili I've ever had." Betty thought so, too, but she liked to hear it anyway. "Can I have some whisky, now?"

"How about a little coffee, first?" She went to get it without waiting for a reply.

After an hour of drinking coffee and watching the games, Frederick fished a quarter out of his pocket. The girl had won again, and her opponent was racking the balls.

"Would you mind if I get in?" Frederick asked.

The boy looked at the girl and shrugged.

"Fine," she said, and Frederick lay his quarter behind two others in the cleft between the rail and the felt surface. The girl played steadily and kept winning. Too often, the boys shot so hard that the balls scattered and left easy chances for her. They dropped quarters in the jukebox and swapped information about their trucks and didn't seem to care if they won or lost. They were playing for a drink, and the girl already had five glasses of wine sitting on her table.

When his turn came, Frederick knelt and injected his quarter into the table's mechanism and the balls rumbled to him. He arranged them into the rack while the girl chalked the end of her cue. Then, she drove the cue ball into the racked balls with a force that scattered them like birdshot. Frederick was still choosing a cue from the rack, and he turned back to the table just in time to see the eight ball drop into a pocket. He looked at her, then back at where the ball had disappeared, then back at her, again.

"Did I just lose?" he asked.

She did her best not to laugh out loud. "Yes. I believe you did."

"Is the eight the only one that went in?"

"Yes." He began to laugh, shaking his head over the congruity of this event with the rest of his day.

"What were we playing for?" he asked.

"We never said."

"Well, you got enough to drink there. How about we make it for a buck?" He fished one out of his pocket and laid it next to the wine. "Do I know you?" he asked.

"My name is Lisa Melendez." She extended her hand and he shook it. It was warm.

"Nope. I don't know any Lisa Melendez."

"It used to be Lisa Breka before I was married."

"Are you related to Frank Breka?"

"He's my dad."

"I know Frank. He's got that little farm on the river."

"That's right. And who are you?"

"Frederick Heinold. I farm three miles north of here."

"Nice to meet you, Frederick." The new challenger had racked the balls and was waiting for Lisa to break.

"I guess I'll have to wait my turn," Frederick said and hung up his cue. The game began and he went over to the bar to get some quarters. "Okay, how about some whisky, now?" he asked Betty. "You darned near got me sobered up."

"Okay. But remember you've still got to drive home."

"Betty, I won't even go home. I'll just spend the night here, sacked out on your pool table." It seemed like an odd reply, but Betty reminded herself that Frederick Heinold had a reputation for being a little odd.

The whisky and the companionship postponed the certain loneliness that waited at the house, and he was grateful to spend the rest of the night drinking and playing pool. Around midnight, the other players left, leaving just Frederick and Lisa. His play got better and he even made a couple of modest runs, but she always managed to clean up the last two or three balls to win. It didn't matter. It was better than going home. At a quarter of two, Betty began to switch off the beer signs.

"Time to close up, folks."

"Can I have one for the road?" he asked.

Betty preferred not to, but she was tired and it was too late to argue.

"Okay. But if the sheriff stops you, you didn't get it here." She made the drink in a paper cup and handed it to him—a local custom, if illegal.

"You better give Lisa one, too."

"I guess they can only take Otis's license once," she said. Lisa poured some of her wine into a cup and they went outside.

They stood by his pickup and looked up at the roof of stars. He was glad that she had lingered, too. He cast about for something to say.

"Do you want to walk down to the bridge?" he asked.

"Sure." They walked the half block to the bridge and leaned against the concrete railing. A quarter mile upstream the river dropped over the modest shelf that gave the town its name. The falling water made a steady, comforting sound in the hollow of the night. "Do you have your crop in?" she asked.

"No," he said. "I'm afraid not." There was a sadness and resignation in the way he said it that revealed his loneliness. "What do you do?" he asked.

"Not much of anything, right now. I'm taking a couple of courses at the college in Lime City and helping dad out when he needs me."

"How is Frank? It's been a while since I've seen him."

"He's fine. He never changes." There was a smile in the way she said it, and Frederick knew exactly what she meant.

"He's one of the old-timers," Frederick said, approvingly. "He farms for the right reasons."

"Yeah, he does." She smiled as she said it.

They fell into a silence until their cups were empty and the cold began to chill them. As they walked back toward their vehicles, Frederick realized that the whisky wasn't going to hold him. They stopped between their pickups and he looked up into the stars, again, trying to think of something to say that would keep her there for a little longer.

"Do you want to come home with me?" she asked. "I've got a little bourbon in the house."

II

Frederick followed Lisa's pickup along the empty township roads, and then they turned into a gravel lane that ran down into the woodlands along the river. Frank Breka was a Bohemian and, like other Bohemians who had settled in the area, he preferred the trees and river and the limestone cliffs and ledges it had carved out to the richer flatlands.

Over the past few years, when land prices had risen so sharply, many of the second generation Bohemians had cleared wooded pastures and planted crops on them, but Frank had not. He had a couple of small, patch-work fields planted in row crops, but he made his life out of the myriad enterprises that had characterized farming twenty-five years before.

Chickens, turkeys, several kinds of ducks, and geese all wandered freely about his farmyard. He had a pasture of sheep from which he sold lambs and wool, and he kept a small herd of cattle for his own milk and meat as well as to market. For years he had burned wood in a capacious furnace that he had designed and built with the help of Oscar Wyborny who operated the repair shop in Rock Falls. Every spring he and his wife planted a huge garden from which they canned a year's supply of food.

Frank had his own vineyard, one of the few in the whole county. Most years he made over a hundred gallons of Concord wine, some of which he distilled into a spirited brandy that he flavored with syrups from his thickets of raspberry bushes and apple, pear, and plum trees. He smoked his own bacon and ribs and even fish that he caught from the river. He owned only one tractor, an ancient John Deere that he had to start by hand.

As Frederick followed her, the lane narrowed into little more than a field rut that wound through the trees down to a small clearing. There, sitting just above the river, was a small trailer house. "This is it," she said. They went inside and she lit an oil lamp.

"I don't have any power out here," she said. "When I want to read at night, I use a Coleman lantern."

"It's nice," he said, looking around.

"I like it, but it won't work this winter. There isn't any insulation in the walls so I'd freeze. I'll move in with the folks when it gets too cold, but for now I prefer it here." She got the bottle of whisky and a glass from the cupboard and set them on the little table. Frederick poured a small amount into the glass and sipped it. He felt himself beginning to sag.

"I'm married," he told her, "and things aren't going too well." Deep in his chest the words were breaking apart and he paused as he tried to hold them together. Lisa waited, her face shining softly in the dim light. "I can't—I can't seem to do anything right."

"Will she be worried about you?" she asked.

He smiled and it hurt his face and throat clear down into his chest. "No. I don't think so," he said.

"Is she at home waiting?" she asked.

"No," he said "she's not home." The words sounded as hopeless as he felt. Her face had begun to shimmer. He took another sip and waited vainly for its steadying bite. He'd done everything he could to stay above the pool of emotion rising in him, but nothing was working anymore.

"Do you want to stay here tonight?" she asked.

"I—I don't know," he said. "I don't know what to do."

"Maybe you should," she said.

"Are you sure?"

"Yes. The couch makes into a bed. Not much of a bed, but a bed."

"I'd really like to not go home tonight." He pushed the glass away. "Guess I had enough of that."

She spread a sleeping bag on the couch. "This should work," she said.

"Thank you."

"Well, goodnight," she said and went back into the tiny bedroom.

Frederick took off his boots and jeans and shirt and crawled into the bag. Here he was with a girl he hardly knew in a tiny house in middle of the night. He felt like he'd been rescued.

As his eyes grew accustomed to the dark, he was suddenly aware that Lisa was standing beside him.

"I brought you a pillow," she said, and her hand went under his head to lift it. As she did, the fragrant darkness of her hair fell against his face, and he reached through it and drew her down beside him.

Not since he was a child had he held someone so tightly, and she held him, too. After a while she pulled the sleeping bag over them and they lay without talking until he fell asleep.

III

A little before dawn the wind came up and the gentle movement of the trailer woke him. Lisa was still beside him, sleeping quietly, her warmth reassuring him that he was not alone. He listened to the stirring trees as they whispered a trembling song of winter soon to come. The faintest first light of the dawn peeked into the little trailer, promising a day that he didn't yet want to think about. Soon, he would have to go home for he could not stay beside this girl who had taken him in like a stray puppy. But for now, he was not alone and that was enough.

SEVENTEEN

When Frederick next woke, it was light and Lisa was at the tiny stove, making coffee. The sky was overcast and the trailer shuddered in a gusting wind. He sat up with the sleeping bag wrapped around him, and she handed him a cup of coffee.

"It looks like our good weather has left us," she said, looking out a window.

"I hope not. I've got over a hundred acres of corn to get in."

"A hundred? Dad had thirty-five altogether."

"Frank's smart. He still runs his farm instead of the other way around."

"He'll never get rich, though."

"None of us will."

"Dad says Eldon Mathews is supposed to be a millionaire."

"Well, Eldon thinks so," he told her. She laughed and Frederick saw how oval her face was with her hair framing it. Unlike JoAnn, she seemed utterly unaware of herself. "Are you married?" he asked her.

She laughed again. "Do I look married?"

"Not particularly, but I thought I'd better ask."

"Actually I am—barely."

"Barely?"

"Yes. We've been separated for almost two years, and I've been trying to get a divorce for most of that time."

"I didn't know it was that hard," he said.

She shook her head. "It is with Sonny. Everything's hard with Sonny."

"Where is he?"

"In Des Moines. He's an ironworker. That's where I've been living. I came up here to get away from the whole mess."

"What kind of troubles did you have?"

She laughed. "Every kind that you can have. Sonny wouldn't know how to be married even if he wanted to be."

"Why no divorce, then?"

"He doesn't want to let go."

"He still loves you?"

"Oh, he loves me alright. After his bike and his buddies, he probably loves me the most." She laughed.

"I wish I could laugh about my predicament."

"It took me a while," she said. "But it's over for me. It has been for a couple of years. I'm ready for something else."

"Like what?"

"Oh, I don't know. Just something that's not Sonny and his crazy life. I need some time to find out, but that's not something I can do while he's around."

Frederick envied the distance she'd established from her old life. If there were scars, they didn't seem that deep. He was still acquiring wounds, still bleeding, and it was hard to imagine not feeling like he did. He picked his jeans up from the floor.

"I'll give you some privacy so you can get dressed," she said and went out.

When she came back, he was dressed and ready to go. He realized that he hadn't even kissed her. "Thanks for bringing me home," he said.

"It's okay," she said, and then he left.

II

When Frederick got back to the house, only Molly was there, tail wagging in her happiness to see him, and his hungry cows.

"Did you get lonesome, girl?" He knelt to give her a scratch and she flopped on her back as she liked to do. "You can come with me today," he told her. He spent the next hour tending to his herd.

The sky had the dingy, swollen look of imminent rain or maybe even snow, an unnecessary reminder that he needed to hurry. He had pissed yesterday away, but it had cleared his mind enough so he could focus on work. When he finished with the cows, he went in the house to change clothes and make a thermos of coffee. As he expected, there was no sign that JoAnn had been there.

It felt good to be back in the combine. There was still plenty to do, but now the end was in sight. His problems with JoAnn were out of his hands, and probably had been for some time. As he thought about it, he realized that her dishonesty wasn't something new, although she had never viewed it that way.

She inflated her sales to anyone who'd listen, and to JoAnn, the housing market was always good even if it wasn't. To keep the peace, he'd accepted her explanation that these exaggerations were just a part of the business, that she was only telling people what they wanted to hear, but after a while he'd noticed that she hedged in other ways, too.

It wasn't as if he hadn't heard white lies before. It was common for farmers to overstate their yields, a habit his father avoided. You grew what you grew, he'd tell his son. Some years it's better than others, but it doesn't always have to be better than the neighbors. For a lot of guys he knew, Eldon chiefly among them, fudging the numbers was automatic. If they actually harvested a hundred thirty bushels of corn to the acre—a good yield—it somehow grew to a hundred and forty or fifty by the time they told you about it.

He had soon found that if he dared question JoAnn about her fibs, there was a price to pay. She'd sputter with indignation. How could he? What did he know about it? And that had worked. He'd stopped questioning her dubious assertions to avoid fighting with her. Even now, when he was pretty sure that she had probably committed adultery, she insisted on seeing herself as the aggrieved, someone who could never do such a thing. The more he thought about it, the more he could see that none of what had happened should have been a surprise. It didn't make it hurt less.

III

That evening Frederick drove his pickup back down through the woods to Lisa's trailer. She looked puzzled when she opened the door.

"Surprised?" he asked.

"Kind of. How are things at home?"

"About the same, I guess. I haven't seen her."

"Has she called?"

"Not that I know of, but I've been in the field all day. That's why I came to see you."

"About what?"

"I want to hire you."

"Hire me? To do what?"

"Help me get my crop in. I can't do it by myself and I'm afraid to hire another green hand from the Labor Office." She looked skeptical. "I mean it, Lisa. Mainly, I need someone to pull wagons and keep an eye on the dryer—someone who's spent some time around a farm—someone like you."

"I don't know, Frederick."

"Lisa, the last guy I hired drove my combine through a fence."

"Really?"

"Really. I'll pay you a buck an hour over the going rate. It would be worth it to get someone I can trust." She turned away to think it over.

"I have classes on Monday, Wednesday and Friday mornings," she said, "but the rest of the time I'm free."

"Well, do it then," he insisted.

"Are you sure it won't just make things worse with your wife? I don't want to get in the middle of anything."

"They couldn't be worse, Lisa. I promise you that. I doubt if she'll even be showing up. But what could she say? You're just helping me out." He paused. "I wouldn't ask if I didn't need you."

"I could sure use the money, there's no doubt about that. My savings are used up, so dad's been helping me out—and he really can't afford to."

"It's a deal, then?"

"I guess—if you're sure it'll be alright."

"Of course it will! When can you start?"

"In the morning?"

"Great! I'll see you then."

IV

The sky cleared during the night, and at six in the morning the thermometer outside Frederick's kitchen window read nineteen above zero. When he fed his cows, he had to break a crust of ice off the waterers. They were fat, almost at market weight, so the cold didn't bother them. The air felt more like January than late October. At least it was clear. A few more days should do it—now that he had some help.

Later in the day he was back in the house, grabbing a sandwich, when Lisa showed up with two bags of groceries.

"I picked up a few things in town," she said. "I hope you don't mind, but that way I can fix some hot meals."

"Thanks," he said. "I haven't taken the time to stock up. I always keep cash here." He opened a drawer to show her. "Just take what you need and leave the receipts."

While she put the groceries away, Frederick filled a thermos with coffee. Man, it was good to have a woman in his kitchen, putting groceries away. Such a small thing, yet it filled him with something akin to elation. She was wearing old jeans and a bulky sweater, and her hair was pulled back like the night he had met her. He remembered how it had fallen over him in the darkness of the trailer.

He was aware that desire was mixed in with his gratitude. He hadn't kissed her that night, and now he wondered how it would feel if he did. It had been so long since he'd even touched a woman other than JoAnn. He'd never imagined that he'd ever want to but now, as he turned the cap onto the thermos, he realized that he might like to kiss Lisa Melendez.

Steady, boy, he thought to himself, she's helping you, and you need that more than anything. Maybe later you can think about her that way, after this crop is finally in—after the dust settles. Maybe then.

"I'd better get back out there," he said as he went out the door. "I'll see you later."

EIGHTEEN

Eldon's men had finished the fall plowing, and he was damned happy about it. Harvest was a crazy time of year, even crazier for him because of all the land he worked. The worst thing about it was the calls he constantly got on his radio from his crew—and his wife. He liked the radio because it kept him in touch with everything that was going on. It let him keep his finger on the pulse, so to speak.

If people would just use it like he told them to—when his advice was needed or there was a problem—it would all work fine, but they didn't. Instead, they called him about stupid goddamned things they should have been able to handle themselves, or they didn't call him when they should have.

In truth, Eldon had assembled a force of the best help around, and Sherry had enough savvy and organizational know-how to run a good sized-company. But he had no confidence in any of them, so he invariably used the slightest problem as an excuse to chew someone out—and the louder the better. Just that morning he'd had to jump on Clyde.

"Goddammit to hell, ain't you got better sense than to move those cows without askin' me first?"

"You told me you wanted to move 'em in the next couple of days, Eldon. I had the time, so I thought I'd—"

"Don't think, Clyde. Thinkin's my job."

Clyde Duncan had worked around cattle since he was six years old and forgotten more about them than Eldon would ever know. But, he was fifty-two years old and his future plans didn't include looking for a new job. That's why he leaned against the pickup, studied his boots, and kept his mouth shut.

There was good reason for Eldon's problems with the radio. After years of verbal abuse, his hired men and Sherry, without ever a shared word of conspiracy, had adopted the practice of using the radio to subtly harass him. Having become finely attuned to his annoyances, they learned to nuance their transmissions with just the right amount of exaggeration or hyperbole to set him bolting over the roads.

Living as he did in a kind of perpetual emergency, Eldon found relief where he could, and that was primarily through the satisfying medium of gossip. Spreading the word about other people's misfortunes nourished his sense of superiority. Of course, he felt immune to these pitfalls. People could talk about him all they liked, but what was there to find fault with? His money? His progressive ideas and methods of farming? Who cared? Of course he and Sherry had their little problems—hell, what couple didn't—but they were smart enough to keep them to themselves.

One of Eldon's chief sources of information was Betty Petrowiak, and he stopped by the Falls Tavern a couple of times a week to find out if she had any new tidbits for him. The two of them had developed an unrehearsed routine: Eldon would stand at the bar, sipping the same RC Cola he ordered every time, likely as not talking crops or whatever with whomever happened to be there. Usually it was Betty who would find opportunity to insert a seemingly innocuous question into the conversation: how had so and so's operation gone? Was it true that so and so had switched churches even though his wife had not? Was the bank really getting close to cutting so and so off?

Not everything came from Betty, though. As he rushed up and down the roads, Eldon constantly monitored the activities of his neighbors. He often knew before anyone else who had bought a new pickup or piece of equipment. He knew every barn and shed that needed painting, how many cattle were being fed, how many hogs were headed for market—and how many nights JoAnn Heinold had not come home.

"Maybe she took a trip," Sherry had replied ingenuously after he mentioned this to her.

"During harvest?" he smirked.

"She works in town, Eldon. From what I've seen, she hasn't

really helped him out for over a year." Despite her unhappiness with her own life, Sherry did not approve of JoAnn's lack of participation. She, herself, had grown up on a farm where fifteen-hour workdays were common. She couldn't see why JoAnn couldn't manage to help Frederick out after she'd finished her own work.

"Maybe she didn't help out, but she always come home at night. Who the hell is cookin' for him?" Eldon was unaware that women existed who did not cook.

"Maybe he does his own," Sherry offered.

"You never know with that odd-ball. He's probably a goddamned vegetarian or something. I wouldn't blame her if she did leave him."

"Eldon, she hasn't come home for a couple of nights. That doesn't mean that she's left him."

"Well, somethin's goin' on. He's been two nights in Rock Falls drinkin' this week, and he's still got corn in the field! I tell you something's goin' on."

The prospect of something wrong with Frederick Heinold's marriage greatly appealed to Eldon. His own domestic milk was so sour that it made him feel better to learn that someone else was having marital problems. But with Frederick there was an even more important reason: when a couple split up in the country, it often meant that land had to be sold off. A shaky marriage was Eldon's best hope for getting his hands on the Oddball's farm. That's why he had to keep his eyes open.

It was with such speculation on his mind that Eldon passed Frederick's pickup later that afternoon. It was slowly towing a heavily loaded grain wagon over to the home place, but when Eldon passed it he saw that it wasn't Frederick or JoAnn behind the wheel.

"Jesus Christ!" he said aloud. It was a woman and a good-looking one, from what he could see, but who? "Goddamn!" he exalted. "No wonder the old lady ain't comin' home!"

II

Late in the afternoon, Frederick took a break to come to the house to feed cattle and get a bite to eat. On the way, he passed Lisa in the middle of a shuttle run but they didn't stop to talk.

When he had finished his chores, he went into the house to make a sandwich and discovered that she had cooked a roast along with potatoes and carrots and some other vegetables. They, along with some fresh-baked rolls, were in the warm oven. It was an oasis.

The kitchen hadn't smelled this good since his mother had died. He loaded a plate with food and sat down at the table. It was nothing but plain country cooking, the kind his neighbors ate every day, but it tasted wonderful. For the first time in a lot of meals, he took his time over it, savoring each mouthful. When he finished and went back outside, he found Lisa by the dryer.

"That was something special," he told her.

"Dinner? It was nothing. "

"It was to me," he said. "Thanks."

As he headed back to the field, he thought about what a major undertaking that meal would have been for JoAnn, and how much it would have obligated him to a ration of compliments. Still, he didn't want to dwell on JoAnn's weaknesses. For now, he wanted to keep his mind off their problems.

III

JoAnn was seething with anger at Frederick's humiliation of her, and within earshot of the receptionist, no less, which meant it was now all over the office. She would never forgive him for that—never. So, he thought he was the injured party, did he, the poor, betrayed husband of an unfaithful wife? Well, he could forget about this wife—and this marriage. He could sleep with his goddamned farm for all she cared.

Too upset to work, she left the office, but as she drove around the town, she had to confront the question—what, what she going to do? She wasn't going to go to the farm, and she couldn't bear the idea of explaining the whole mess to her mother who was probably going to side with Frederick, anyway.

Her office was the only place she felt was truly hers, but she couldn't stay there. She had to find a place of her own. It was time. She had already given some thought to buying a house, but there wasn't time for that now. She needed something right away, and that meant an apartment.

By six-thirty, a little less than nine hours after her fight with Frederick, JoAnn had rented a furnished efficiency apartment. It was small and most of the furniture appeared to be made of plastic, but it was a place to stay for now. Most important, it gave her independence from Frederick.

With the apartment rented, she went to the mall and bought some towels and enough clothes to get her through a couple of days. In another day or two, she'd go out to the farm and get her things, but for now she wanted to avoid her husband.

By the time she got around to stopping at her office, it was dark. She had only two messages, both from Miles asking her to call him back at his room at the motel. She'd had a long day, and the thought of seeing him brought out the weariness that her activities had masked.

While she'd been confronting her problems, he had undoubtedly slept, probably past noon. That was Miles: stay up most of the night and sleep most of the day. She couldn't live like that and work, too. She didn't know how he managed it.

Although they had only known each other a few weeks, it seemed longer. It had all begun as a lark. He would leave in a few weeks then her life would go back to its old routine. But he hadn't left, and her life was never going to be the way it was.

And now he'd told her that he loved her. She was having some doubts about that. He was beautiful, by far the most handsome man she'd ever known, and that alone made him exciting, but there was a strained quality to his life that she doubted she could ever adapt to.

Miles could exhaust a day, or a week, like no one she'd ever known. When she was with him, they always seemed to be drinking and eating too much, spending too much time in bed, putting too much of that white powder up their noses. God, she couldn't believe that she was actually doing that, even after she told him she'd never to do it again.

Realistically, she knew she'd be better off with him gone, but tonight she was too tired to think about it. Everything had happened so quickly, and she needed time to collect herself and think. She'd face her first night in the apartment by herself. She knew she ought to at least call her mother, but that could wait, too. Everything could wait until tomorrow.

IV

Miles had slept into the afternoon and then spent several hours waiting for JoAnn to call him back. He was uneasy with the lack of communication and not knowing what was going on between JoAnn and her husband. Around five-thirty, he drove by her office but her car wasn't there.

The whole idea of trying to facilitate a divorce between JoAnn and her husband was a long shot to begin with, and he wasn't even sure he wanted to hang around long enough to make it work. But there was a lot of money involved, maybe three-quarters of a million, and he didn't have to risk arrest to get his hands on it.

If there was one thing he knew how to work, it was a woman. He'd done it before, and with someone a hell of a lot less attractive than JoAnn. If she were to come into a chunk of money, he was certain he could get his hands on at least part of it. But where the hell was she, and why didn't she call?

V

JoAnn was in when Miles called the next morning, and the receptionist put him right through.

"I missed you yesterday," he said first thing. She noticed without enthusiasm that he sounded as bright and confident as usual.

"I'm sorry, but you wouldn't believe how bad my day was."

"Aw, that's too bad. Why don't I take you to lunch and you can tell me all about it."

She hesitated as she tried to build some firmness into her reply. "I can't, Miles. I've got too much to do."

Now, it was he who hesitated. "Are you trying to avoid me?"

She would liked to have said yes. "No. It's not that."

"What then?"

"My marriage is coming apart. I need some time to think."

"Come on, then. It will do you good to talk to someone. You don't have to carry all of this by yourself, you know."

"Miles, I don't think so."

"I'll pick you up in ten minutes," he said and hung up.

She slumped in her chair. She'd lost ground again. During the long, sleepless night in the overly warm apartment she had decided not to see him for at least one more day—and he was already on his way to pick her up. Did she have control over any part of her life? It didn't feel like it.

VI

"And he told you that someone called him?" Miles asked as he drove to the restaurant.

"Yes."

"But he didn't tell you who?"

"I didn't ask," she said. "But Frederick saw my car in the parking lot."

So, it was him, Miles thought. "But you don't think he knows for sure?"

"Well, he didn't actually see us there. How could he?"

"That's good, isn't it? It's one thing to suspect something and another to know it." Miles was speaking from a depth of experience.

"I don't even care," she said, glumly. "He was such an ass—coming to my office like that."

"So you wouldn't care if he knew?"

JoAnn hesitated. "That would make all of this seem like my fault," she said after a moment, "and it's not." Miles noticed that she had not answered him directly. "Maybe we shouldn't see one another for a while," she told him. "It had to be somebody who knew me; probably someone who knows me from business. That's the problem. Too many people know who I am."

"But, you've got a good reason for being with me. I'm a client. You're showing me properties."

"At a motel? In the middle of the night? I don't think so." He'd never seen this side of her, this persistent skepticism. He had a sense of slippage, and he tried not to let it show but it must have. She put her hand on his arm. "It would just be for a while," she said, "until things settle down a little."

"Yeah. Sure," he said.

She could hear the disappointment in his voice. She leaned closer. "We just need to slow things down a little," she said, but it didn't make him feel better. "I rented an apartment," she said more softly. He looked at her. "Last night." That seemed to help.

VII

After spending a second night in the apartment, JoAnn knew that she could no longer avoid going to the farm. She was out of clothes, for one thing, and there were other things she wanted to get, like a radio.

It would also give her an opportunity to tell Frederick about the apartment, something she was looking forward to. She promised Miles to meet him later for dinner and left the office about four o'clock. As she drove, she touched up her make-up and added perfume. She wanted to make this as difficult for Frederick as she could.

When she pulled into the yard, his pickup was not there but another, which she did not recognize, was. Don't tell me he's finally hired some help, she thought, and after all the whining.

When she walked into the kitchen, the woman standing by the stove turned in surprise. JoAnn stopped dead.

"Who are you?" she asked. The tone of her voice was unrelated to any she might have chosen. She looked around the room as if to assure herself that she was where she thought she was, and then back at Lisa who had not moved from the stove.

"You must be Frederick's wife," Lisa said. JoAnn stared at her, still trying to comprehend this unexpected presence.

"That's right, I am," she finally said.

"I was just cleaning up." Lisa wiped her hands on a towel. "I've got some pork chops in the oven—I hope you don't mind—I mean using your kitchen."

"Who are you?"

"My name is Lisa Melendez."

"What are you doing here?"

"I'm helping Frederick. He hired me." JoAnn only stared at her. "Oh, not to do this. To haul wagons—and run the dryer. I'm just doing this," Lisa looked at the stove as if it would explain everything, "because I—."

The awkwardness of the moment was eroding her composure, and the words trailed off in the strained tension. There wasn't the slightest indication on JoAnn's face that she comprehended this explanation, and Lisa felt trapped in the swelling tension. JoAnn's arrival may not have been completely unexpected, but this reaction certainly was. Lisa had never encountered anything quite like it.

"It's nice to meet you," she finally said and extended her hand to JoAnn who stared mutely at it. Then, just as Lisa thought she might say something, JoAnn Heinold fled from her own kitchen.

VIII

Eldon Mathews had never seen JoAnn Heinold drive so recklessly. She came right down the center of the road, so he had to move almost to the shoulder to make room.

When he drove by Frederick's, the strange pickup was still parked there. Something was going on, that was for damned sure. He'd have to stop in Rock Falls to see if Betty had heard anything.

IX

"She was here," Lisa told him when Frederick got back to the house.

"Here?" he asked.

"Yes, and she was really upset."

"What did she say?"

"She asked who I was. Otherwise, nothing."

"Nothing?" That didn't sound like JoAnn.

"I think she assumed the worst, Frederick." He nodded. "I tried to tell her that I was only helping you out, but I don't think she believed me. She didn't act like it, anyway." Lisa was obviously upset, herself but he didn't know what to say to her. Things had gone to hell without his participation. "I'm going to go now," she told him. He walked out to her truck with her.

"I'm sorry," he said.

"I am, too. It was hard to see her upset like that."

"Lisa, I know this has been tough but I hope you'll come back in the morning. We're almost finished."

"I guess the damage has been done," she said. "I'll come over after my class. But I better stay out of the kitchen."

After she left, Frederick ate the meal she'd fixed and tried to figure what had happened. He'd made a mistake to not expect JoAnn to show up. He'd been so happy to have Lisa's help that he

143

hadn't even thought about it. The more he thought about it, the worse he felt. What if JoAnn had taken the first step toward some kind of understanding between them and been rewarded with a strange woman in her house?

X

In the morning Frederick decided to drive into town to see JoAnn. When he got to her office, she was there. Without a word of greeting, she stepped around him, closed the door, and sat back down at her desk.

"I heard that you stopped out, yesterday," he said. "I was surprised."

"I can see why."

"JoAnn, I hired her to help me out."

"I see. With your household chores?"

"I hired her to help with the wagons and the dryer. She just happened to be in the kitchen when you got there."

"How convenient."

"Look. She's doing pretty much what you used to do when you helped me out."

"I'll bet she is."

"There's no reason for you to be upset over this."

"There isn't? Look how upset you got because you heard I was doing something wrong! And did you even give me a chance to explain?"

"I guess not."

"But you think I should give you one!"

"Look. I didn't come here to get into all that. I realized that you'd come out to talk things over, and it must have been awkward to find someone in the house. I came to tell you that there's nothing to her being there."

"That's very big of you, Frederick."

"I didn't come here to fight. I'm sick of fighting. You made the first move, and I thought you would appreciate my coming here to set things right."

"I didn't make the first move, Frederick. I didn't go out there to talk to you, I went there to get my things. I've rented my own apartment!"

"You've what?"

"I've rented an apartment."

"You've moved out?"

"Yes."

Everything inside him was twisting, again. "Couldn't we have talked it over first?" he asked.

"After the way you walked in here and humiliated me?"

"You? How the hell do you think I felt?"

"Oh, you felt like God himself—accusing me—judging me!"

"You were in a motel room in the middle of the night—with another man!" The lid was coming off again.

"That's not true!" she said quite loudly. "Someone called you in the middle of the night and told you that, and you believed them without even talking to me!"

"Your car was there! I saw it!"

"That doesn't mean that I was with someone!"

"And it doesn't mean you weren't!"

"I saw the woman in your kitchen!"

"I hired her to help me because you wouldn't! You kept telling me to hire someone and I did!"

"A woman?"

"She was raised on a farm! She knows what she's doing!"

"You ought to be happy, then! You finally got yourself a little farm girl who'll stay home and do the chores!"

"That's right, JoAnn, she does! She even turns the oven on once in a while!"

"I'll bet that's not all she turns on!"

It's going to hell again, he thought. He hadn't wanted it to, but there it was.

"I'm sorry," he said, almost softly.

"I'm not," JoAnn said. He stood for a few more moments, but he could think of nothing else to say. It was time to go, but his hope—his need—to make things better held him there.

"I'm sorry," he said again and turned and left.

JoAnn sat down and stared at the place where he had been standing. Now she knew that renting the apartment had been the right thing. She couldn't imagine their being together again. There was nothing left of them but anger and blame—ashes from a fire that hadn't been very bright to begin with. It was time to move toward whatever the future held.

Now she could talk with her mother. She had found another

woman in the house and Loretta would take her side against that. And now that she could tell people that she and Frederick were separated, it would be easier to be seen in public with Miles. She was on her own. It would be nice to have him stay around for a while to keep her company. Maybe they could even take a trip together—maybe to Florida.

NINETEEN

Two days after his fight with JoAnn, on the second of November, with less than sixty acres left to harvest, the storm hit. It had begun as the last tropical storm of the season, sucking itself out of the Gulf of Mexico and squalling north toward a collision with a mass of cold air stalled over the northern plains. As Frederick finished his chores, an anemic dawn leached slowly out of a sky swollen with jaundiced clouds. It was a dangerous sky and the air was thick with the ominous smell of rain. This would not miss him. Whatever was to come was already up there, a vast ocean of trapped water and wind, straining for release.

It hung above, through the morning, while he anxiously worked the rows of the last field. Then, just before noon, the sky grew so dark that he had to turn on his lights. As he finished a pass and turned back toward the east, the face of it came across the road and hurtled toward him, a furious tantrum of driven rain that slammed against the machine with a fury that forced him to stop.

He could barely see past the platform where the flailed corn was drowning in a grand mal of maddened water. The cab kept him dry, but the harvester rocked violently in the shearing wind, and he had to shield his eyes from the lightning that lit the sky with blinding discharge. He could do nothing but sit and hope— and then he heard what he hoped he would not hear—the rattle of hail against the metal of the combine, first one then another and another until they blended into a din of battering ice.

Although he couldn't see through the blear of water, he could tell from the sharp sounds that the stones were big—and they were pounding his combine with a frightening intensity. He feared they'd smash the glass of the compartment he sat in.

Instinctively, he leaned back from the windshield, but there was no escaping the roar of ice and water that was destroying his crop. He hoped that Lisa had not been caught in the open. Although he had never seen it, he had heard of large hail stripping trees and even killing small animals. His father had told him of being forced into the back seat of his car while hail broke out the windshield and covered the front seat with knobby, gray hailstones the size of baseballs. He was grateful that his soybeans and most of his corn were safely stored in bins.

In less than fifteen minutes, the storm passed as quickly as it had come, and Frederick stepped out into the desolation. He had never seen anything like it. Millions of tons of water and ice had been dumped on the field, too much for the earth to swallow. Water stood ankle deep, a strange, shocked lake, scummed with shattered plants and ice. Here and there, broken corn stocks jutted out of the water like compound fractures, but most had been pounded flat.

The roof and sides of the harvester were peppered with thousands of dents and much of the paint was gone. It was as if someone had taken a large hammer to it. The wheels of the heavy machine had already sunk to the axles in the mud beneath them. He couldn't have moved it if he'd wanted to. Since there was nothing more he could do, he shut off the engine and waded through the cold muck to his truck.

It was just as badly dented as the harvester and the windshield had been cracked. He locked the hubs on the wheels into four-wheel drive, then churned across the field to the driveway. There were a couple of places where his wheels went down so far that he didn't know if he'd make it, but they somehow found purchase and kept him moving until he reached the road.

When he got to the house, the yard was littered with hail and leaves and small limbs, but he couldn't see anything more major. As he walked toward the porch, Lisa came out to meet him.

"I saw it coming," she said. "I just got my truck into the shed before it hit. Thank God Molly was with me." The dog huddled against her leg, still scared. "I thought it was going to tear the roof off."

"It did a number on my combine," he told her. "I better take a look around to see what else is damaged."

"I'm going to run home and see how Dad made out," she said. As she walked toward her truck, Molly stayed at her side.

"You may have a new dog," he said.

"She's just scared. She may as well ride over with me."

After Lisa left, Frederick toured his buildings. He could see plenty of damage to roofs, but not to anything else. The wind was swinging to the northeast and the temperature was still dropping. Lisa called to say that some of her father's chickens had been killed and she was staying to help him dress them out.

"I'm finished in the field," he told her. "I don't know when I'll even be able to get the combine out. There's nothing I can do now but run these last wagons through the dryer. Come over when you get a chance."

By nightfall, the temperature had dropped thirty-five degrees and a heavy snow began to fall. It was early in the season but this looked serious. It was still coming down when he got out of bed at six-thirty. By then it was over a foot deep. He spent part of the morning mounting a front loader on his tractor and the rest pushing snow out of his driveway and from around the buildings. This was work he was accustomed to doing in December and January, but not in early November.

Lisa came over at noon. The storm had ended the reason they had for working together, and Frederick was already regretting it. They sat at the kitchen table drinking coffee while he figured up what he owed her and wrote a check. Molly had calmed down and sprawled under the table, napping.

"She's going to miss you," Frederick told Lisa when he handed her the check.

"I'm going to miss her, too." She knelt down to scratch the collie behind an ear.

"I'm sorry things came to such a sudden halt," he said.

"I am, too," she said. "I'd forgotten how much I love doing this kind of work."

"You're good at it, too," he said. "The best help I've had in a long time."

She smiled and almost blushed. The dog lay blissfully beneath her stroking fingers, oblivious to the changes going on around her. It's too quick, Lisa thought to herself. She had known the work was only going to last so long, but now that it was over she regretted it.

She knew that she'd made Frederick's life a little easier since they'd met, but now he was going to have to go back to being by himself, and she wasn't sure how that would go. It looked to her as if this was shaping up to be an ugly divorce. She thought about saying something to reassure him but she didn't. She patted the dog and stood up.

"I'd better go," she said. He walked her out to her truck, and she said good bye and drove off.

II

After the snow finally stopped, the sky cleared and the temperature dipped near zero. Light winds had begun to worry the snow into restless tendrils that sent little drifts across the roads and began to fill the ditches. He knew the drifts would get larger in a hurry if the winds should rise. In years past his road had been closed many times by drifting snow, and it looked like it would be happening again, and soon.

Two days after the storm, Frederick drove into Lime City to stock up on groceries. He drove by JoAnn's office but didn't see her car. It made him feel like he was back in high school, driving by some girl's house just to check her out, but he knew that he needed to stay away. Besides groceries, he stocked up at the liquor store, buying more than he'd ever had in the house before.

Frederick adjusted as well as he could to the sudden changes the storm had brought. Except for tending his cattle, he stayed mostly in the house, trying to catch up on his paper work and picking at a book that he'd been meaning to read. He cooked big pots of spaghetti and soups that provided lots of leftovers.

Just a few days before he had been harried by work, but now he had too little of it to fill the hours. He hoped for a warm-up, something to delay winter a while longer, but there was nothing in the forecasts to indicate one was on the way. It looked like a long winter, ahead.

Two days later, at nightfall, the wind rose, blowing snow into a fine powder that obscured headlights and made the road difficult to see. It was a bad night to be driving, which is why he was surprised when the Cadillac came fishtailing up the driveway and stopped in front of the house. He was just finishing loading silage into a feed bunker, when it drove in and two people got out and hurried into the house. Who the hell did he know who drove a Cadillac?

When he walked into the kitchen, JoAnn had thrown her coat over the back of a chair and was rubbing her hands together to warm them.

"Frederick!" she said a bit gaily. He was discouraged to see how good she looked. Just then, a man that he did not know came into the room. "Frederick, I want you to meet a friend of mine—Miles Richards. He offered to drive me out." Miles extended a hand.

"I was just using your bathroom," he said pleasantly. "It's getting kind of bad out there isn't it?"

Frederick was still surprised by their sudden appearance and he probably showed it. Incredibly, the man was dressed in an open-necked shirt and sports jacket—as if it were summer.

"It is," Frederick answered, "especially if you're driving a car." He turned to JoAnn. "You should have called. I would have come and got you with the truck."

"Oh, I didn't want to bother you while you were so busy. I just needed to pick up some things."

Her cheerfulness confused him. She'd been so bitter the last time. He wondered if she'd been drinking, but mostly he wondered who this guy was.

"Are you from Lime City?" Frederick asked him.

"Oh no," the man said, smiling at the idea. "I'm from Florida—Fort Lauderdale."

"Florida? What are you doing here?"

"You know, I've been asking myself the same question." He smiled at JoAnn.

"I'm going upstairs," JoAnn interrupted, "to get some things together." The man watched her go with the same pleasant expression he'd worn since he arrived.

"Can I get you something?" Frederick asked him. "A beer or a drink? I've got some wine, too."

"Wine would be fine," Miles told him.

Frederick had bought a half-gallon of red wine, and he set it on the table along with three glasses. "I'm afraid I don't keep much of a selection," he said.

"You seem to have an adequate supply."

Frederick missed the amusement in the remark. "How do you know JoAnn?" he asked.

"I've been looking at some real estate with her."

"You're thinking about buying a house in Lime City?"

"Yes, thinking about it."

"You'd move here—from Florida?"

"Not full-time, of course. For just part of the year."

"Why would you want to do that?"

"I deal in antiques. I buy them here and ship them to Florida."

"There's money in that?"

"If I do enough volume. I also do some importing."

"What do you import?"

"Mexican and South American pottery, leather, some jewelry...you know, whatever sells."

"What sells?"

"Right now? Very little. The peso's worth too much."

"So, you're mostly in the antique business."

"Right now, yes." He paused to sip some wine.

"Has JoAnn found you a house?"

"There's one I'm interested in."

"So you're going to stay around awhile."

"Perhaps. I'm trying to decide."

JoAnn called down from upstairs: "Miles, could you help me with these?"

"Excuse me," he said pleasantly and left.

Frederick had a bad feeling that he was sharing a glass of wine with the man who was sleeping with his wife. He wasn't short on guts, that was for sure. Miles returned, carrying two suitcases.

"Let me take those out," Frederick offered. "I'm better dressed for the weather." When he came back in from outside, JoAnn had put her coat on. The visit was ending as abruptly as it had begun. "Be careful," he told them. "That road will be drifting shut."

"Miles can handle it," she assured him, and then they were gone.

Their arrival and departure had been so sudden that

Frederick had hardly been able to collect himself, but now the reality of the empty kitchen set in. He needed something stronger than wine, so he got out a bottle of whisky and poured some into a glass. They had seemed as comfortable and happy as he had not. He would have bet that this was the guy she was with at the motel that night. Except for in movies, Frederick had never seen anyone dressed like that.

He was a good-looking son-of-a-bitch, he'd give him that, but he wasn't impressed with his intelligence, driving around on a night like this on roads he didn't know, wearing clothes that wouldn't keep him alive ten minutes if they ended up in a ditch. JoAnn had been dressed almost as foolishly in a light coat and high-heeled shoes—and she knew better. And what was with that flippant giddiness of hers?

None of these disparagements made him feel any better. He sipped the whisky and tried not to think of the long night ahead, but it was hard to ignore the sharp edge of loneliness. Just then, the porch door banged and Miles Richards walked in. Everything—his clothes and hair—even his eyebrows—were coated with snow, and his face and hands were red with cold.

"Stuck," he said. "Went in the ditch." He was shivering so hard that he could barely get the words out.

"Where's JoAnn?" Frederick asked. "Did she stay in the car?"

"Y-y-yes," Miles replied. Early stages of hypothermia had turned his glibness into imbecility. While Frederick pulled on his heavy coveralls, Miles crouched over the heating register and tried to get warm.

Frederick headed slowly down the road which was fast disappearing under drifting snow. Once in a while he caught a glimpse of the Cadillac's tire prints, but otherwise he could see nothing. He tried to keep to the center to avoid drifting off into the ditch—all the while looking for the car. He didn't even know which side of the road they'd gone in.

Less than a half mile from the house, he came upon the big rear end of the Cadillac, jutting up from the ditch like a torpedoed ship. The ditch was full of snow and the car had plunged into it, burying the front end almost to the windshield. He swung the truck around so its lights shined on it, then got out and climbed down to the driver's door. He forced it open enough to get his head in. JoAnn huddled on the front seat. She looked

153

desperate.

"Can you pull us out?" She could barely talk.

"There wouldn't be much point. You'd just get stuck again. Besides, you need to get warm—fast."

"I don't want to spend the night at the farm."

"I don't think you have a choice. Come on. I'll help you out."

She crawled across the seat and squeezed out the door.

"My God!" she said as the wind hit her. He picked her up and staggered up out of the ditch. "I don't want you to carry me, Frederick." He ignored her and carried her to the truck.

She huddled against the heater vent as he carefully turned the truck around and started back.

"Why didn't you run the heater in the car?" he asked.

"The engine killed and he couldn't get it started. Is he okay?"

"Yeah, he's alright," he said with disgust. "He's damned lucky he found the house. The wind chill must be twenty-five below."

"Thank God," she said.

When they got to the house, she was shivering so hard she could barely talk.

"I'm so glad you're alright," she said to Miles. He had drawn a chair up to the register and was holding a glass of whiskey.

"This heat feels good," he said.

"Come on, JoAnn. I'll run you a bath," Frederick said. He led her up the stairs to the bedroom, then ran the water in the tub as hot as he thought she could stand it. "I'll make you something hot to drink," he told her then went downstairs.

He boiled up a kettle of water. "Do you want something hot?" he asked.

"No. This'll do," Miles said. He was preoccupied with getting warm. Frederick made tea in a large mug, then added honey, lemon and a generous shot of bourbon, and went back upstairs with it.

He knocked on the bathroom door.

"Yes?" JoAnn asked.

"I made you a toddy," he said.

"I'm in the tub, Frederick. I'll be down in a few—"

He opened the door and went in. She frowned, but was too exhausted to argue. "Here," he said, handing her the mug. "How are you feeling?" He couldn't help but look at her nakedness with longing.

"I'm okay." Her voice was going drowsy. He sat down on the stool and felt the water near her knee. It was too hot for him to have sat in.

"Do you want me to wash anything?" he asked in an attempt at humor.

"I'm not dirty, I'm just cold." It was a rebuff, to be sure, but at least it was the JoAnn he knew and it reassured him.

"Do you remember when I used to make you toddies like that?" he asked.

"Yes." She held the mug above the water in both hands. He loved the way she cradled it with her fingers, so delicate and feminine that it made him ache. She closed her eyes and sank until the water touched her chin. She knew that he was looking at her body and wishing that he could have it.

"You'd better go down and see how Miles is doing," she said without opening her eyes.

"We hit a big drift," Miles explained to Frederick. He had moved his chair back from the register and his smile had returned, flushed now by the whiskey.

"It can happen," Frederick said.

"Winter came kind of sudden, huh?"

"Yeah, kinda," Frederick said. His mind was upstairs by the tub and he didn't feel like talking to this guy.

Just then JoAnn came into the room wearing a sweater and some old jeans. "I look kind of grubby," she said to Miles.

"You look lovely," he said with such enthusiasm that Frederick looked at him. The man had no sense of his own foolishness—or how the two of them might have frozen to death because of it. He was back in his routine.

JoAnn pulled a chair up to the table and sat down. "What are we going to do?" she asked Miles.

"I'm at your disposal," he said and lifted his glass in a little salute. Frederick watched them, painfully aware of their restored intimacy. JoAnn glowed from the warmth of her bath. Had she ever been so desirable to him? Had she ever been so distant?

She looked at him. "Will your truck make it?" she asked.

"I don't know. I doubt it. And what if we all get stuck out there? What do we do then?"

"I don't want to stay here," she said stubbornly but he didn't bother to argue. It was all out of his hands, anyway. She'd walk, if she decided to walk. Naked, if she felt like it. It would have nothing to do with anything but what she wanted to do.

Frederick sipped the whiskey, which was beginning to take effect. Miles reached to take her hand.

"Why don't we stay here until tomorrow," he suggested.

"Are you sure?" she wondered.

Without letting go of her hand he turned to smile at Frederick. "What do you think?"

"I've stopped doing that," Frederick said ironically.

"We'd better stay then," Miles said with his odd pleasantness. He picked up JoAnn's mug. "I'll fix you another."

For the next several hours the three of them sat at the table drinking while Miles talked constantly and expansively, as if he had designated himself the featured speaker. He focused on JoAnn, surrounding her with talk, caressing her with his enormous enthusiasm for the things he was telling her, and as she drank more, she began to respond with a coy flirtatiousness that Frederick had never seen before.

As their enjoyment of each other grew more exclusive and more enthusiastic, Frederick felt as if he were receding further and further from them into the embracing companionship of the whiskey. It was his only hope of surviving the disappointment and loneliness of this increasingly surreal night.

By midnight, they were all drunk, none more than JoAnn who rose suddenly to her feet. "I'm going to bed," she announced and walked uncertainly out of the kitchen. Miles remained in his seat, smiling down at the table, still pleasantly absorbed in whatever it was he had been relating to her. After a few moments, he realized that his audience had left. He and Frederick silently sat for some time in their respective stupors.

"Guess it's time to hit the old sack," Miles said after a while. He got up and went into the living room and crashed on the couch. At least they're not sharing a bed, Frederick thought. He remained at the table for a while, listening to the wind and feeling miserable. He wished that they had left, but it was too late now. He hoped he was drunk enough to sleep.

He went upstairs. The door to their bedroom was closed and he paused by it, leaning heavily on the jamb, longing to go in but remembering the last time he'd transgressed. Instead, he went into the bedroom across the hall and fell into bed. He was asleep and snoring in minutes.

III

JoAnn had not been sleeping long before she was gradually awakened by the clumsy efforts of someone trying to undo the clasps of the brassiere she had worn to bed. Her brain did its best to ignore the bothersome fumbling and the raspy chin against her neck, but they persisted until she was awake enough to realize where she was and what was going on.

"Frederick!" she hissed. "Get out of this bed!"

"Shhhhh," Miles whispered back. "It's me."

"Miles! What are you doing here?"

"What do you think?" he giggled.

"Where's Frederick?"

"Damned if I know."

"You've got to get out of here! He'll hear us!"

He squeezed her breast for a reply. "Shhhhh," he repeated, "he'll hear us." He was trying to push the bra off without undoing it.

She rolled over to face him. "Miles, I mean it! You've got to get out of here!"

"How do you get this thing off?"

She tried to stop him as she listened for a sound that would tell her if Frederick was awake. Miles pulled free and began to paw her.

"Get out of here before you wake him up!" she hissed.

"Do you know any good farmer's daughters jokes?" he asked.

JoAnn was completely awake, now, and she realized that he was drunker than she had ever seen him. He didn't care who heard him.

"Please, Miles. Would you just leave?"

"If you'd shut up, he wouldn't hear nothin'."

"Please stop, Miles. Please."

"Just relax," he said, and he began to mouth her nipples. She thought she heard Frederick's snoring from down the hallway. Miles was not going to give this up. If she kept resisting, the noise might wake her husband.

"Okay, okay let me get it," she said, accepting the inevitable.

She reached to unsnap the bra. "But for God's sake, be quiet!"

As she slipped it off, she hoped that he would be content to finish this quietly—and quickly—but her sudden cooperation only encouraged his aggressiveness. He grasped her panties with surprising roughness until the fabric pulled up into her. "Miles," she gasped. It sounded much louder than she intended, but he still ignored her.

Just as she was about to cry out in pain, they tore away and he tossed the remnant away. Then he was after her, his mouth roving her body with sucking kisses and sharp little bites. He took a nipple between his teeth and held it just above the threshold of pain, and she responded with an unintended moan.

She tried to keep him quiet, but her body was insurrecting to his determined efforts to excite her. She found herself barely holding on. He wanted nothing less than total surrender and he was driving her toward it as he never had before, and she was giving way, crumbling, her body breaking into pieces, each a tiny cry that fluttered into the darkness. Then it was all past holding and there was nothing she could do but crush a pillow against her mouth.

TWENTY

Much as he might have liked to have slept on, Frederick woke at dawn and went downstairs. The visitor was asleep on the couch, his clothes as rumpled as the newspaper he slept on. So the previous night hadn't been a bad dream—and it was still going on.

He made coffee and drank a cup, then went outside. As he expected, a lot of snow had blown in during the night. After he fed his cows, he spent the next two hours on the tractor, clearing it out. It was a job he was already tired of—with maybe four months of winter still ahead. When he went back inside, his visitors were still asleep. Although the sun was shining brightly, the day was anything but promising.

He had another cup of coffee, then decided to take the tractor and a log chain down to the Cadillac. When he got there, he found that the snow had erased all signs of last night's activity. The car's rear end thrust skyward from a perfect drift like the centerpiece of a museum tableau. Only a little snow was now moving in the faint breeze, but everywhere he saw the perfection of sculpted drifts. It would have been beautiful if it hadn't meant so much inconvenience and work—and that his wife and another man had spent the night.

He hooked one end of the chain to the tractor and the other to the car's rear axle and easily dragged it up onto the road. Afterwards, he rehooked the chain and towed the Caddie slowly down the road and into his yard.

The kitchen was still empty when he got back, but he could hear water running in the upstairs bathroom. After a while

JoAnn came down, wrapped in a bathrobe and looking pale and unsteady. She sat at the table.

"You still can't drink," he told her.

"Where's Miles?" She spoke softly and carefully as she tried out her first words of the morning.

"In the living room, I think, still asleep."

She carefully brushed her hand through her hair. "I feel awful," she said.

"Do you want some coffee?"

"No. It wouldn't stay down."

He knew that her hangover was crushing her. She looked forlorn—hopeless. Drinking did that to her. "I got the car out," he told her.

"Good," she said without conviction.

"Do you want me to call your office?"

She thought it over. "No." She stroked a temple and he watched her and the room filled with silence, again. "I've got to sleep some more," she finally said and slowly climbed the stairs.

The house was too quiet, so Frederick went back outside and pushed more snow from around the feed bunks. The cattle milled against the side of the barn, their backs covered in powdered snow. Somehow they had adapted to the sudden change in weather. As long as he kept them well fed, they'd generate enough heat to stay warm. They were plenty fat, he was just waiting for prices to improve so he could sell them. Right now, he was happy they were giving him something to do.

When he went back in, they were both in the kitchen. JoAnn didn't look much better. The man's clothes were irreparably rumpled, but he seemed to have recovered, somewhat. "I made some more coffee," he told Frederick. "I think it's a little strong."

"How are you feeling?" Frederick asked JoAnn. She only nodded, slowly. She was wearing her clothes, now, and they looked slept in, too.

"Well, we appreciate your help," Miles said to Frederick. "I guess it's time we got back to town."

Frederick had known they would be going, even welcomed it last night, but still he asked her: "Do you want to stay? You don't look so good."

"No. I've got to go," she said, and then they were gone.

II

He began to drink—by himself—in the house. There was too much time to fill—too much silence—too much loneliness. He tried to recall how he'd lived in the years after his father died. Had he been this lonely? He didn't remember, but he'd been someone else, then, someone that he wasn't now and someone that he wouldn't be again. Bad as his marriage had gotten, he didn't want to be single again. Why, he wondered, would JoAnn want that? Maybe she didn't. Maybe she didn't plan to be. Maybe she was planning to marry this guy. How could she replace him so soon? He couldn't see how he ever could, but she didn't seem as unhappy as he felt and that made him feel worse. He drank.

The days went on with agonizing slowness, the light shrinking and the darkness growing as the solstice, the nadir of the sun's light grew nearer. The snow's brightness bounced the sun's paltry warmth back out into space, and the temperatures stayed far below normal. It snowed every couple of days and the wind haunted the fields, scouring plowed fields down to anthracitic clods of frozen earth and building substantial drifts everywhere it found a lee. Blue shadows stretched across the snow.

Every morning he had to clear the yard again. He had to feed his cattle more to keep weight on them. His wife did not call him nor did anyone else. He went to Lime City once a week to buy food and whiskey and did not drive past her office. Sometime during the second week he began to view his drinking as something other than a character flaw: it was a necessity, a substitute for everything that was gone and not coming back, and necessities were not flaws.

During the third week he didn't shave for a couple of days and the stubble grew out and he decided it would be a beard. He had never grown a beard before, but it seemed like a good time for one.

One evening in the fourth week someone knocked on his door. It was Lisa. He could see that she was as surprised by the beard as he was by her arrival.

"How are you?" she asked as she slid her coat off.

"I'm making it." His voice sounded strange to him—unused. Fortunately, the kitchen was actually kind of presentable.

"Would you like something to drink? I'm afraid I don't have any wine."

She looked at the half-full bottle of bourbon on the table. "I'll have a little of that," she said.

He put some ice in a glass and poured some of the whiskey over it.

"Some weather, huh?" he asked.

"It's terrible. I had to move in with Dad a couple of weeks ago. The snow got too high."

"Shot any pool lately?"

"Not much. The snow keeps drifting our lane shut, and I've been afraid to leave after dark. How about you?"

"The same. It's pretty much been just Molly and me."

The dog had come in from the living room when she'd arrived and was standing next to her, begging a pet. Lisa leaned down to rub her head.

"I'd heard you were sort of doing the hermit thing," she said.

"I'll bet I know where."

"No bet," she said. "It was Betty."

He took another sip. "So, what did she say?"

Lisa hesitated. "She said that your wife ran out on you." Frederick shook his head at the joke. The world knew. "I guess they're right," he said.

"I'm sorry, Frederick."

"Me, too," he said, "but there's no getting around it."

"I've been thinking about coming to see you, but I didn't want to cause problems—especially after what happened last time."

"It's awfully good to see you. Don't worry. She's gone for good."

"You're sure?"

"I'm sure. She came out one night to get her clothes and brought the new boyfriend with her."

"Oh, Frederick. That had to be pretty rough."

"I don't think it's going to kill me," he said, "although some nights I wish it would. It's just going to take me some time. Enough of that, though, how's school?"

"Okay. I just finished finals."

"Good for you, Lisa."

"I think I'm going to be leaving soon."

"You are?" The dismay in his face was pretty evident.

"Sonny has been calling me a lot. He wants us to get back together."

"And you're thinking about it?"

She laughed. "Hell no. But he won't take no for an answer. Sonny doesn't understand the concept of no. I'm afraid he's going to come up here, and I want to be gone when he does."

"Where are you headed?"

"Arizona. I've got a friend who lives in Tucson. She'll put me up until I get situated." He couldn't think of anything to say. "I wanted to see you before I left," she said.

"I hate to see you go," he said. "You're the only thing that seemed half right the past few months." His sadness filled the room, and she reached and took his hand in both of hers. He looked at her and found her looking at him. When he leaned to kiss her, she came to him.

The kiss reminded him of the night in her trailer when she had rescued him. Her mouth was warm and giving and he savored it. "I'm sorry about the whiskers," he said.

"It's okay."

"If I'd known you were coming, I'd have shaved."

She saw the smile and was glad for it. "Sure you would have."

"I won't always be like this."

"I know. Things will get better for you. It'll just take some time."

"Will you stay with me tonight?"

"Yes."

They stood next to the bed and he undressed her. He kissed her again and again, savoring the warmth of her mouth, the tenderness of the kisses she gave back, the subtle joy of their mutual discoveries. When he slid next to her under the covers, a wave of repose washed over him. He found her mouth in the darkness and kissed her for a long time and felt the lightness that had nothing to do with whiskey. Each tenderness was a rediscovery of things he had forgotten and for these few precious hours he felt as if he'd been saved.

III

"I don't want you to leave," he told her in the morning. They had made love again in the first light, and were lying under the covers with their bodies touching.

"Oh, please don't ask me, Frederick. It's hard enough. If I stay any longer I may not be able to leave at all."

"You don't have to," he told her. She turned to look at him, their eyes only inches apart.

"It's not good for us, right now," she said. "I've just gotten myself unmixed with Sonny, and you're all mixed up with JoAnn."

"It's over."

"You don't know that. It's not necessarily over just because you say it is or you want it to be. Sometimes not even when the judge says it is. A marriage has its own life and it dies when it's ready to die, and until it does, you can't see clearly ahead. Some people never seem to get clear of it. They're with someone else, but they're still tangled up with the past because they never got it settled or let it go. It won't work if you haven't left the other person behind."

He knew that she was speaking this last thing directly to him. "I need you," he said.

She turned from him and stared up at the ceiling. "I know you do, Frederick, and I love being there for you when you need me, but I'd like something more than need, I guess." There was nothing he could say to argue it. It was out of his hands—like everything else. "Timing is a big thing in life." She said it as much to herself as to him.

"I guess. I never thought of anything beyond JoAnn. I never thought that I'd have to. I thought we'd go on and on—and yet, here I am."

"I know."

"Leaving sounds awfully nice, but I've got to stay and see this through. My whole life is here. I don't know what I'd do without this farm. With everything else falling apart, it's still something to hold onto. It's like when my mom died and my dad had to go on after all those years with her. The farm helped him through it. I'm hoping it'll help me, too."

Lisa kissed him. "You'll be all right," she said, and she knew that he would be, that what he had said was absolutely true. The farm would help him through all this loneliness.

"It's all I know and all I am," he said. "I guess I better take care of it."

IV

A few days after Lisa left, Frederick went into Rock Falls to socialize at the tavern. Several people kidded him about the beard, but no one brought up the subject of his absent wife. Encouraged by this civility, he decided to hang around and shoot some pool.

He had won a couple of games and was bent over the table, lining up a shot, when an enormous figure in a snowmobile suit and helmet strode through the door and began to talk—loudly. Without looking up, Frederick recognized the voice as Eldon's. He paused, recalibrated the shot and made it.

"Betty, I need a schnapps!" Eldon ordered.

Eldon rarely drank anything alcoholic at the tavern, except when he was out on his snowmobile, like tonight. Two of its major effects on him were that he got louder and more aggressive, and he was manifesting at least one of them right now. Frederick decided to ignore this stridence and focus on the game, but when Eldon turned to survey the room, he saw him.

"I'll be goddamned! The hippie farmer is out tonight!" He strode toward the table in a flourish of jerked zippers and Velcro, as he tried to ventilate the hot suit.

Frederick stood up. "Eldon," he replied with a slight nod. A snowmobile suit becomes a sauna in any temperature above thirty degrees, and Eldon's face was already looking poached.

"Lookin' a little shaggy, ain't you Freddy?" He seemed delighted with the beard.

"Just a little."

"Just bought me a new sled, today. Fastest one they make—the Eliminator."

"I see," Frederick replied. He lined up the six and shot it into a side pocket.

"You don't have snowmobiles, do you Frederick?"

"Nope." Frederick moved toward his next shot.

"You ought to. Nothin' like a ride on a fast sled to blow the stink off a man. It's good for you."

Like most farm kids, the one playing Frederick was obsessed with machines and speed. "How fast will she go, Eldon?" the kid asked.

"She's supposed to top out somewheres around a hunderd,

165

but I ain't had her over eighty-five."

"Man," the kid said. It was his turn to shoot, but Frederick could see that his concentration had been lost to the conversation with Eldon. He knew that he'd beat him for sure, now, but he regretted the loss of competition.

"Why don't you shoot a game, Eldon?" he asked. Frederick knew that he didn't like to play pool so why not ask him. "Put your quarter up."

"Naw. Pool's a goddamn waste of time. If I'm gonna relax, I wanna do it out in the fresh air, not in a smoky old beer joint." Just then the kid carelessly knocked the eight ball in. "See, there. One little mistake and there goes another fuckin' quarter."

"Watch the language, Eldon," Betty chided him from behind the bar.

"Whoops. Sorry Betty."

The kid looked at the clock that hung over the back bar. "I got to go," he said and picked his coat off a chair. As Frederick went over to put up his cue, Eldon followed.

"I ain't seen the old lady around, Frederick."

It was not entirely unexpected, but Frederick felt the flush of heat in his stomach, anyway. He turned and faced him.

"She's moved into town."

"For good?"

"Maybe."

"Who's the guy with the Cadillac?"

"A friend, I guess." He leaned against the pool table, wishing he'd go away and knowing that he wouldn't. The meat of Eldon's face was basted in sweat and strands of hair stuck to his forehead.

"You don't look so good, Frederick. You been eatin' okay?"

"Yeah, I think so."

"Maybe you should hire you a cook. I hear that Breka girl's lookin' for work."

"Where did you hear that, Eldon?"

"I dunno. Around, I guess."

"Is there some point you're trying to make?"

"Naw. I'm just tryin' to be neighborly. I figured it was kind of tough to have your wife run off like that."

So, here it was. Frederick stood up. "It sounds like the schnapps is running your mouth tonight," he said.

Eldon smiled the smile of a man picking a fight he knew he couldn't lose. "I figure I can back up anything it says," he replied.

Frederick thought it over. He should have seen this little ambush coming and cleared out before Eldon got his chance, but he'd stayed and got suckered. Now it had come down to Eldon's terms—fight or get laughed at. Frederick was angry enough to fight. Life had been kicking him around, and now this asshole wanted to rub his nose in it. One good punch in that arrogant mouth might be worth getting his ass kicked. But if he hit him, he would surely get it kicked. Eldon waited as did a couple of others who had overheard their exchange.

"I'll shoot you one game of eight ball for a hundred dollars." Frederick said it quite loudly.

"What the hell are you talkin' about?"

"Just what it sounds like," Frederick told him. "I want to play you for a hundred bucks. A hundred bucks couldn't mean much to a big operator like you."

Several customers eased over from the bar to watch this play out.

"I told you. It's a goddamn useless game, and I don't want nothin' to do with it."

"Well, it's put up or shut up," Frederick told him. He could see a large artery throbbing in Eldon's neck.

Eldon slammed a fist on the table. "Goddammit, we wasn't talkin' about shootin' pool!"

Frederick walked over and picked his coat up from the chair where he'd left it. "You disappoint me, Eldon. I guess you talk a better game than you play." He could hear the laughter as he went through the door.

As Frederick stepped into the cold night, he almost stumbled into the snowmobile where Eldon had left it, right in front of the door. Built purely for speed, the Eliminator was little more than a huge engine with windshield, skis, handlebars, and a seat attached. He could imagine the staccato racket it would scatter over a quiet winter landscape. You could hear the damned things for miles.

A crisp slice of moon threw light on the snow so brightly that Frederick could have driven home without his headlights. Once again he was soothed by the moon's peacefulness and his anger at Eldon ebbed in the reverie he felt.

When he drove into the yard, Molly came out of the barn to greet him. There wasn't a whisper of wind and he lingered under the moon's subtle smile. The snow had changed the shapes of Frederick's world, and the moonlight changed them more. Far off in the quiet night he heard the metallic slap of a hog feeder. If he lingered long enough, he'd probably hear the obnoxious whine of Eldon's snowmobile coming down the river. He went inside.

TWENTY-ONE

By the time early December arrived, Frederick had found a rhythm for his life alone. He spent most of his days working on his equipment in his shop or hauling corn to the elevator in Rock Falls. And he still had his cows to care for. The temperature rarely went above fifteen degrees, and most nights went below zero. Every few days there was another snow, which would now have measured almost four feet on the level—but of course it was never level. A great deal of it was piled around his driveway and yard, which he still had to clear almost every day.

He had not heard from JoAnn and he had not tried to call her. For a time, at least, the problem had gone away. Sooner or later he would have to do something, but for now doing nothing seemed okay. He had a tough winter to get through, at least three more months of it, and that was going to take most of the energy and will he had.

The letter showed up in his mailbox the day before Christmas. It was from a Des Moines attorney, informing him of JoAnn's petition to dissolve the marriage. He had to smile at her timing.

A few days later he took the letter into Lime City to his attorney, Nate LaPointe, who had handled the probate of his father's will. Nate was a little older than Frederick, and he'd built a practice on probates and divorces. When the attorney met him at the door, Frederick could see the surprise and curiosity in his face.

"What's up, Frederick?" the attorney asked him as he went

around his desk and sat down. There was a clutter of papers and photographs on it. Behind him were plaques recognizing the various things he volunteered for, most of them having to do with his children.

Frederick handed him the letter, and LaPointe took it out of the envelope and began to read. "Jesus, Frederick," he said when he had finished. "I thought you and JoAnn were getting along okay."

"It came on kind of sudden," Frederick told him.

"Is there any chance of patching this up?"

"I don't think so. I haven't even seen her in over a month." LaPointe looked at him. "She's hired Thomas McKenna from Des Moines," he said.

"Yeah. I saw that."

"Do you have any idea who he is?"

"No."

"He's a divorce specialist—a heavy hitter."

"What does that mean?" Frederick asked.

"It means she may be going for a big settlement."

"Settlement. Of what?"

"Property." He looked at Frederick over the top of his glasses. "You do own a farm, you know."

"Farm? What the hell would JoAnn want with the farm? She doesn't even like it. That's one of the reasons why we're breaking up!"

"I can't say for sure what she wants, Frederick. I only know that she's hired an attorney who's built a statewide reputation for winning large settlements in divorce cases."

Frederick almost came out of his chair. "Jesus, Nate! She couldn't get a part of the farm, could she?"

"Calm down, now. There's no use jumping to conclusions. The first thing you need to do is sit down with JoAnn and discuss this thing. And you need to do it calmly." For emphasis, he leaned a little across the desk. "It's in your best interest."

Calm was the last thing on Frederick's mind. His heart was pounding in his throat. "I never thought that something like this could happen. Do you think she has a chance of getting any of my land?"

"Now, settle down. We don't even know that she wants it."

"But what if she does? She can't get it, can she?"

"Well, not over half, at any rate."

"Half! Jesus Christ! That farm is part of my family! How could she get any of it?"

"These things are argued before a judge who decides on the disposition of property. All sorts of things come into it and you have all kinds of judges. There is no way to absolutely predict an outcome."

"But there is the matter of what's right and fair."

"Yes."

"Then, he wouldn't give it to her. The judge I mean."

"I can't guarantee that. Besides, it won't necessarily be a him."

II

When Frederick left LaPointe's office, he was barely hanging onto his self-control. As much as he wanted to confront JoAnn at that moment, he knew it would be stupid in his present state of mind. As he drove home, he told himself over and over that he was probably worrying needlessly, but that didn't work.

There was a reason why she'd hired an out-of-town hotshot, and he knew what it was. He was half way home when he turned the truck around and headed back to Lime City. Fuck it, he thought. It's my life and my farm.

When he got to JoAnn's office, her car was not in the parking lot, but he went in anyway.

The receptionist looked a little startled. "She's not in," she told him.

"I figured that. When will she be back?"

"We expect her on Monday."

"Monday? Where in hell is she?"

"I believe she's in Jamaica."

"Jamaica?"

"Yes. She's been there all week."

On the road, again, Frederick could feel the panic jumping in his stomach. Christ! His wife was in Jamaica with that smiling son-of-a-bitch and they were planning to take his farm—or at least half of it. And he'd hoped that doing nothing would take care of everything. But JoAnn had done something, and now she was off where he couldn't even find out what!

He could never have imagined she'd have an interest in the farm. She hated it. She'd told him as much. It just didn't seem like JoAnn. But maybe it wasn't her idea. Maybe it was the guy she was in Jamaica with, the guy with the flashy clothes who didn't have enough sense to stay out of a ditch. Maybe he was whispering in her ear. Maybe, maybe. Until he talked with her, it's all he had to go on.

III

Frederick was right. JoAnn had not thought about going after the farm on her own. She was not thinking on her own, these days, just as she was not lying on a tropical beach by herself. When the idea had "occurred" to her, it had been after several weeks of helpful suggestions from Miles.

It was also Miles who had helped her past her reluctance to file for divorce, then sensibly pointed out that, as long as there was going to be a divorce, she'd be wise to make the best of it. There was no sense in looking back and wishing she'd done things differently. That was how they'd come to hire Tom McKenna, the meanest son-of-a-bitch in the valley of divorce. Miles had come up with his name, too.

Despite these developments, she still had doubts about the whole thing and several times she'd threatened to just forget about the farm, but Miles was there to shore up her fortitude. Remember that woman standing in your kitchen, he reminded her. By now she was probably living in her house and sharing their bed. Those images rekindled her anger and resolve, at least for a while, but—although she couldn't confide it to Miles—she still had her doubts.

Maybe there was no going back, as Miles put it, but what lay ahead? There was too much about him that she didn't know, perhaps even things that she didn't want to know. How could she possibly think about a life with him? The questions hung over her like a weight that grew increasingly heavy.

Her mother's opinion swerved between a thin, conditional support and strident criticism for leaving Frederick. It seemed to depend mostly on how much she'd had to drink. After a while, JoAnn could hardly go over there. She felt trapped with these thoughts, these questions, so complicated and unsolvable that at times she wanted only for the whole mess to be over. She began to drink more than she usually did.

But now, lying on the beach next to Miles in the healing warmth of the Jamaican sun, she felt that things were looking up. Even Miles was happier and more relaxed. He hated the oppressive winter, and this getaway was a tonic. She'd wondered aloud why they didn't just go to Florida, but he'd convinced her to come to this island where she'd never been before. She wasn't sorry.

Mile was feeling more relaxed because the trip allowed him some respite from the vigilance her vacillation required. Over the past weeks his biggest fear had been that she would drive out to the farm to confront Frederick. Miles knew that such a meeting might produce a far different outcome than the one she envisioned—and he couldn't risk reconciliation between them, even though she would have insisted that was the furthest thing from her mind. He had too much at stake to risk letting them talk things out, especially if he wasn't there—and even if he was.

Talking her into retaining McKenna had been part of his insurance policy. Naturally, she had balked at first. "Why do we have to get an attorney in Des Moines?" she asked. "Isn't he going to be expensive?"

"Just talk to him," he told her. "If you don't like him, you can get someone else."

Finally, she relented. As it turned out, she almost instantly liked the man whose success had a great deal to do with his ease with women. He had the biggest office JoAnn had ever seen, and an enormous desk behind which he presided over their meeting. He hadn't wasted any time.

"You've probably heard that I'm expensive," he told her. "It's true. I am—but I'm worth it. You can ask any of my previous clients. I think you'll find that my services are a good investment, perhaps one of the best you'll ever make. Most women divorcing men of means—especially the wives of farmers—at first avoid even the mention of settlement. They're raised to be grateful for anything they have, and they give their husbands most, if not all, of the credit for their success—and, of course, their husbands are all too happy to take the credit.

"They—like you—forget the part they played in the accumulation of wealth, the countless hours spent in the background supporting him, always being there for him, raising the children, putting food on the table, moral support—I think you know what I mean." Although most of this did not apply to her, JoAnn nodded in assent anyway.

It was breathtaking the way he explained it. "Before they talk with me, these women—like you—are perfectly willing to sit meekly by—in the background, just like always—and accept whatever the husband is willing to grant them. Once in a while, a great while I might add, the man recognizes her contributions to his success and treats her with fairness. But this is rare. Usually, he considers success the product of *his* labor and forgets her part in it."

McKenna's explanation was so wonderfully polished that JoAnn hesitated to interrupt him, but she was worried that she didn't fit the characteristics of his typical client. "But, my husband inherited his land," she finally interposed in a rare pause.

"Doesn't matter. You've been married—he paused to glance at his notes—five years. Do you have any idea how much his net worth increased during that period of time? No, no, inheritance changes nothing. Only a prenuptial agreement might mitigate it, to some extent, but my understanding is that no such agreement exists."

"That's right," she said, feeling better about her question.

"I'm sure you've noticed in the papers how European royalty or American millionaires are always making substantial settlements with spouses, and some of those fortunes have been inherited for centuries. No, don't worry, inheritance has nothing to do with it." He paused to assess her reaction to what he had said so far, before he went on to the final part of a presentation that he'd made so often he could do it in his sleep. A glance at his watch told him that he was right on schedule for his next appointment.

"Of course, he will be upset, even angry, but that's to be expected," he went on. "That's human nature. No one gives up anything happily. If they did, there'd be no need for divorce lawyers." He laughed a short professional laugh that invited them to join in, and they did, JoAnn out of relief more than anything. Miles had watched her carefully during the meeting and he could see that McKenna had completely convinced her.

174

The lawyer rose from his chair and came around the desk and took one of JoAnn's hands in his. "I want you to put the entire matter in my hands," he said. "You will have moments of doubt, everyone does. That's why you've retained me, to carry the battle for you—and I will."

Almost on signal, the door behind them opened and McKenna's secretary waited to see them out. "If I can be of any help—he gently squeezed JoAnn's hand for emphasis—I want you to call me." The man is good, Miles thought to himself, and he'd known a few lawyers.

It had been Miles' idea to take the Jamaican trip during the week that Frederick would get his divorce papers, and when he had privately mentioned it to McKenna, he had concurred. JoAnn was ecstatic with relief. She did not want to be anywhere near that look on Frederick's face when he got the news. As Miles had suggested, the delay would give him time to settle down before she got back. Now, she was lying on a beach two thousand miles from the cold and feeling as if the worst might be over.

She felt an intense gratitude to Miles for remaining by her side through the dismal Iowa winter rather than going back to Florida. She couldn't imagine getting through this on her own. At first, he had stayed with her a few nights as she struggled to adjust to being alone in the apartment, but it wasn't long before he had moved in. She'd criticized other people for living like this—shacking up, people called it—but she didn't care. She needed him close by.

Miles hated the winter cold and went out less and less. His clothes were pitifully inadequate for the harsh cold, but he refused to buy anything more practical. "I'm not going to be here long enough to need it," he told her somewhat defiantly, and went about in the same clothes.

At first, he actually made a few half-hearted trips to auctions to look for antiques, but the cold made the Cadillac balky and he grew tired of jumping the battery to get it started. Finally, he just let it sit on the street near JoAnn's apartment, and parking tickets began to accumulate under the wipers. The snowplows gradually walled it in with dirty snow and ice until he couldn't have moved it if he'd wanted to. He drove JoAnn's car when he needed to.

The discomfort and inconvenience only fueled his open

disparagement of the frozen city and his determination to see this divorce through and claim what, he was more and more coming to believe, was owed him. By now he knew JoAnn well enough to think that she would never have embarked on this course by herself. She neither had the will nor the strength, so, he was doing her a favor, bringing about what was going to eventually happen anyway. But he wasn't doing it for nothing. He expected to be paid, and he was going to be paid. And he was going to enjoy his reward in Florida.

He knew that he'd probably have to take her with him. She wasn't going to just give him the money out of the goodness of her heart. She wasn't that spellbound. It might even mean getting married again, but that wasn't a big deal. He'd done it twice before. He wasn't sure if he was divorced yet from the second one. He hadn't stuck around to find out.

It didn't matter. It was strictly for convenience, anyway. He was certain he could get enough money from her to get back in business. He'd given up on Iowa. There was too much bullshit to put up with—and the fucking weather! No, from now on, he'd take his chances in Florida, but he wouldn't be back here again, not ever.

IV

On their third afternoon they were having lunch at an outdoor café, and JoAnn was basking in the sheer beauty of the place. "Wouldn't it be wonderful to live like this all the time?" she asked.

"Maybe you'll be able to," he said.

She laughed. "Miles, it takes money to live like this."

"Well, you're going to have money, aren't you?"

"Well, maybe some, but not enough to live like this."

"What if it's half?" he wondered aloud.

"You mean of the land?"

"Yes."

"That would be a lot," she said.

"How much?"

"Well, he owns two hundred and forty acres. I guess it would be half of whatever that's worth." Miles just managed not to choke on the salad he was eating.

"I thought I remembered another figure—something a little more than that."

"No," she said with maddening pleasantness. "It's always been two hundred and forty."

Miles couldn't say anything for a moment. Something in the order of three-quarters of a million dollars had just been subtracted from his plans, and their departure left him shaken. That fucking Roland, he thought, but he knew it was his own fault. He should have known better than to listen to a fucking drug dealer!

He dabbed at the corners of his mouth with the cloth napkin and observed JoAnn who had leaned back in the sun's warmth and closed her eyes. Rationally, this wasn't her fault, but that did little to diminish the frustration and disappointment he felt. Beyond her, in the harbor, a collection of expensive yachts nodded on their moorings. Until a few moments ago, even the larger ones had seemed possible.

JoAnn reached to touch his arm. "Are you okay?" she asked.

What a luxury it would have been to tell her how he really felt. "Why do I remember your talking about something like five hundred acres?" he asked. "Did I just imagine that?"

"Oh," she said, finally understanding. "He farms that much, but he only owns two hundred and forty. He rents the rest from other people." She smiled and laid her head against his shoulder. "Did you think I was married to a rich farmer?"

V

JoAnn had not been back in her office an hour when Frederick called. "How was your trip?" His voice was too taut to carry the intended civility. He's upset, she thought.

"Fine," she said.

"I got your letter."

"My letter?"

"The one from your attorney."

"Oh, yes."

"It wasn't exactly a postcard."

"No. It wasn't."

"Couldn't we have done this on a little more personal level?"

"This is the way they do it."

"Does it have to be the way we do it? It's still us, isn't it?"

Despite his intent to remain composed, she could hear a sharpness creeping into his words. She felt the heat rising in her own throat. Still, he was calmer than she might have expected.

"The lawyer thought it would be best if we kept it formal—so it won't get overly emotional." She'd borrowed the last two words from McKenna.

"I see. So nobody gets their feelings hurt. Is that the idea?"

"I guess it's something like that." He didn't say anything for a few seconds, and she knew he was shifting gears.

"I want to see you," he said.

"I don't know about that, Frederick. I just got back. I have a million things to do."

"JoAnn. We're still married. Sooner or later we're going to have to sit down and talk."

"I don't know. I—." She wasn't ready for this. McKenna hadn't said anything about this!

"How about lunch today?"

"No. Not today. I couldn't possibly."

"Tomorrow, then, at the Tailfeathers. I know you like it there. I'll make a reservation. Do you want me to pick you up?"

"Frederick, I don't know."

"JoAnn, it's just to talk. Would you prefer that I come to your place?"

"No—the Tailfeathers would be better." Her mind was racing. She felt tremendous pressure. "Okay, the Tailfeathers, but I'll meet you there at one."

"Okay," he said, his voice sounding lighter.

"I don't want you to get upset."

"I won't. I promise. I'll see you tomorrow."

He hung up. That had gone miserably she thought. Without wanting to she had agreed to see him. Somehow she'd gotten the impression that she wouldn't have to except in the safe neutrality of the courtroom, and now she was meeting him for lunch. She called Miles.

"Why didn't you just tell him no?" he asked. Since their vacation he'd grown less patient with almost everything.

"You don't know him like I do. If I didn't agree, he'd just come to the office or the apartment."

"Well, we can't have that." She caught the sarcasm.

"I don't care what you think, Miles. I'm still married."

"So what?"

"So, I don't want people thinking that I'm being unfaithful!"

"But you are being unfaithful."

"I'm not! I wouldn't have gotten the apartment if he hadn't behaved the way he did, and you know that!" She was near tears. They'd been over this before and always with the same results. "I can see that you're not going to be any help," she said and hung up.

She called McKenna but his secretary said he was busy. By the time he got back to her later in the afternoon, she had grown more upset, and the moment they connected, she began to cry. Since he was billing her at over a hundred dollars an hour, she found him more patient than Miles. "I don't think it's anything to worry about," he soothed.

"But I don't want to see him," she said. "Isn't there any way you can just keep him away?"

"Not unless he's harassing you. He's not doing that, is he?"

"No. He's not harassing me."

"But you're worried about seeing him?"

"Of course I am! I don't want him getting all upset with me!"

"It's good that you're meeting publicly, then. I'm sure he'll keep himself under control."

"But what if he brings up things I don't want to talk about? What if he wants to get back together?"

McKenna paused to think this over. She had a point. More than one client had called to tell him the divorce was off, that they'd decided to try it again. He was as much for reconciliation as any man, but it seldom worked out. Too often it lapsed into a futile activity that only embittered the principals and prolonged the struggle. He knew couples who had been separated for years, because they'd never managed to get entirely quit of each other. They lived in social and economic limbo, their resources squandered by their inability to control their emotions.

He saw the possible danger in this situation. His client sounded frightened and unsure. Maybe she lacked the strength to do what was right for herself. "Well," he finally suggested. "Maybe you should take your friend—er—."

"Miles."

"Yes, Miles. Would that make you feel better?"

"Yes, it would." She hesitated. "But would it be okay?"

"Oh, I think so. It is just lunch, isn't it?"

"Oh yes, just lunch."

He could hear the relief in her voice. "It should be fine, then."

"I'll do that, then. Thank you Mr. McKenna. Sorry to bother you."

After she hung up, McKenna had to smile. You are worth a hundred bucks an hour, he thought.

VI

Frederick was already seated at the table when they arrived. He almost did not recognize JoAnn with her deep tan. She'd also lost some weight and her hair was shorter. Right behind her was the guy. They looked like they'd just stepped out of a travel poster. She stopped and looked around the tables, searching for him.

I'm right here in front of you, he thought, and then he remembered the beard. He waved and she saw him.

"How long have you had that?" she asked as Miles seated her.

"A month, I guess." He could see her disapproval. It was difficult for him not to stare, they looked so goddamned healthy. JoAnn was discouragingly beautiful.

"You remember Miles, don't you?" she asked. Miles smiled at him.

"Yeah—Miles." He looked at her. "I didn't expect two of you."

"I didn't think you'd mind."

The waitress came and brought them menus, and they ordered drinks. It was Frederick's third. The waitress greeted JoAnn and Miles like old friends and gushed over their tans, and they went on about the delights of Jamaica. It gave Frederick opportunity to notice his hands, which looked like lumps on the white table cloth. The nails were stubbed and uneven, and oil and grease were worn deep into the calluses. He shifted them to his lap.

The waitress went away and the two smiled pleasantly at Frederick. "So, Frederick, how are things?" JoAnn asked.

"I got thirty acres of corn snowed in," he said, exaggerating the damage. She nodded. He was mounting an effort to be sociable, but his nervousness gave him away.

His face was the face of every farmer she'd ever known: cheeks chapped red by wind and sun and cold, his forehead pale as a corpse where the cap covered it. And now there was also the beard. Compared with Miles, he looked like a hobo, but then no one looked like Miles. Everywhere they went, women looked at him with undisguised desire, but he was hers and just being with him made her feel better, especially now.

Miles was relaxed and happy. He had nothing to do but enjoy the meal. He didn't need to say a word, if he chose not to. It was enough to merely sit and observe and provide a devastating contrast to the shabby husband—and wonder where this lunch was headed.

In the midst of their next drink, the waitress brought the food and they began to eat in the style of their respective moods: Miles with expansive ease, JoAnn picking nervously at her salad, Frederick chewing mouthfuls with bovine determination. He was better at eating than talking—at least with these two. Their small talk was utterly useless to him, irrelevant to any aspect of his existence. How could he join in that? They could have been speaking different languages.

The last drink was improving things, though. He felt much less nervous, less apt to do something that might unravel the moment and lead it off to—he hadn't an idea where. But what if he did? What would be so horrible about saying what was on his mind? That's why he'd wanted to see her. He didn't care if they were enjoying themselves or not; he was the one with something to say, so why wasn't he saying it?

"You're not trying to take my farm, are you?" They weren't the exact words he had intended, but close enough.

JoAnn looked as if he'd slapped her, her face frozen in a grimace of mortification, a forkful of salad poised between the plate and her mouth. Miles was watching him, too, the smile bemused—waiting.

"We weren't going to talk about that!" she hissed.

"Who said?" Frederick asked.

"We did, didn't we Miles?"

"What the hell does he have to say about it?" Frederick demanded.

"I talk to him about things!"

"About my farm?"

"I told you I'm not talking about that!" She glared at Miles for not chiming in.

"What the hell's going on?" Frederick demanded.

"Nothing's going on," she said. "We were just going to have lunch and not talk about this!" She was getting louder.

"You're planning to steal part of my farm, aren't you!" Now, it was out.

Miles smiled. The couple at the next table had risen and abandoned their coffee. JoAnn's face was a carotid flower, the flush overwhelming the tan.

Frederick couldn't stop. "You never even liked the farm!"

"We're—not—talking—about this!" She stood and braced herself against the chair with both hands. The napkin slid from her lap.

"You got what you wanted," he said, looking at Miles then back at her, "now leave me alone!"

And just like that she had left, leaving food, drink, husband, and lover in the silence of her vacated anger. Frederick stared at his half-finished plate. Miles did not move. Very slowly, the accoutremental sounds of eating and small talk crept up around them like timid children. Without speaking, the waitress brought the bill to the table and set it between them.

Miles took a sip from his glass. "They can be difficult," he said. Frederick got up and left.

TWENTY-TWO

The particulars were mailed to him two weeks after the disastrous lunch. He did not need LaPointe to interpret them: "the Southwest quarter and the West one-half of the Southeast quarter of Section 13, Tier 10 North, Range 27 West of the Principal Meridian in Lime River County, Iowa, consisting of two hundred forty acres, more or less." The letter did not state which half she wanted.

"Of course," LaPointe said quite unnecessarily when Frederick showed it to him, "she really doesn't want the land."

"Of course not," Frederick agreed. "She's only holding it for ransom."

"Frederick, being melodramatic about this isn't going to help."

"Of course not," he said and walked out.

In the days that followed, he could not work enough to displace his anger or his fear, but he tried. Always on this or any other farm there was something undone, tines or shares or blades to be sharpened or replaced, draw bars or hitches to be welded, viscosities to be checked or changed, vaccines and medications to be given, feed to be ground, manure to be forked and hauled, bedding to be spread, boards to be nailed, wire to be wrapped. But now, for the first time in its history, human energy almost matched that which the farm exacted and absorbed as massively as sunlight falling on plowed earth.

The weather kept him hard, alert, alone. He gave up trying to keep the beard trimmed, and it blossomed into irregular tufts of fur. When he was outside, the vapors of his breath froze in it, then dripped into his coffee as he sat in the kitchen and ate. He did not call even LaPointe and stopped answering the phone, which rarely rang, anyway.

There were moments when he was visited by impractical fantasies of protecting his land by force. He oiled up his old Winchester twenty-two pump with the magazine missing but couldn't find any shells. When the work wasn't distracting him, he felt besieged and fearful and could not sleep well. Out there, things were happening that he was not stopping, probably could not stop.

He dug out an old pair of snowshoes that had hung forever on the wall of a shed and replaced the rotted leather webbing with nylon line and refitted the bindings to fit his feet and hiked off across the farm into his woods. Wind and cold and snow had reduced the landscape to the barest elements of texture and line and black and white and gray. Sometimes he was walking across bare frozen earth and at others he was climbing enormous, dirty, wind-fluted drifts that curled high above his fences like calcified surf that he could cross without leaving a footprint. In his whole life he had never seen drifts as huge as these.

By late January, more than seven feet of snow had fallen and collected and some drifts had grown to twenty feet high. The county snow plows ran day and night, their crews exhausted by the need to open, over and over again, roads that kept drifting shut. With their budgets exhausted, the commissioners decided to stop plowing those not essential for travel or safety. These included the road west of Frederick's driveway, where JoAnn and Miles had gotten stuck.

Long, striated drifts ran for miles over the open country like spindrift on a grayish sea. Frederick's windbreak had trapped a huge breaker of snow that kept the hard edge of the wind off his house and buildings, but almost every day he was obliged to clear the powder that unfurled in its eddy. It was gritty with dust blown off unprotected fields.

In many places roads had been reduced to narrow, one-lane trenches cut through the drifts that snow quickly filled, and going to town for even a short time carried the risk of being cut off or stranded. The mailman ground doggedly through his rounds, the rear tires of his car wrapped in chains. He had already burned up one transmission rocking it out of a drift. It would have been okay with Frederick if he'd never made it. The mail had become an instrument of threat.

Despite the weather, a second letter arrived from LaPointe, explaining that a date had been set for the dissolution. "I have been trying to call you," he'd written in longhand at the bottom. "Please call at your earliest convenience." Despite his hermetics, it was all going on.

"Why haven't you called me?" LaPointe chided when Frederick finally called him.

"I've been busy." His voice sounded strange to him. The phone was sucking his vitality.

"This is your life, you know," LaPointe said, annoyed, but Frederick began to laugh. "Did I say something funny?"

"Yes."

"Would you mind telling me what?"

"For one thing, it's not my life."

"Like it or not, Frederick, it is."

"My life is here. I'm not bothering anyone."

"You can't make this go away by ignoring it."

"Don't I have anything to say? I'm being robbed, you know."

"You're not being robbed. Your wife is trying to obtain part of your property through a divorce settlement. It's completely legal."

"It's robbery! The only difference is she's using the law instead of a gun. She even has an accomplice, the pretty boy she left me for. She's screwing him, you know. It's time we stopped pretending that it's all reasonable and face the truth."

"Even if that should be true, Iowa no longer recognizes adultery as a factor in divorce."

"No one seems to. No wonder there's so much shooting."

"That's nonsense, Frederick. The law has come a long way from adultery and cruel and inhuman treatment as grounds for divorce. It's no-fault, now."

"Has it improved my chances?"

That broke LaPointe's rhythm. "No," he said, "but they haven't gotten any worse either."

"What is there to do, then? I tried begging."

"That's not exactly how it was described to me. It didn't help, you know. Anger doesn't help."

185

"Just because I'm forced to eat shit doesn't mean I have to call it a delicacy."

"Look, Frederick. I'm your attorney. You're paying me to give you the best advice I can. Why not listen to what I have to say?"

"And that would be?"

"You need to take the initiative."

"The initiative."

"Yes."

"How?"

"I think you should try to negotiate a settlement."

"Negotiate."

"Yes, negotiate. JoAnn is suffering the same risks that you are. A judge could conceivably award her just a fraction of what she is seeking—or even nothing. It's happened before. If you go to her with an offer, she might take it. You might be able to settle this on terms favorable to you."

"By offering her some part of what she has no right to, I might persuade her not to try to take all of it. Is that your best advice?"

"Yes, Frederick, it is."

"I guess I wouldn't have come up with that on my own."

"Sarcasm won't change anything."

"Are they expecting something like that?" he asked.

There was another of LaPointe's expensive pauses. "I've discussed it with McKenna," he said.

"I see."

"He and I have to talk, even if you and JoAnn can't. Otherwise, it's just warfare."

"Yeah, I guess."

"So, what do you think?"

"I'll get back to you."

"Frederick, are you alright? You don't sound alright."

This time he didn't laugh.

II

After the phone call Frederick tried to think practically, the way LaPointe wanted him to, but it didn't work. He couldn't imagine bargaining away a part of the farm any more than he could imagine losing an arm or a leg. LaPointe wouldn't understand that. Probably nobody else would either, except another farmer. Sure, JoAnn only wanted the money and not the land, and that made it less onerous to LaPointe. But Frederick simply couldn't accept that rationale.

He didn't reconsider and he didn't call LaPointe. Instead, he retreated back into his isolation, letting winter swallow him, sealing off the unthinkable possibilities their talk had festered in his mind. He even stopped going to Lime City for groceries, preferring to make the longer drive to Austin, Minnesota where he wouldn't chance upon someone he knew. He didn't want to talk to anyone about anything. His telephone dangled at the end of its cord.

Despite these measures, the fears came on him anew, and even the work couldn't save him. The bourbon numbed his thoughts, sometimes starting in the mornings after he had fed his cattle and continuing through the afternoons and nights which began to blur into a long continuum of inebriation that lacked ends and beginnings. When he went out to do his chores in the morning, the cold cauterized his hangovers, but he was soon at it, again, the obliterating haze barely holding his troubles at bay.

One morning he decided it to sell his cows. He called Dalton Homrig, a cattle buyer who occasionally bought stock from him. Dalton was a southerner from Texas or Missouri or someplace, who wore his disdain for the Iowa cold in a broad-brimmed 5X beaver felt, J.B. Stetson hat that Frederick had never seen him without, even on the bitterest days.

"I wonder if you can get into my driveway?" Frederick asked him.

"I have no idea," Homrig told him. "If we can't, we'll drive them to where we can load. How many you got?"

"A hundred and twenty-seven head."

"I'll see you in the morning."

Homrig arrived at first light and the two of them walked among the milling animals while the buyer looked them over. It was fifteen below, but he still wore only the hat while his ears grew red and his nose began to drip.

"They're in good shape," he told him. "The best I've seen in a while."

That's why Frederick liked him. If you had fat cattle, he'd tell you so and pay you for them. He didn't try to whittle a fair price down to something less. "We've spent a lot of time together," Frederick replied. "I'm kinda going to miss 'em."

Homrig liked Frederick because his cattle were always in prime shape, and he judged people by the condition of their stock. But he could see that the man had problems. He looked like hell, for one thing, and he could already smell the booze on him at eight in the morning, but they didn't know each other well enough for him to say anything.

That afternoon two semis backed down the road and stopped by the driveway. Because of the snow, they couldn't make the turn into the yard, so the two drivers and Frederick cut small bands out of the herd and drove them across the yard and into the trucks. Homrig stood by, supervising the loading and marking his ledger with a stubby pencil. When the last of them were loaded, the two of them tallied and he wrote Frederick a check and left.

Usually, it was good to sell cattle, both for the money they brought and the relief from the work they required, but this time he felt little satisfaction with their departure. It wasn't that he felt remorse for raising them for slaughter. That was an old covenant between them, one he'd first learned about when he was only four and his father had led a young steer into the barn and shot her, then hung her up by her back legs and butchered her into meat that had filled their table for months.

That's how it was on a farm. You raised animals for the milk or eggs or meat they'd provide. No matter how much you might come to like an animal, they were not pets. Nothing was, really. A dog was expected to protect the place and keep the varmints down and maybe work cattle or sheep. Cats were there to kill the mice that could otherwise overrun a granary. Everyone and everything had a purpose.

At the very least, his cows had provided a sense of purpose for him, albeit sometimes a grudging one, a reason to get out of bed in the mornings and come home in the evenings. Maybe, too, it was the reassurance of an old, old routine. It would be some months before he'd buy calves to replace them, and in the meantime the farm would be completely silent.

With nothing to do in the mornings, he drank harder. He

began to wake up in inappropriate rooms like the kitchen and discover tumblers—some with bourbon still in them—at odd places around the house where he had left them. After neglecting to wash dishes for a few days, he began to drink from coffee mugs. One morning he woke at three A.M. in the bathtub half-filled with chilly water that had apparently been warm when he'd gotten into it. Eventually this random existence overwhelmed his diurnal urge and he began to sleep through much of the day and get up at one or two in the morning.

One morning, not long after midnight, when he was not quite drunk, he grew restless. He dressed in his heavy clothes and went out, with Molly following behind. There was a half-moon high overhead, its bright light mottled by scudding clouds. A light breeze curled snow around his boots, but he was warm in his clothes.

He strapped on the snowshoes and headed west across a half mile of open field toward the river pasture beyond, the dog trotting along. As he cleared the windbreak, a northwest wind blew snow against his face so sharply that he pulled the drawstring on the hooded sweatshirt even tighter. Even so, the cold felt bitter on his nose and cheeks.

He went on for some distance until his face became so cold that he turned around and began to walk backwards. The snowshoes were too clumsy, though, and the pointed backs kept catching on the snow until they finally tripped him and he fell backwards on the steep, hardpan face of a large drift. He sat, for a moment, catching his breath. Molly came up and nuzzled his face, and he pulled her against him. "Good girl," he reassured her.

It was then that he noticed he could no longer see the lights of the house. He thought he was facing toward where they should have been, but they weren't there. He couldn't see them anywhere. How far had he come? He hadn't yet realized that it wasn't distance that obscured them.

When he got to his feet, the coveralls flapped against his legs. The wind was blowing snow and grit into a blinding ground blizzard, and he could see barely forty feet in any direction. Although he probably wasn't more than a quarter mile from the house, he had no idea in which direction it lay.

The collie hunched against his legs, ready to be off for home.

She could probably find her way back, but she didn't know that he couldn't. By now the wind was blowing at least thirty-five or forty and still rising. This was getting ugly and he had to move, but in which direction? His only frame of reference was the shape of the drift, which should be lying from northwest to southeast, the direction the wind usually blew, but how dependable was that?

If he walked north, and he couldn't be certain which direction that was, he should cut the road which he could then follow home. That is if he could recognize it as a road, buried under the drifts as it was, and if his body heat lasted long enough to get him that far. He wasn't cold yet, but that was coming quickly as the wind carried his heat away. Gradually, his body would cool and at some point he would begin to shiver. Not long after that his core temperature would fall to where he'd begin to lose consciousness. Then, he'd stagger on until he fell or just sat down—and then he'd go to sleep.

The shortest way would be directly to the house, but if he guessed wrong, by even a few degrees, he'd miss his buildings and wander in empty fields until he couldn't go on. Now he was feeling a different fear than the one that had driven him into paralyzing self-pity, and this fear carried a sense of urgency: if he didn't do something—and do it immediately—there was a very good chance that he was going to die.

Taking his bearings from the direction of the drift, he began to walk in what he could only hope was the direction of the house. The wind was thrashing, now, threatening to gust him off his feet. The snowshoes slowed him so he knelt and took them off. Molly waited, eager now to be someplace warm. What was he up to, she wondered.

He headed off into the roiling blast toward where he hoped the house to be. He could picture it clearly and expected at any moment for it to emerge from the maelstrom.

As the moments went by, the effects of the whiskey he'd drunk earlier wore off and a great fear of his predicament took their place. Drunk, he'd been concerned, but now he was frightened. Where the hell was the house? He should have come to it by now. He was sure. But he hadn't.

And then he heard another voice. Why are you so frightened? it asked. You've given up on your life anyway. You're in this jam because you've been drinking for days and now you've gotten careless and there's a good chance you're going to die. That should make you happy, shouldn't it? Are you happy now, Frederick?

He stumbled on under the lash of this realization, driven almost to the point of panic. Suddenly, he found himself climbing a drift that was much larger than any he'd encountered before. He paused on the top of it. The thing was huge. He was sure he hadn't crossed it before. Surely, he would have remembered it. That could only mean he hadn't been this way before—and that meant he wasn't retracing his route. He was lost.

Part of him was willing to give up. He'd done his best, hadn't he? He could simply sit down where he was and curl up, or keep walking aimlessly. Either way, he'd eventually grow colder until there was nothing more to worry about. Those who'd experienced it, people who had frozen to death and then been revived, claimed that it wasn't bad. It was just like going to sleep.

Even as these thoughts absorbed him, others were trying to solve the problem of how not to die. Why was this drift here? Drifts usually grew in the lee of objects like trees, fences, buildings—maybe something recognizable that would give him a better sense of where he was. But as he peered about, he could see nothing. Crouching low against the blast, he began to search the drift's flanks, but he found nothing there. Even if there were something, he might not see it in all this blowing snow. He could be standing on it and not know.

He stumbled down the sheltered side and sank to his waist in the soft snow that had accumulated. There, the drift protected him somewhat from the wind, a better place to make his next decision. But, he needed information—and he didn't have any. He was completely lost, without a hope of finding his way, and growing colder by the minute.

He might as well make the best of where he was. It was probably as much shelter as he was going to find. With one of the snowshoes he began to dig out a hollow, something he could huddle in for protection from the wind. Molly had sat down a few feet away and was chewing at the ice that had collected between her toes.

The snow dug easily and as the depression got deeper, he felt warmer. He stopped digging and crouched in the space he had hollowed out. It was much better, but it didn't seem like enough to keep him warm. But what if he dug a hole into the drift itself? He'd dug snow caves as a kid, but those had just been for fun. He'd never needed one to stay alive. It was worth a try.

Using the narrow end of a snowshoe, he began to hack his way into the solid outer surface of the drift. The first foot or so was so compacted that it broke into chunks that he could toss away, but, as he had hoped, the snow behind was much softer and easier to dig. He hacked away at the opening until it was just wide enough to crawl through, and then he began pulling snow through it with both hands, widening a cavity big enough for him and the dog. When it seemed large enough, he crawled in to find that he was completely sheltered from the wind.

"Come on, Molly. Come on girl," he called, and she came eagerly through the entrance and curled up beside him.

While Molly licked the melting snow from her coat, Frederick packed snow around the entrance until there was barely an opening. Only when the work was finished did he lay back. It was dark in there but not as completely black as he might have expected. What struck him was the stillness. A few minutes before, he had been struggling through a howling blizzard but now, except for the sound of Molly's tongue on her fur, there was silence.

The fear that had driven him was subsiding. He didn't know if he'd saved his life or not, but he'd greatly increased his chances of surviving until daylight. As the anxiety drained away, a warmth flowed through him that bordered on euphoria. Only minutes after being perilously close to death, he was alive.

The dog finished her grooming, gave a deep sigh, and went to sleep. She had complete confidence in Frederick. Had she ever questioned his ability to get them to some place warm? He doubted it. She might have died out there with him. As he relaxed, he began to feel sleepy. Was it okay for him to doze off? What if the warmth flowing through him was some deceptive final stage of hypothermia from which he'd never wake? But it was too much to think about. He'd just have to trust that he was okay. He closed his eyes and drifted off.

III

Molly woke him with her nose. Bright light was shining through the opening. He rubbed her head and she whined happily. He pushed the snow away from around the opening and they crawled out. The sun was well above the horizon, the light so bright that he had to shield his eyes. There was no wind, and he could see for miles. The house was less than a hundred yards away.

TWENTY-THREE

After Frederick got back to the warmth of his kitchen, he made coffee and a big breakfast. He was just cleaning up when a pickup drove into the yard. He wiped his hands and went to answer the door. It was Eldon. He had a nervous smile on his face and was carrying a suitcase.

"Frederick. Can I come in?"

Frederick stepped back and Eldon came in, stamping snow from his boots. He carried the suitcase over to the kitchen table and looked down at the breakfast dishes which had not been cleared away.

"What's going on, Eldon?"

"I need a place to set this," he said, "where I can open it up."

Frederick still didn't understand. What the hell was going on with the suitcase? What was he doing here?

"I need to set it on the table," Eldon said.

"Okay," Frederick replied, and he set the dishes in the sink. Eldon set the suitcase on the table and took a moment to regard it with a strange mixture of anticipation and slyness. Then, almost ceremoniously, he undid the latches, and the lid popped slightly open from the pressure of the contents. He flipped it open and stepped back. It was filled with bundles of money.

"Jesus!" Frederick said. "What'd you do? Rob a bank?"

"Nope. It's all yours if you want it."

Frederick couldn't help but stare at it, a suitcase full of money on his kitchen table. Eldon was elated. This was exactly the reaction he'd hoped for. The poor sap had his mouth half open with surprise, not that he could blame him. It looked impressive, that was for sure.

"If I want it?" Frederick asked, looking at him again.

"That's right."

"For what?"

It was time for the punch line, the one Eldon had savored for days. "It's for the farm, Frederick."

"The farm?"

"Yes. The farm." His voice rose with excitement. "There's seven hundred thousand dollars in that pile. I'm offering you top dollar for the place, here and now. No goddamned real estate agents and no goddamned lawyers! Just you and me shakin' hands on the deal like two real men!"

Frederick stared at the money, trying to absorb this surreal turn of events. Released from the compression of the suitcase, the money actually appeared to be swelling.

"I know that you and JoAnn are splittin' the sheets—hell, everyone knows—and I know you're probably gonna hafta sell the place, and I wanna buy it. I know you and me ain't always been the best of friends, but you know that I'm a neighbor, not some goddamned outsider, for chrissakes. I'll take care of the place, Frederick, just like Emmett would've wanted."

Eldon paused to evaluate the effect of this on Frederick, but he couldn't read anything but surprise in his expression. He had the same dumb-ass look on his face as he always did, except now the beard made him look even dumber. This was important, though, real important, and Eldon knew that he had to give it his best shot.

"I mean, how would feel about havin' a stranger farmin' the place? It could happen, you know. I heard that an A-rab just bought six hundred acres north of Osage! Six hundred acres! How would you like to have your farm owned by a fuckin' A-rab?"

Eldon was distressed by this prospect. For years he'd pictured himself owning this farm. He already knew all the changes he was going to make to it, but now, in this crazy land market, anybody could buy it—even a foreigner! It wasn't right but that's the way it was, and that's why he was taking this shot.

"It's not for sale," Frederick said, calmly.

"You and JoAnn ain't splittin' up?"

"We are splitting up, Eldon, but the farm is not for sale. Not to you, not to the Arabs—not to anybody."

Eldon's face turned sour. "If the judge gives her half, you won't have nothin' to say about it, buddy boy. They'll sell it at an auction to the highest bidder and you won't have nothin' to say about who buys it. It might bring a few bucks more than I'm offerin' but I doubt it."

"I wouldn't know about that," Frederick said. "I only know that it isn't for sale."

Eldon wasn't liking this, but he'd already thought about the possibility of this glitch. He reached into the pockets of the coveralls he was wearing and pulled out two more bundles of money.

"Here's another ten thousand," he said and threw one of the bundles onto the table. "And ten thousand more for good measure." He threw that one, too.

"You could throw another hundred thousand on there and it wouldn't be for sale." Frederick told him.

"You're crazy if you don't take this!"

"I'm not crazy enough to sell my farm!"

"Nobody is going to offer you more money than this!"

"I don't want more money than this! I want my farm, and I want people to leave me alone!"

"You always were an odd-ball son-of-a-bitch!"

"And you were always a bully, Eldon, a guy that does his best to make life miserable for everyone else! And now you're a greedy shithead, as well. Well, I'm tired of being pushed around by you or anybody else! Take your fucking money and get out of here!"

Eldon forced the lid of the suitcase down and latched it. "She's gonna stick it to you," he said, "and I'm gonna be there waitin'! And after I buy it, I'm gonna burn down this fuckin' house and piss on the ashes!" He snatched the suitcase from the table and rushed out. Frederick was right behind.

"Emmett always thought you were a jerk!" he yelled after him.

II

It was a Sunday morning when Frederick went to see Loretta. At first, she wouldn't tell him where JoAnn was living. "I don't want to get into the middle," she told him.

"You won't," he said.

"You're not going to do anything rash, are you?" His beard made him look a little desperate.

"I'm just going to talk to her."

"It's a little late for that."

"Maybe, but better late than not at all."

He had not been in the city for weeks, and it looked as if it had succumbed to the long winter. Dirty snow covered everything, and the city's plows had pushed snow and ice into huge piles that were spilling back into the streets and narrowing many of them into single, rutted lanes.

When he knocked on the door to the apartment it was almost eleven. No one answered, but JoAnn's car was in the parking lot and he was pretty sure that it was the Cadillac buried under a pile of snow in front of the building. He knocked again, harder.

"Who is it?" It was her voice, cautious and tentative.

"It's Frederick."

"Who?"

"Frederick. Your husband." He said this quite loudly and almost immediately she unlocked the door and opened it a little.

She was wearing a robe and looked unhappy to see him. "What do you want?"

"I want to talk."

"No."

"Please."

"We tried this. It didn't work."

"I want to try again."

"No."

"JoAnn—."

"No, Frederick. I don't want to. I don't want you here. You're just trying to bully me."

"I just want to talk."

"I don't want you here. Please leave." She closed the door, and he heard the lock close.

"We can talk face to face or I can yell through the door."

She opened it, again. "I'll call the police, if you don't leave.

"JoAnn, we need to talk to each other."

"No!"

"I want to stop this—now. I want you to come home."

She was startled. "What?"

"I've been wrong about a lot of things. I know that. I'm willing to try to change."

"It's too late for that," she said, and he pushed suddenly through the door. It surprised Miles who had been standing a few feet behind her. The place was small and dark and crowded with furniture.

"Is this what you want? To live like this?"

"Frederick!" Her neck was turning red and he knew he didn't have much time.

"JoAnn, we've never really talked since this whole mess started. We're married to each other! There ought to be some way for us to talk other than through an attorney!"

"There's no talking to you," she said bitterly. "Look at you! You look like you've just crawled out of a cave! And you keep pressuring me!"

"Is it pressure to want to talk about our marriage? What kind of people would just let it die without at least talking?"

"You're upsetting her," Miles said.

Frederick almost laughed at the theatrical self-importance with which he said it, but he needed to reach her, and arguing with this guy wouldn't help.

"JoAnn, we've never really talked through anything difficult because it always upsets you. Maybe if we had, things wouldn't have come to this."

"So, you're blaming me for everything."

"I'm not. I'm saying that it might have been better for us if we'd been more direct—more honest with each other. That's what I'm trying to be right now."

"I was never dishonest with you."

"It doesn't matter if you were."

"I was never dishonest!"

He lowered his voice as he tried to keep this from running away, again. "I didn't say you were. We had a life together. It wasn't perfect, but it was our life."

"I didn't like it out there."

"I know you didn't, and I know that I should have been more understanding, but was it bad enough to bring us to this? Our lives are falling apart and we're not doing anything to stop it."

"It's too late."

"Why?"

"I want a different kind of life. I have a different life."

"We can have a different kind of life," he told her. "I know we can."

"There's nothing left, Frederick."

"Maybe that's for the best," he said. "We know it all, now." He looked at Miles. "Everything."

"I haven't been unfaithful!" she cried.

"You know what you've been."

"You're accusing me!"

"No, I'm not! It's doesn't matter, anyway."

"It does! I won't have you thinking that!"

"It doesn't matter!"

"Yes. It does matter—to me!"

It was falling apart, again. "Then stop denying it! Stop lying about it!"

"I'm not lying!"

"Don't you understand? I don't care if you are! Whatever you did, you did for a reason, maybe a good reason, I don't know, but at some point we've got to admit our mistakes so we can go on and find some honesty!"

"I am honest! I haven't lied!"

"Yes, you did! You lied to me, JoAnn! You lied! And you went to bed with him! You can't stand to admit it to yourself, but you did! And you're lying now, just to hold onto something that doesn't mean anything to anybody but you!"

"I didn't—I didn't!" She was desperate, now, and if she could have run away she would have, but there was no place to go. Frederick had let his anger out, but at the same time he wanted to hold her, to reassure her in a way that his words couldn't, but he knew it would only make her more desperate.

"Admit it and then let it go. Whether we're going to be together or not, let it go. Give yourself a chance to live with some honesty."

She'd backed away from him and he'd followed, trying not to spook her altogether, but he could see that he'd come as far as he could. She began to cry, forlornly, like a devastated child.

"I didn't—I didn't—I didn't," she protested. Miles put his arms around her, and she collapsed against him.

"You'd better go now," he said to Frederick without anger.

"What are you going to do when he leaves you?" Frederick asked.

"I'm not going to leave her," Miles said.

"Yes, you are."

JoAnn turned toward him. "You don't know anything about him," she said. "He's more understanding than you ever were. You're only here because you're worried about your farm. Just like always."

TWENTY-FOUR

The day after his final disaster with JoAnn, Frederick went to see his commodities broker, Louie Bates. He found him standing in the trader's area just outside his office.

"Frederick, how are you?" No matter how good or how bad business was, Louie always greeted him with the same Chamber of Commerce joviality. "What are you up to today? Gonna short the beans?"

Frederick looked up at the big mechanical board that covered almost an entire wall. The market had closed an hour before, so the board was still.

"No, I've got something else in mind," he said.

"Come on into my office and we'll talk about it."

Frederick followed him into the cubicle and sat down in one of the two chairs. Louie sat down in the other, an aged swivel that squeaked every time he moved. There was a computer screen on the desk with which he could summon information on any commodity sold in the world. If you wanted to buy coconuts in Borneo, Louie could arrange it.

Most of his desk was covered with slips of paper, hundreds of them, and even more were taped or tacked to the walls. It was the nearest thing he had to a filing system. More paper was stacked in piles or lying where Louie had dropped it, hours, weeks or months before. It was a miracle that he hadn't set the place on fire with one of the cigars he was always smoking.

"So, tell me, Frederick, what's up?"

"I need a lot of money in a hurry."

Louie laughed. "Who doesn't, but why—and why now?"

Until these last few days, Frederick couldn't have imagined talking to anybody else about his problems but things had changed. "JoAnn's left me and she wants half the farm."

Louie was on his third marriage, but he still hated to hear it. "I'm sorry to hear that, Frederick, but what's it got to do with trading commodities?"

"I want to make enough to pay her off so I can keep the farm in one piece."

Louie liked a commission as well as the next broker, but he also knew trouble when he heard it. "That sounds pretty risky. Maybe you ought to think this over."

"I have thought about it."

"You could lose the whole thing. Don't you think half is better than nothing?"

"Call me desperate, but that's the way I'm going to do it. If I can't keep it together, then I'll lose it all."

Louie puffed thoughtfully on the cigar. "How much is it worth?" he asked.

"Someone just offered me seven hundred and twenty thousand, cash."

"How much would be net?"

"All of it. I just paid off the inheritance tax. The place is clear."

"So, her half would be something like three hundred and sixty thousand," Louie said. "That is serious money."

"Serious enough to try the gold," Frederick told him.

"Gold! Man, gold is brutal—up the limit five times and down four during the last month alone."

"What did it do today?"

"Up the limit—" he punched keys and the computer screen bloomed with numbers "to seven hundred and eighty-three dollars an ounce."

"A contract is a hundred ounces, right?"

"Yeah. That's seventy-eight thousand three hundred dollars a contract."

"How much of that do I have to pay to control the contract?"

"Twenty percent, which comes to fifteen thousand six hundred and sixty bucks. But that's just to get in. You've also got to be ready to answer margin calls."

Frederick was rolling the numbers around in his head. He

stood up.

"I'll be back, Louie."

"Think it over, Frederick. It's a hell of a risk."

II

Darwin Kittleson had been Frederick's banker for the past five years. They'd been classmates in high school, and then Darwin had gone off to Iowa State to party and major in finance. He was an ambitious young man who had already worked his way up to vice-president in charge of Agricultural Lending at the Farmers National Bank, which stood on a corner across from the square in Lime City. A lot of people thought he was a sure thing for the big office on the first floor.

Darwin loved his work, which these days consisted of lending impressive sums of money to farmers at double-digit interest rates. As far as he was concerned, the golden age of farming had finally arrived—and it was long overdue. The old-time farmers he had grown up with had mostly been replaced by men who rightly viewed agriculture as a business and were using bigger equipment and chemicals to expand as fast as they could.

As they sought to buy more acres, they competed furiously for any land that came up for sale, driving its price far higher than it could ever return in income. But that little impracticality didn't matter. As the saying went, "They're not making land anymore." Adding to the mix were cash-rich foreigners like the Germans and Saudis who were buying it, too.

When land prices rose to where farm income could no longer support the purchase of a farm, most lenders solved the problem by basing loans on a farmer's net worth, most of which consisted of the equity of his land—its current value minus what he owed on it. If for some reason land prices fell significantly, as they had several times earlier in the century, the equity would vanish and every leveraged mortgage would be in default. That would result in massive foreclosures, as it had in the Great Depression. The failed loans, in turn, would collapse on the banks, eventually exhausting their reserves and bringing on their insolvency and failure.

That was the thinking of many of the old timers who could still remember the twenties and thirties when that very scenario had unfolded, but it was not the thinking of Darwin Kittleson or the Farmers National Bank. Agribusiness had become a way of life, and Farmers intended to stay at its forefront. Of course the bank recognized that there would be casualties, just as there were in every major economic change, but that was the price you paid for progress.

How much risk could there be if federally mandated institutions like Federal Land Bank and Production Credit were pushing money even more aggressively than Farmers? The Lime City Federal Land Bank office had actually fired a loan officer for telling a big client that he was overextended. The client had gotten angry and come right over to Farmers, and Darwin had loaned him the money. The bank got a big new account and Darwin got a raise.

Darwin always had to shake his head when Frederick Heinold came to see him. Here was a guy in his thirties, who had the outlook of someone in his seventies. There weren't many like him, thank God. Usually a guy Frederick's age would be charging hard, leveraging everything he had to buy or rent more land, but not him. He'd had to borrow to pay off the inheritance taxes on his farm, but nothing else until this year when he'd rented that extra ground. But then, just when Darwin thought Frederick was finally getting with the program, he dug in his heels and refused to buy the equipment he needed to farm it.

A lot of Frederick's neighbors thought his backward ways were pretty comical, especially Eldon Mathews who was Darwin's biggest customer. Every time they talked, Eldon had another Frederick Heinold story to tell. The latest was that his wife was leaving him, apparently for some flashy guy with a Cadillac. But the topper was when Eldon came in last week and borrowed all that cash—in five-dollar bills, for crying out loud—and tried to buy the Heinold farm.

If that wasn't the damnedest thing. Everybody in the bank was still laughing about it. It took a little doing to get seven hundred and twenty thousand in five dollar bills together, but that's what Eldon wanted—for better effect, he said. Before he came to pick it up, they piled it on Darwin's desk and took a picture.

He wasn't sure Eldon was actually going through with it until he walked in with the suitcase. Darwin tried to talk him into having a cop or deputy go along just to make sure that he didn't get held up or something, but Eldon showed Darwin the pistol stuck inside his coat and signed the papers for the money and left.

Then, Frederick wouldn't sell and Eldon had to bring it all back in and Darwin had to have the girls come into his office and count it, and Darwin ended up making a seven hundred and twenty thousand dollar loan for one day. In his own way, Eldon Mathews was as much of a character as Frederick Heinold—and an asshole to boot.

Of course, Frederick was unaware of Darwin's involvement in Eldon's scheme when he came into the bank to borrow the money for his own big gamble. He was wearing the beard that Darwin had heard about.

"That's a lot of money to be risking on a pretty crazy idea," Darwin told him after Frederick explained why he wanted it.

"You've been after me for years to take more risk, Darwin. I'm just taking you up on it."

"Gambling your farm in the commodities isn't what I had in mind, Frederick. I was thinking a little more along the lines of newer equipment or machinery, maybe expanding your herd. I can't recall anybody ever coming in here and outright asking for a loan to play the futures."

Even as he asserted that, Darwin could think of several times when farmers had done exactly that. They just hadn't been honest enough to tell him why they really wanted the money.

"If I had the cash, I wouldn't be here," Frederick told him. "But I don't. All I have is a paid-for farm."

"And a damned good one, Frederick. Why don't you just sell off part of it, just to get through this. Later, when you're back on your feet, you might be able to buy it back." He could see Frederick's body stiffen as he suggested this. He'd known him since they'd been in second grade together, but this was the first time he'd ever seen him angry.

"No, Darwin. I don't want to sell it. I want to keep it. That's why I'm willing to take this risk." The banker could see that he'd made up his mind. If he refused him, he'd just go somewhere else.

"How much do you want?"

"As much as I can get."

"I'll need an appraisal first."

"I don't have time for that. I want it in the morning."

"There's no way my board will approve it without an appraisal."

"Eldon Mathews just offered me seven hundred and twenty thousand for it. It ought to be worth at least that much."

For effect, Darwin paused and swiveled his chair slightly away. He knew he could approve this without waiting for the board. He did it all the time with his big customers while he made all the little ones jump through hoops.

Frederick Heinold was definitely small potatoes, but there was another aspect to consider: if Frederick gambled this farm away, as Darwin was pretty sure he would, the bank would get it. That would put him in a position to make sure that his biggest customer—Eldon Mathews—got it and at a premium price, and that would make everybody, including his board of directors, happy.

Darwin swiveled around to the credenza behind him, and his left hand went to the electronic calculator. His fingers tapped expertly on the keys and a number registered on the machine's display. "I can lend you five hundred and forty thousand," he said. "Seventy-five percent of its value. I'll do the appraisal myself, this afternoon."

Frederick stood up. "Good. I want it in a cashier's check," he said. "I'll pick it up tomorrow."

After he had left, Darwin picked up the phone and dialed a number he had memorized. "Eldon. I'm glad I caught you in. You'll never guess who just walked out of my office."

III

Frederick arrived at Louie's office a little after noon and gave him the check. Then sat down in one of the overstuffed chairs in the traders' room. Up on the board, the mechanical clackers were already displaying changes in the prices of the various commodities posted there: corn, soybeans, oats, live cattle, pork bellies, sugar, and Frederick's new interest—gold—as they were directly relayed from the trading floor of the Chicago Board of Trade.

The Board had been established to provide a more stable,

year-round market for farmers and producers of other commodities such as metals—including gold—to sell their products. It also guaranteed that the commercial consumers of these products, like meat packers, bakers, brewers, and smelters, had a dependable supply of raw materials. When it worked right, it diminished drastic fluctuations in the market.

Over the years, Frederick, like many farmers, had used the Board to sell portions of a crop he hadn't even planted for better prices than he could have gotten later at harvest. The only thing was, if he contracted to sell twenty thousand bushels of corn for delivery in December, while he was still planting that crop in May, he'd damn well better produce it. So far, he always had.

Such a system was bound to attract speculators who gambled, as Frederick was doing now, that the value of a commodity would gain or lose value over a specific period of time. He was betting that the price of gold would continue to increase, but he could as easily have shorted it—gambled that it would lose value. Somewhere in the world another trader was willing to bet against him. For every winner there was a loser, and for every loser, a winner. It was a simple game, but it could be financially devastating.

Sitting in the stuffed chairs or on the couch or moving nervously about the room were other traders. Among these were the habitués, the men who arrived just before the market opened at 7:30 and often didn't leave until just after it closed at three. Lunch was sandwiches they made themselves from the cold cuts Louie kept in a refrigerator.

Most were day traders, players whose major assets had vanished long ago but in whom the fever to beat the Board still burned. Often, their credit was shaky and Louie kept a close eye on their small orders. He'd been burned too many times by guys who couldn't make margin calls.

They were always poring over the charts that Louie's company put out, trying to predict the direction and strength of the next move, speaking in the arcane jargon of the traders. The talk was part of the excitement, and they shared it enthusiastically, its pitch rising and falling as the big board registered their successes or failures. Only when the session was over did they finally give up and go home.

Frederick knew only one of them, a tall, lanky farmer by the name of Ben Kramer who lived on the other side of Rock Falls. When Frederick came in, Kramer was leaning forward in one of the big chairs, angrily following the fate of the pork bellies as the board clattered a sudden decline in their price.

"Goddamn it!" he suddenly shouted. "Those sons-a-bitches almost hit my stop, then there they go!" He slapped the Naugahyde and pushed himself out of the chair. "Louie," he yelled as he walked toward the cubicle, "take me out!"

In a few seconds he was back, cussing good-naturedly and still shaking his head. He would have killed for a cigar, but he had diabetes and they weren't good for him. He'd been forced to give up drinking, too. The market was the only vice left to him.

"Those sons-a-bitches," he said to Frederick as he sat down in a chair next to him. Ben Kramer was six feet five and as good-natured as anyone Frederick knew.

"Trouble, Ben?" Frederick inquired.

"Aw, it's those fucking bellies," he replied. Pork bellies were to commodity traders what heroin was to addicts, and he was hooked on their volatility. "What are you up to, Frederick?"

"I thought maybe I'd try the gold, Ben. What do you think?"

"Dangerous, Frederick, scary," he said with a kind of eagerness. "Let's take a look." He picked through the pile of large charts that were scattered on a coffee table in front of them until he came to the one he wanted. It was a graph which plotted the ups and downs of gold over the previous five years, right through the day before.

"As you can see, it's been trending up for months, and a lot of people think there's no end in sight, with this economy. But there's also been signs that it might be peakin'. A couple of times it's dropped back to here, see?"

He poked the chart with his long fingers. "That's the bottom, right now. She's tested it a couple of times over the past month, but always rallied back and gone higher, yet. But that's where the resistance is. If she ever breaks down through that, look out. You could get poor in a hurry."

"Have you ever tried it?" Frederick asked him.

"Gold? Not me. Too rich for my blood. But I follow it. Of course, I follow a lot of things." He did, too. He kept up on events in Iran or Saudi Arabia or Argentina and how they affected the market. "Can you imagine," he went on, "Seven hundred and ninety dollars for an ounce of gold?" He shook his head. "Christ, I can remember all those years when the government held it at thirty-six bucks."

"You should have bought some," Frederick told him and went into Louie's office.

"Well?" Louie asked him.

"Time to try it," he said.

"Gold?"

"Yes."

"How much?"

"I want to buy twenty contracts."

"Whew. That's pretty steep, Frederick. Maybe you should start out with something smaller."

"I want twenty, Louie." The broker shrugged.

"You're the boss," he said and picked up his phone.

Frederick's order filled at seven hundred and ninety-two dollars an ounce. Louie transferred three hundred and sixteen thousand dollars from his account, giving Frederick control of one million five hundred and eighty-four thousand dollars of gold.

After months of wondering and worrying what would happen to his life, of trying to hide from the possibilities, he was doing something. Some day he might look back and see that it was the wrong thing, but right now he didn't think so. Whatever happened from this point on would be his doing, not JoAnn's, not Eldon's, not some attorney's. He hadn't wanted this and he hadn't done anything to bring it to pass, but he was facing it and doing his best to save the farm and maybe himself.

IV

By the end of the trading day, the price of gold had risen to seven ninety-seven. It opened strong the next morning and quickly moved past eight hundred on government news that inflation was up again.

Twenty-four hours after he'd bought the contracts their value had risen to eight twenty-one and he was up sixty-one thousand dollars. It closed at eight twenty-five. By ten the next morning gold was up the fifty dollar limit to eight seventy-five. The contracts were worth a hundred and seventy thousand more than he'd paid for them, a lot of money but not enough.

Through the afternoon it backed off forty points. Ben Kramer had been nursing a bean contract all day long, and just before the close he got off it and sat down next to Frederick. "Well, I picked up a hundred and twenty bucks," he declared. "How you doin'?"

"It was up strong this morning, but then it backed off forty bucks."

"It's been doin' that over the last week or so. Up strong, then down again, but always trending up. You got to keep an eye on it, though, and if it starts through the bottom—get out."

"I will, Ben," Frederick told him and went back to watching the clacking board. Louie came out of the cubicle and stood near him for a while, puffing on his cigar and watching. He didn't say anything.

The next morning gold started dropping at the open and didn't stop until it was down the limit to seven eighty-five and Frederick was losing money. Louie asked him if he wanted to put in a stop to avoid bigger losses.

"No," Frederick told him. "It can't do this two days in a row."

"Who says?" Louie asked.

The morning news was full of bad consumer index news that should have turned it around, but it kept falling, anyway, another fifty points before eleven o'clock. Early on he'd been able to keep track of the numbers in his head, but now he checked them with a pocket calculator. His hands shook as he figured. He was down a hundred and fourteen thousand.

V

At the end of ten days of trading and just five days before he was scheduled to meet JoAnn in front of a judge, Frederick had lost a little over six hundred thousand dollars, Louie Bates had added another blister to his ulcer, and the value of a good Iowa farm had been dispersed into the accounts of various gold traders around the world.

Some would later speculate that he'd recklessly thrown it away out of spitefulness toward JoAnn, but that wasn't true. He had, in fact, applied himself to the endeavor with all of the care and focused attention he could muster. Losing it so quickly and decisively only reinforced his belief that his plan could have worked. He could have made six hundred thousand just as fast as he'd lost it.

TWENTY-FIVE

Nate LaPointe sat behind his desk in silence. He had heard a few stories in his years as a lawyer, but never one like this.

"Is there anything I should do now?" Frederick asked him after he'd explained things.

"No, Frederick. You don't have to do anything. You signed a thirty-day note with the bank and they'll want their money when it's due. When you don't pay them, they'll foreclose to recover it and use the remainder to pay Louie and the IRS what you owe them.

"There might not be enough."

"Then they'll auction your equipment and personal possessions if they have to. If those don't cover it, they'll come after your gold teeth."

"They can have it all," Frederick said without rancor. "I won't need it anymore."

That's right, LaPointe thought to himself, you won't. The whole thing seemed devastating to him, although his client didn't look devastated. He couldn't tell what was going through his mind.

"I guess I'll get going," Frederick said.

"What are you going to do?"

"I don't know, Nate. I never thought about what might happen if it didn't work out."

LaPointe stood and extended his hand. "Take care of yourself, Frederick." It was the only thing he could think to say.

II

By the time that he had driven back to the farm, Frederick had decided some things. Molly came out of the barn to greet him, happy as always. He knelt to scratch her. "I kind of messed it up for both of us, girl" he said, and went into the house.

He was on automatic, focused only on the few things he had to do. He didn't want to think. He went up to the bedroom and pulled socks and underwear from the drawers and threw them into his only suitcase. On top of them went a couple of shirts and pairs of jeans, the few clothes he'd need in the new life he'd already begun to live, but not yet thought about.

Molly stayed close, watching, trying to puzzle it out. When he went out, she followed. He threw the suitcase into the back of the truck, then opened the door and motioned her in. She leapt onto the seat and took up her station by the passenger side window, delighted to be going along.

It was a ten minute drive to the Breka place. The whole time Molly stood at her window and alertly observed the countryside as they drove through it. Frank and his wife had just finished dinner when he knocked on their door. Frank answered.

"Frederick, come in." He was obviously surprised by this visit, but his cordiality was genuine. The kitchen smelled of the just finished meal and wood smoke. Bessie Breka was at the sink, washing the dinner dishes.

"Hello, Frederick," she said. "Have you had your dinner yet?"

"I have, Bessie. Thanks."

"I made an apple pie," she said.

"No, thank you. I came to ask you and Frank a favor."

There was something in the way he said it that caused Frank to look at his wife.

"Sit down, Frederick," she said and the three of them sat at the table.

"I'm afraid I've lost the farm," he told them. The Brekas looked at each other in disbelief. Other than death, this was maybe the worse possible news. "I lost it trading commodities," he went on. "JoAnn had left me and was trying to take half of it, so I tried to save it."

"My God!" Bessie said. She was almost in tears.

"It's all gone?" Frank asked.

"Everything. The bank owns it, now."

"We heard that you were havin' troubles, but we never dreamed it would be anything like this."

"I did my best," he said. "I didn't know what else to do."

"What are you going to do, now?" Bessie asked.

"I'm going away," he said.

"Where to?" Frank asked.

"I'm not sure. Some place that won't remind me of here." This was drawing out longer than he'd thought it would, and he was beginning to worry that he wouldn't hold it together.

"What's the favor do you need?" Bessie asked.

"I'd like you to take my dog Molly in. I want her to be able to stay close to the place she knows, with people who will take care of her."

"You don't want to take her with you?" Frank asked.

"I don't even know where I'm going," Frederick told him. "I don't think it would be fair to her."

Frank looked at his wife. "What do you think?" he asked her.

She looked at Frederick. "She's not a chicken killer, is she?"

"No, Bessie. She's got a good head on her shoulders, and she's pretty good with cows—and she'll look after the place."

Frank Breka searched his wife's face for some indication of what she thought of this idea. Almost from the beginning of the marriage he'd made every important decision with her. He looked back at Frederick.

"She'll have to live outside—sleep in the barn," Frank said.

"That's what she does now," Frederick told him.

The Brekas looked at one another, again. "Okay, Frederick," Bessie said, "we'll take care of her—until you get back."

"I have to be honest," he told them. "That might be a while."

"As long as it takes," Bessie said.

Frederick took out his wallet and counted out ten fifty dollar bills and pushed them across the table. Frank reacted as if he had put a snake there.

"No, Frederick," he said quite firmly. "We don't need any money for this."

"I know you don't, but this is for her, Frank. This way you can feed her good. If she needs a vet, you can just call one without worrying about the money. When the time comes, you can put her down. She's probably going to keep going back home for a while, so you're going to have to make some trips to fetch her. I don't want Eldon running over her or shooting her. This'll help pay for your gas and time—and I'll feel better about it."

"I don't know, Frederick," Frank said.

Frederick's offer was more awkward than insulting, even if it did make sense. Being neighbors meant that you helped people out when they needed it without ever a thought of being paid for it. In the old days, Frank had helped neighbors with haying or harvest, and they'd helped him. People were more independent now, but the old ethic still applied. Being offered money to do what he'd do for nothing didn't sit comfortably.

"Maybe we should," Bessie said. Frank looked at her, a little surprised. Bessie had the business sense between them, and he knew it. "Frederick's right," she went on. "This way we'd never begrudge her anything, because he'd already paid for it." Bessie didn't really believe this explanation herself, but she had recognized something that her husband didn't—that Frederick needed to do this, to feel that he was taking care of the dog.

"But he's a neighbor," Frank replied.

"And that's why I don't want to burden you," Frederick said. He looked at Bessie and then at Frank. "She's taken care of me and my farm," he told them. "I owe her this." He pushed his chair back and stood up, needing to be gone.

Frank Breka lingered for a moment, looking ruefully at the money, and then he stood up, too. "Come on, Bessie," he said. "Let's go meet our new dog."

The three of them put on their coats and walked out to the truck. Frederick opened the door and Molly got out, tail wagging. She rubbed against him and inspected the Brekas.

"Thanks," he said and climbed into the truck. The dog followed, waiting as she always did for him to invite her in. Without another word, he started it and drove off. He knew they would be talking to her, trying to reassure her, but that she had probably started down the lane after him, looking for the brake lights to come on.

He drove as fast as he could, not glancing at the mirrors until the narrow road turned up through the trees and there was no longer anything to see and everything that had happened began to fall behind.

III

Right after Frederick had left his office, Nate LaPointe had put in a call to Joe McKenna, but the receptionist told him that the attorney was in court and not expected back in the office until the next day. LaPointe was a little disappointed. He was curious to see how McKenna would take the news that JoAnn Heinold no longer had the prospect of a four hundred thousand dollar settlement. He doubted that she knew, yet, but word would travel fast.

What, he wondered, would happen to Frederick? He didn't seem like a man who might kill himself, but he hadn't seemed like a man who might gamble his life away, either. Farmers had taken their lives over a lost farm. That might not make much sense to outsiders, but how many of them had been born on, lived, made a living, raised a family, grew old and maybe even died on the same plot of earth? It was a particular context for a life, and it came with particular emotional attachments.

IV

Eldon had just come into the house when the phone began to ring. Since Sherry was gone off to Lime City, he had to answer it.

"Hello," he barked.

"Eldon. I hear you're buyin' another farm."

"What the hell are you talkin' about, Darwin?" He was still pretty peeved over his aborted effort, and not in the mood to be kidded about it.

"Now, you didn't hear this from me," the banker explained, "but Frederick Heinold's farm is going to be sold."

"What? You're crazy!"

"No, Eldon, I'm not. He lost it playing the gold futures."

"Frederick Heinold playin' the futures—in gold? You are completely full of shit, Darwin."

"I'm serious as a heart attack, Eldon. He thought JoAnn was gonna take him for half of it so he gambled the whole goddamned thing!"

Eldon had to sit down. "I can't believe it. Nobody's that stupid," he said.

"He was," Darwin told him.

"Jesus!"

"The bank and Louie Bates own it now," Darwin went on, "and the IRS."

"Are you sure about this?"

"Yes, Eldon, I'm sure. The papers for the loan are lying right in front of me."

"Well, when can I get my hands on it?"

"Our note's due in about seventeen days. We'll foreclose, which will take another thirty, then we'll pay Louie and the government and sell it to the highest bidder. And I guess we know who'll that'll be, don't we?"

"We sure as fuck do, Darwin. We sure as fuck do."

After he hung up, Eldon walked into the living room and looked out across the road at the farm he had coveted for so long. A few short minutes before he'd thought that he'd never get it, that he'd spend the rest of his life aching to own it and hating the son-of-a-bitch who did and now, suddenly, it was going to be his—two hundred and forty of the best acres in the township and all lying just across the road. He felt almost light-headed with reverence and gratitude. He smiled as he thought of the promise he'd made to Frederick Heinold.

V

Joe McKenna returned Nate LaPointe's phone call the next morning and got the bad news.

"I'll call my client," he said crisply, then hung up and called JoAnn at her office.

"Have you talked with your husband since yesterday?" he asked.

"No. I haven't. Is there something wrong?"

"I just had a call from his attorney. It seems that Mr. Heinold has lost the farm playing the commodities market." There was an understandable silence at the other end of the phone.

"He did what?"

McKenna moved the phone away from his ear. "Mr. LaPointe told me that your husband gambled six hundred thousand dollars that the price of gold would go up, but it didn't."

"Gold? Frederick? That's impossible!"

Here it comes, he thought, looking at his watch. "I'm only

relaying what LaPointe told me."

"That's crazy! Frederick would never do that! The farm is his whole life!"

McKenna now realized that JoAnn Heinold was adding minutes to a fee that she might not be able to pay. "Perhaps Mr. LaPointe can provide more details. Why don't you give him a call."

"He couldn't do that, could he?" she persisted. "It isn't legal, is it? Wouldn't it be like stealing?"

"I'm afraid that there's nothing illegal about squandering jointly held assets. People do it every day, although seldom so precipitously."

"Can't you make him give it back? I had counted on this! You told me I have a right to it!"

"You did when he possessed it, Mrs. Heinold, but it sounds as if he no longer does."

She began to cry, mournfully—hopelessly. "What can I do? Can I sue him?" she asked between sobs.

"I suppose you could, but for what? No, I'm afraid there's nothing you can do. Just hope there is enough left to pay the IRS." JoAnn was sobbing uncontrollably, now. She lay the phone down and searched through her purse for something to wipe her nose. By the time she picked it up, again, McKenna had hung up. She called Miles. He was, of course, still in bed but she rang the phone until he answered it.

"He's lost the farm," she wailed.

Miles tried to clear his head and light a cigarette at the same time. "He what?" he asked.

"He lost the farm?"

"JoAnn, you're hysterical. Now calm down and tell me what's going on."

"I am telling you!" she screamed. "My goddamned husband gambled everything away!"

He took a long drag from the cigarette. "You'd better come home and tell me about it," he said. He was completely awake.

VI

By the time JoAnn got to the apartment, she hadn't calmed at all. Despite her hysterics, Miles was still skeptical of what she was telling him. It didn't make sense.

"Look," he said after listening to twenty minutes of rant, "why don't you call his attorney and see if you can find out what's going on."

She called LaPointe who confirmed everything McKenna had told her, while Miles sat nearby and grimly smoked one cigarette after another. As it all sank in, the hysteria drained away until she was limp with defeat.

"Where is he?" she asked after she'd heard everything.

"I don't know," LaPointe told her. "I haven't seen him since yesterday. As a matter of fact, I'm concerned about him."

"You should be," she said, "because if I see him, I'll kill him myself." She hung up and began to cry, again, a hopeless, repetitive, dirge of recrimination and regret.

If things hadn't been so dismal, Miles would have found her funny. Crushed as she was, she couldn't begin to understand how disappointing this was for him. She had talked at length about her plans to invest the money and let it grow for the security she valued so much, but Miles had already spent it on dreams.

As always, the TV was on in the corner and he appeared to be watching it, but he was not. Instead, he searched through the possibilities that her husband's stupidity had left him, and they were few and unappealing. His money had dwindled to a little more than three thousand dollars, and he had to replenish it soon.

JoAnn finally stopped crying, and he knew that she was watching him, hoping he would look up and smile and tell her everything was all going to be alright. But he did not. Things were not alright—and might never be again.

TWENTY-SIX

After he left Breka's, Frederick drove the truck west to Highway 65 and turned south. It seemed as good a direction as any. He didn't have a specific destination in mind, only some place without memories. Memories were his enemies now, bearers of pain he might not be able to endure. He would drive until he escaped them.

After sunset a huge moon rose, at first tarnished by the earth's atmosphere, but growing whiter as it climbed into the frigid sky. God might or might not be up there, but the moon certainly was, presiding over the world's misery, a talisman of the night and those who fled by night.

The life that Frederick had lived was over, as finally as if he had died. To have stayed would have been to live as a ghost in his own past. People would know him not for who he was, but who he had been, what he had done. Gone, he would pass quickly from their thoughts.

JoAnn's unforgiveness might endure longer, but she, too, had to go on. Life didn't provide breathers. Clinging to memories was a luxury none could afford. Life kept coming, and one lived it or perished in some way.

II

The evening of the day after JoAnn got the bad news, Miles went to Antonio's by himself. Roland Higgins was at his customary table.

"Sit down," Roland told him. Miles wasn't exhibiting his

usual nonchalance. "How's it going?"

"So, so," Miles said.

"Woman trouble?"

"In a way."

"Women are the worst trouble a man can have," Roland said with considerable conviction. It was the most forthcoming he'd been, but Miles was too preoccupied to notice. "Goin' back to Florida?"

"Thinking about it."

"Palm trees, sunshine—it sounds good, man."

"If it sounds so good, why don't you go?"

"I go to Jamaica. All the ganja in the world and the cops don't give a shit. I stay stoned for a week at a time."

Normally, Miles thrived on this kind of small talk, but not tonight. And he hadn't forgotten how Roland had set him on the path to this eventual fiasco.

"I guess things aren't working out for you here," Roland went on. Miles looked at him. "You know, the antique business."

"Yeah," Miles said. "Too bad."

Roland laughed.

"What's so funny?" Miles asked him.

"Let's go for a ride."

"Where to?" Miles asked, but Roland was already pulling on his coat and heading out the door.

Just north of town, Roland turned off the highway onto a gravel road and drove into the buried countryside. The headlights were hemmed in by drifts that towered over the car. After he had driven about a mile, he stopped and turned off the lights. He adjusted the rear view mirror so he could watch the road behind.

"What's going on?" Miles asked.

"I've got a big order of coke coming, and I have to lay some of it off. Are you interested?"

"I might be. How much?"

"A half a kilo. Twenty-five thousand."

"That's hardly wholesale."

"We're at the bottom of the food chain, here. What can I do?" A familiar edge had come back into his voice.

Miles looked out the window at the wall of snow. He felt

hemmed in by it—by everything. "I'll let you know," he said.

"I got to know now."

"Why?"

"If you don't want it, I'll find someone else." He started the car.

"I'm only saying it's short notice."

"It's always short notice," Roland said.

It was, Miles thought. He had to do something. "I'll take ten," he said.

"That's all?"

"Yes."

So much for the big shot from Florida, Roland thought. "Okay, ten."

III

"It's just a loan—and just for a few weeks."

"Miles, it's all the money I have."

"I'm only borrowing it, JoAnn. I'm going to pay you back."

"I know that, but—couldn't you get it from the bank?"

"Okay," he said. He got his coat from the closet and put it on.

"Where are you going?"

"Where I have friends who trust me."

"Miles! I trust you. It's just that—."

"Just what, JoAnn?"

He was at the door, ready to leave. She went to him. "Don't leave."

"I don't want to, JoAnn, but I need this money."

She wanted to explain to him, again, why this troubled her, but she was afraid he'd only get angry and leave—and she couldn't bear that. It really wasn't a choice.

"Okay, Miles. I'll do it."

IV

It was Wednesday, and Sherry Mathews was getting her hair done just like every other Wednesday. Eldon had seen her off with his usual disparaging remark.

"It's a waste of money," he said. "It's supposed to improve your looks, and I ain't seein' no change." It was another way to tell her he wasn't getting enough sex.

Sherry had come to the Cut N Curl for years, continuing even after the previous owner had retired and sold it to Grace Miller who had moved back to Iowa from somewhere in the east. Grace was somewhere around fifty and possessed a kind of worn beauty.

She was quiet and revealed little about her previous life except that she was divorced and had two grown children. Sherry liked the way she did her hair, which was all that mattered. Unlike some of Grace's customers, she wasn't interested in gossip. She liked to look nice, even if it was wasted on Eldon, but it was the soothing ritual of getting her hair washed and trimmed that she really looked forward to. Grace provided the most relaxing hours of Sherry's life.

She also used her time in town to pay bills, buy groceries and pick up parts for Eldon when he needed them. She preferred to get her hair done later in the afternoon after she'd finished those tasks, and over time that had become her regular time. She also liked that the shop was quieter, then, and Grace took more time with her.

It had been less than a week since Eldon had triumphantly learned he was getting his hands on the Heinold farm, and she couldn't remember when he'd been so happy. His good mood had ignited his libido and that brought on a period of civility, but it no longer worked. She had learned her lessons years before, and no matter how much he cajoled or cursed, she refused to share a bed with him. She would have been delighted if someone had promised she'd never have sex again.

As usual, the delicate touch of Grace's hands had brought on a lavish drowsiness, and Sherry's eyes closed and her head nodded slightly. As Grace drew a comb through her hair, she slid a hand under the back of Sherry's neck and slowly tilted her head back.

"Is that comfortable?" Grace asked.

"Mmm, yes," Sherry replied. Grace kept her hand there, combing one side and then the other, and an exquisite tingling radiated down Sherry's neck and across her shoulders. Her mouth fell slightly open and she could hear the relaxed cadence of her own breathing. She might have fallen completely asleep if Grace had not leaned over with her own trembling heart and kissed her.

V

JoAnn drew six thousand dollars from her savings account, then wrote a check for a thousand more. She took it all in hundred dollar bills as Miles had requested. What had the teller thought about that? The hell with her, she thought. She could think what she liked. Word of Frederick's stupidity had spread, and she knew people were talking about it and maybe having a laugh at her expense. To hell with them, too. Frederick had disappeared and left her with this mess, and she couldn't waste time worrying about what they thought.

She had dismissed McKenna and hired a much cheaper local attorney to handle the divorce. He had hired an accountant to figure out what was owed the IRS. Fortunately her business was okay. Thank God, Miles had stayed. With prospects for the farm squashed, she'd feared he would go back to Florida, but he hadn't.

They seldom went out now, and he really hadn't been his old self until he'd come upon the investment she loaned him the money for. She didn't really want to, but she could see how important it was to him. And he was putting up twenty thousand of his own, so they were in it together.

She couldn't bear to have him leave. She needed him, and she had convinced herself that he needed her—perhaps he still loved her, even though he had not told her so for some time. Why else would he have stayed through this dreadful winter? She dropped the money off at the apartment before going out to show houses.

The sheaf of bills felt comforting to Miles. He was back in business. He might have taken the money and gone to Florida, but the Cadillac was entombed in a bank of snow and ice. And once there, he'd have to do what he was doing here with people just as questionable as Roland—probably with even more risk. Roland was suspicious of everyone, and that was a good thing. He might as well stick around and try to make this work.

At eight-thirty he took a cab to the motel. He went into the bar and ordered a scotch, which he drank too quickly. He ordered another. He was nervous. Take it easy, he told himself, at least you're not out in a dark field with a head case like Billy

Meyers.

That made him think of the gun he'd left out there. It had cost him four hundred dollars because it was supposed to be untraceable. He hoped it was. If Billy got careless and shot somebody, Miles didn't want it traced back to him. The scotch was beginning to relax him, and he ordered another.

At nine, he paid his tab and walked through the lobby and down to Room 42. He took a breath and knocked and the door opened right away. "Roland told me there was going to be a party here," he said. The man who'd opened the doorway was tall, in his thirties, with blonde hair, cut closely like an athlete.

"We're just getting started," he said easily and Miles went in. Another guy sat at a small round table with a lamp hanging over it. A can of beer sat on the table in front of him. He was thin and dark with long hair that fell forward across his shoulders.

"That's Tony," the blonde guy said, "and I'm Ed." Tony merely nodded and sipped from the can. "You want a beer?" Ed asked him.

"No thanks," Miles said. Nothing about these guys seemed sinister. His nerves started to settle down.

"Have a seat," Ed said and motioned for him to take the one opposite Tony. He sat down and Ed got another and sat down with them. "I guess Roland told you it would be a small party."

"Yes," Miles said. "He did."

"I prefer small parties."

"I do, too," Miles said.

"So, did you bring us something?"

"I followed his instructions."

"Good. Good." He looked at Tony, and Tony brought something out of his pocket and put it on the table and pushed it over to Miles. It was a clear plastic bag, plump with white powder.

"Okay if I have a taste?" Miles asked.

"Of course," Ed said.

Miles undid the rubber band that kept the bag closed and took a tiny spoon from a coat pocket. He worked it down into the center of the powder and drew out a sample. He tapped off the excess and inhaled what was left into his right nostril. The effect was instantaneous and satisfying.

He set the spoon down and resealed the bag, then took a

small portable scale from his coat pocket and hung the bag from it.

"It looks good," he said and set the bag down. He took the folded bills from another pocket and pushed them over to Ed. Ed picked them up, pulled the rubber band off, and quickly counted. Then, he refolded the bills, slipped the rubber band over them, and put them in a pocket.

"Nice doing business with you," Ed said.

"Same here," Miles replied. He put the scale in one pocket and the bag in another, and left.

Each step Miles took down the hallway seemed lighter than the one before. He felt great, like jogging. His right hand was around the bag. A half kilo. Beautiful. That was more like it—no punk like Billy Meyers to screw things up. Maybe he could get used to this place after all.

He went into the bar and called JoAnn, but she didn't answer. He called a cab and ordered another scotch.

By the time he finished the drink, the cab hadn't arrived yet, so he went outside to wait. It was cold, but it didn't bother him. A half kilo, he thought, holding the bag in his hand in the pocket. It felt substantial. He could do big things with a half kilo.

The cab pulled up and he opened the back door and got in. Before he could tell the driver where to go, both doors opened and a voice very near said, "Don't move. You are under arrest."

VI

It had taken Frederick fifteen hours to drive down US 65 to Little Rock, Arkansas, stopping only for fuel and finally, something to eat. He had left the last remnants of snow behind in central Missouri, but there was little appeal to the dripping southern winter he had entered. The trees were bare and the fields gray and sodden. Even this far from Iowa, corn and soybean stubble pricked memories of his own fields. He would have to go farther, but not today. He was too tired.

He found a motel on a grimy strip on the edge of the city and checked in. The couple who ran it lived in a room behind the office, and the air was thick with the smells of frying pork and cigarettes.

"Thirty-five even," the heavy-set man told him. He was wearing an undershirt and the cigarette bobbed in his mouth as he talked. "Iowa," he said, looking at Frederick's driver's license, "must be cold up there." Frederick nodded and took the key. He wasn't ready to talk.

The room was cheap and cold. There was a single thin blanket on the bed along with the thread-bare spread. He turned on the TV and found Bob Barker steering a contestant through the hysteria. Frederick didn't care. It was distraction.

He pulled off his boots and stretched out on the bed. Everything in him sagged. He closed his eyes and his mind focused half-heartedly on the program. Somewhere he had read that Barker did not eat meat because of his love of animals. No cows or pigs. Not even a chicken. Just the thing for a fugitive Iowa farmer.

Sometime during the afternoon he woke up, cold. He pulled the blanket and spread over himself and fell back into a deep sleep. He dreamed that JoAnn was leaving him and he was in despair. Then, she was leaving him again and he was shattered anew. When the last dream woke him, the room was hot and the ten o'clock news was on the TV. His clothes were sweaty and he was hungry. When he went out to get his suitcase from the truck, it was raining.

He showered and put on fresh clothes and went in search of a place to eat. He found a truck stop, noisy with the bustle of waitresses and the clatter of dishes.

He read a newspaper while he ate roast beef and potatoes. Little had changed in the past few days. Jimmy Carter was foolishly defending Bert Lance, and gold was still falling. He could have lost the farm, again. At least it hadn't been a close call.

He drove back to the motel through heavy rain. He was grateful not to be on the road. It was just after midnight when he got back. He turned on the TV and searched through the handful of available channels for something to watch, but there was nothing. He felt an urgent need for distraction. Why hadn't he found a place with cable?

The room was still too warm, so he fiddled with the controls on the window unit. It began to clank noisily, but the temperature stayed the same. He undressed to his underwear and stretched out on the bed, his head propped on the pathetic pillows, and tried again to find something to watch. Why hadn't he brought something to read? He finally settled on a movie he'd seen before.

At one o'clock, the movie ended and was replaced by the Star Spangled Banner and then by a test pattern. It was the same on the other channels, except one where a preacher was energetically urging the faithful to accept the inevitability of their sins and subsequent damnation. He was well into it when Frederick tuned in, his hair tossed wildly by the vigor of his exhortations. Normally, he would not have spent a minute watching this, but he had no other options and he needed some kind of distraction, no matter how bizarre.

At a quarter of two the preacher skillfully segued into a pitch for donations. He was pretty good, Frederick thought, splicing his sermon seamlessly to requests for "five, ten, twenty-five dollars—whatever you can to help me do God's work." And then he, too, was gone, replaced by another version of the national anthem.

Now he was left to himself and the bottle of bourbon he'd packed in the suitcase. There was no ice, and he wasn't going to brave the rain to get some, so he poured one of the plastic cups that came with the room half full and added some water. It did not taste good and wouldn't have even with the ice, but he drank it anyway, with the faith he'd developed in the months before. With the dawn he'd move on, but first there were five hours of darkness and silence to surmount.

He finished that glass and poured another, studying the room as he did, noting with approval the functional cheapness in which he couldn't detect a trace of sentiment. Once it had probably enjoyed a middle-class respectability and been furnished with some commercial approximation of hominess, but all of that had succumbed long ago to the tawdry neglect of those who stayed there. Everything about the room was worn or soiled or damaged and smelled of a thousand cigarettes. It was wonderfully appropriate for the first night of his new life.

As the warmth of the whiskey spread through him, the dreaded, elongate shape of time evolved into something less threatening. The glass was empty, so he replenished it without getting off the bed so that a little spilled on the spread. Certainly not the first time, he reflected.

He drank without tasting it and when it was gone he poured some more. This time he raised the glass and solemnly gestured to the right and then the left. The time had come for a benediction, but when he tried to speak, the words lodged in his throat like a bone, and he struggled to push them out. But they were stuck there and hopeless. Then the room was aqueous and tasted like salt.

TWENTY-SEVEN

Eldon finally did get Frederick Heinold's farm, but it took longer than Darwin Kittleson had said it would and cost more than Eldon had hoped.

It was late February before the county sheriff held the auction at the courthouse in Lime City. JoAnn Heinold had signed off on her interest, but no one knew where the hell her husband was or even if he was still alive, so the bank had to go ahead and foreclose, anyway. Two other men bid on the farm, but it was a foregone conclusion that Eldon would go as high as necessary to get it. It cost him seven hundred and sixty-eight thousand dollars, the most ever paid for a farm in the entire county.

A week after the closing, he made arrangements with the Rock Falls Volunteer Fire Department to come out and burn the house. It was a cheap, legal way for Eldon to get rid of it, and the department got to practice its skills. The Saturday they burned it was cold but sunny, with almost no wind. Eldon was waiting for them, along with his crew and a big Caterpillar tractor he'd hired.

While the others waited outside, Eldon and the chief went into the house to look it over. The door had been left open and it was as cold inside as out. Since no one had bothered to shut off the water, it had frozen in the pipes and burst them.

JoAnn had taken only a few things and sold the rest to a secondhand dealer who had removed the rest of the furniture and whatever else of value. Shelves and drawers were emptied and scattered.

"This is a shame," the chief said, shaking his head. "A

perfectly good house."

"Next spring I'll plant corn right here," Eldon told him. "You won't be able to tell it was ever here."

That didn't make the chief feel better, and he went back outside, leaving Eldon in the living room. Through the windows he could see them standing around the fire truck, stamping their feet to keep warm. Good as his word, he urinated on the floor, then went outside.

Eldon got a five-gallon can of diesel fuel from the back of his pickup. "Where's the best place to light it?" he asked the chief.

"Anywhere on the first floor. One can should do it, if you spread it around good." Eldon carried the can into the living room and began to spread the fuel around. He felt a kind of thrill while he was doing it. The chief came back in as he was pouring out the last.

"Should I light it?" Eldon asked.

"Go ahead," the chief said. The sooner it was over, the better he'd like it. He went back out.

Eldon stood in the doorway between the two rooms, and began to light matches and throw them on the soaked carpet. The diesel began to burn, slowly at first, then gaining momentum from the growing heat and the draft that it created. He watched for a moment in fascination as the accumulating heat warmed his face, then he picked up the empty can and went outside.

In a few minutes smoke began to seep out of the open door. The fire crew had laid its hoses out on the snow and now they stood around waiting. So far no flames could be seen through the windows, only smoke roiling viscously behind the panes. But after a short while, intermittent tongues of orange began to flicker in the smoke and they could see that the fire was growing quickly. Then, a window broke and then another, and the fire began to draw air through the hole.

Eldon was transfixed with awe and happiness. When he looked at the second story windows, he could see that the fire had climbed the stairs and was burning aggressively in all the rooms. Gray smoke leaked from the shingles. The only thing containing the fire, now, was the house.

More windows broke and smoke and flames streamed from every crack and breaking window and it began to growl as it sucked the air around it into a twisting vortex of flame and smoke. Then it broke everywhere, through walls and roof, and the house disappeared.

Disheartened by the spectacle, the chief and his men only watched and didn't bother with any drills. Usually the houses they burned were decrepit and unsalvageable and the fire they set only hastened a demise well under way, but that was not the case here. For a hundred years this house had provided a home to people who had taken care of it, and now it was being needlessly destroyed. Eldon Mathews could have burned it down without any help from them—and they wished that he had.

II

It took Eldon's crew another two days to crush the other buildings and push them into burn piles.

"There was a lot of salvage there," Clyde remarked with some regret, as he oversaw the burning of the last pile. Eldon had tired of the razing and left, but his crew leaned on their shovels and nodded in agreement with Clyde. "I guess if you got money you can afford to burn a good house," he said.

The following day, after the ashes were cold, the Cat pushed the foundation of the house down into the basement along with anything that had not burned. Loads of soil were hauled in and used to fill the hole, until the place where the house had sat was level.

Eldon supervised the last of the operation himself, and when the crawler had finished and backed away, he walked out into the middle of the fresh dirt and surveyed the result. Except for two grain bins and some fences his crew would tear out after the ground thawed, there was little left to remind him that Frederick Heinold had ever lived there.

III

Miles Richards was one of seven people arrested in the county that night, all given up by Roland Higgins who had been quietly arrested two weeks before and offered reduced charges for the names he gave the police. Miles had been the first to come to Roland's mind, and he hoped that would appease the cops enough to let him off the hook, but it hadn't. Even though their interest in Miles was piqued, when they found that he was from Florida and had come to Iowa to traffic, they wanted more and Roland had to give them additional names.

In his first meeting with his attorney, Miles learned what he had suspected—that the two buyers in the motel were DCI agents. He wouldn't figure out Roland's complicity until later, after he'd begun his ten-year sentence in the Iowa State Reformatory.

JoAnn learned of Miles arrest only minutes after it occurred, when other agents brandishing weapons and a search warrant started pounding on her door. After they found the marijuana that Miles had hidden in a drawer under his underwear, she was handcuffed and read her Miranda rights. She was taken to the county jail where she was booked and then allowed to call her mother. Loretta paid her bail, then drove her home in a condemning silence. Once again they'd been betrayed by a man.

IV

As surprised as she had been by Grace's kiss, Sherry had been even more surprised by her reaction to it. Never in twenty years of marriage had Eldon kissed her so tenderly, and even in the brief shock of Grace's lips on hers, she felt something she'd never felt before. She had wanted it to go on.

But those feelings were overcome by her confusion and disbelief. A woman had kissed her! She virtually leapt from the chair. "What are you doing, Grace?"

Grace backed away, mortified by her own audacity. "My God! What am I doing?" she cried. "I'm so sorry! I don't know what came over me."

"Well—I've never! What were you thinking?"

"Sherry, I'm so sorry," Grace insisted. "I can't understand what came over me. Can you ever forgive me?"

She was truly frightened. The kiss had jeopardized not only her business relationship with Sherry but her reputation, her work—everything!

Sherry could see the two of them reflected in the mirror behind Grace. Grace was in the foreground, her shoulders shaking with emotion, and Sherry stood almost protectively behind her. She did not seem to be upset.

"Have you ever done anything like that before?" she asked. "Kissed a woman?"

"Me? Oh, no! Please believe me! I don't know what came over me!"

"So, you're not a—lesbian?"

"My God, no! I was married for over fifteen years! I have children!"

"Did you love him?" Sherry asked.

"Love him? You mean my husband? I don't remember. I must have, musn't I?"

"Not necessarily," Sherry said. "I've been married for twenty-three years to a man I can't stand." She looked at Grace. "Never once did he kiss me like you just did. I didn't know that anybody could."

"So, you're not mad?" Grace asked.

"No. I'm not mad," Sherry said. "Confused, maybe, but not mad." She glanced back at the image in the mirror. She looked pretty. People used to tell her all the time how pretty she was, but she never felt pretty. Mostly she felt nothing—until that kiss. That kiss had unleashed a swirl of feelings in her head, her stomach—her heart!

She could see that Grace had once been pretty, but somewhere along the line she'd stopped caring about her own looks. Instead, she spent her days helping other women look pretty. Her hands were reddened from the chemicals she used in the permanents. Veins stood out on the backs of her legs from so many years of standing, and now tears streaked her face.

She looked forlorn and alone—and suddenly vulnerable and terribly dear to Sherry. "It's going to be all right," she told her. "It's going to be all right."

V

From Little Rock, Frederick headed southeast toward the Gulf of Mexico, managing each night to find a room as shabby as the one before. He didn't hurry. There was no point in hurrying when he didn't know where he was going. He had money to buy what he needed which was whiskey, which, for all its shortcomings, the South understood and provided in generous quantity.

Sometimes in the evenings he'd go to bars where he sat, speaking to no one, listening to the drawling voices that told him he was a stranger. Mostly, he drank alone, in the room, trying to hold his thoughts at bay.

As he descended through Louisiana, the air grew warm and bayou smells rose out of the matted pastures and hung like Spanish moss in the sad, southern trees. Louisiana seemed as decrepit and unkempt as a beggar: old trees and shacks and dark listless water waiting for God knew what. Old folks—black and white—shuffled along the side of the road, and children pedaled rickety bicycles and congregated at the tiny stores he passed.

The roads took their time through the countryside, unconcerned with symmetry or the need to get somewhere. Farther south, the state flattened into a landscape of lakes and bayous, more water than land. The highway turned one way and then another to avoid an inlet or estuary or bayou until it seemed it wasn't going anywhere. The entire south edge of the state was beset by the relentless waters of the Gulf of Mexico, which he had smelled but not yet seen.

As he drove the last few miles, a vast space began to open behind the trees, and he thought it must be the sea, and he was coming to the end of land. He turned off the highway onto a narrow shell road, and followed it down to a deserted beach. He got out of the truck and walked down to where small, dirty waves nuzzled the darkened sand.

The shore stretched in either direction, littered as far as he could see with every kind of bottle and piece of plastic. In most places only a few feet of sand lay between the low, eroded banks and the water, and in some places there wasn't even that, so the trees and shrubs grew at the very edge. A log lay near the water, and he got the bottle from his suitcase and sat on it. The sun was warmer than he had felt it in a long time, its light filtered into various shades of silver by the high overcast.

Despite the profaning trash that lay everywhere, he felt some elevation of his spirits as the morning warmed. The bottle was almost full, and he screwed the cap off and took a sip. Far out on the water he could see the silhouette of a boat, but he couldn't tell what kind. It was a good place to sit and enjoy the sun and drink from the bottle.

VI

He woke the next morning on the beach, the almost-empty bottle lying next to him. A few feet away, small waves still slapped at the sand. The sea was flat. There was sand on his clothes and on his cheek where he'd slept on it. His head felt hot and ached when he moved. The air was mild, although the sun was not quite up. He wasn't making progress.

He undid his shirt and took it and the rest of his clothes off and waded slowly in. The water was warmer than he had expected. It was shallow for some distance, and a gentle swell rose and fell like the sea was breathing. When the water came to his shoulders, he leaned forward and began an easy breaststroke toward the south.

He went on for some time, until the sun lifted clear of the horizon and glazed the water with metallic light. He rolled onto his back and sculled with his arms. When he paused to look toward the beach, the truck had gotten tiny. There was nothing beneath his feet but water. He turned and began to swim, again.

After a half hour, the water began to chill him. When he looked again, he couldn't see the truck at first. The water had changed color as the sun went higher. When he felt out of breath, he rolled onto his back and studied the clouds. They seemed familiar. Except for the quiet splash of his swimming, the world was still and silent.

Some part of his brain tried to tell him he should go back. After all, he was a landsman, a great distance from land, farther than he might be able to swim. But he wasn't frightened. He stopped again and looked south. Sky and water merged so he couldn't tell where either ended or began.

His arms sculled back and forth like insufficient wings. He was flying over a land that lay far below. If he faltered, he would sink in a languid, spiral until he touched down like an exquisite ballerina. Would his memories follow? It would be nice not to remember.

But as he lay on the back of the sea, it was clear that he could not outrun any part of himself, dreams or otherwise, nor should he want to. He did not exist in parts but as a whole. He was not separate from anything in the world, not even the sea which he barely knew. It was time to stop.

TWENTY-EIGHT

In early August, Eldon Mathews received a registered letter from a Des Moines law firm informing him that Sherry was suing him for divorce. It was the stupidest thing he'd ever heard of, and he would have told her so if he could have found her, but she had anticipated this by secretly moving to a Des Moines apartment.

"You mean I don't even get to talk to her?" he demanded of his attorney.

"Not if she doesn't want you to," the attorney told him. After taking an inventory of Eldon's wealth, he also concluded that her terms—one million in cash—would not be considered unreasonable by any judge he could think of.

"A million dollars! She's fuckin' nuts!" Eldon protested. He truly thought she was, and if he could just talk to her he'd straighten her out. He was also convinced that someone had put her up to this. "She's not smart enough to think this up on her own," he told the attorney. "She's got a man. I know it! She's gonna take me for a million and then blow it on a goddamned boyfriend!"

Eldon was partly right. It was not an idea the woman he had been married to all those years would come up with. That woman wouldn't have left him for any reason, because women like that didn't leave. They made the best of what they'd been handed, bad lot or not, and went on.

But all of that had changed when Grace Miller kissed her, and Sherry began to discover the vast country of her own longings and the possibility of actually living a happy life. That single, awkward kiss had opened the door to all that, and when she stepped through it, her marriage was doomed.

After that afternoon, she and Grace had spent the next few months secretly getting to know each other. Grace would close the shop after her appointment with Sherry and they'd meet again at her apartment. More and more, Sherry found other reasons to travel into Lime City, but Eldon hardly noticed.

Although it was Grace who had taken that first audacious step, it was Sherry who was most eager to explore the emotions the kiss had set loose in her. They would sit together on Grace's couch, sipping wine, and Sherry would gently kiss her, her eyes closed, lips barely parted, slow, savoring kisses.

It was as if she had tasted some wonderful new food that she'd never dreamed existed, and now she couldn't get enough of it. Grace was shyer and less adventurous, but drawn to Sherry's physical beauty. The kisses brought her closer to another person than she'd ever been.

Each was falling in love as she'd never fallen before. They were adolescents again, discovering what they might have discovered when they were sixteen if they had lived different lives with different people. They felt the world opening for them, and their old lives falling away like husks.

The sheer audacity of their relationship spawned new possibilities; if they could find one another like this, they could do anything. They could go anywhere and live as they liked. They could be together openly, not hiding like this.

In July, Eldon went on a two-day junket with a seed corn company, and Sherry and Grace drove to Des Moines so Sherry could talk to an attorney. She had not thought much about what a divorce might mean to her financially. She had been required to sign purchase agreements for the farms Eldon had bought, and there were large numbers on those agreements, but Eldon had also borrowed a lot of money so it was hard to know exactly what they were worth.

The lawyer thought that she should ask for at least two million, but she decided on one million, the current value of the three hundred and twenty acres she had inherited from her parents. Even though Eldon thought her demands outrageous and talked openly about fighting her in court, he followed the advice of his lawyer and borrowed the money from The Farmers State Bank and paid her off.

"You won't be sorry," the attorney told him.

"I'm already sorry," Eldon replied. "She shouldn't have gotten a fuckin' cent!"

Darwin Kittleson pointed out that time was on Eldon's side. The price of land was still rising. "Look at it this way," he suggested. "She could have gone after the farm itself. This way you got the land, and it's just going to go up and up in value."

Later that year, Grace told her customers that she was selling the shop and moving to Florida, where the winters weren't so hard. Without anyone in Lime City ever getting a whiff of their relationship, she and Sherry moved to Sarasota.

When Eldon heard that Sherry had moved, he was more convinced than ever that she was with another man. Somewhat defiantly, he began to date, but the few available women were either too plain or had other shortcomings. For the first time he began to see how attractive and capable Sherry had been, but he was too embittered to admit it. She never let me have any of it anyway, he consoled himself. It's not like it was a big loss.

Kittleson was right. The price of land did keep rising, so much that by early 1981 appreciation had replaced almost half of the money Eldon had given to Sherry—at least on paper.

But the frenzy to buy land had finally reached an unsupportable level, and the balloon began to deflate. At first it was gradual and not alarming—there were always corrections with these things, some said—but it wasn't long before the losses began to grow and that set off a fatal set of events.

The price of an acre of land began to slide, and within a year it was in free-fall. It wouldn't bottom out until the spring of 1987, when it had shed three thousand dollars of value.

It didn't have to drop nearly that much to erase Eldon's equity, and in 1985 the bank foreclosed on every acre he owned. The debt he had incurred to pay Sherry was a burden he couldn't survive, and he suffered the fate of tens of thousands of other farmers.

When it became evident that Farmer's Bank was drowning in all of its bad farm loans, Darwin Kittleson was fired. But it was too late. In 1986 the bank was declared insolvent and sold.

Eldon's home had been protected from foreclosure by Iowa's

bankruptcy laws, and he continued to live in it for several years, surrounded by his old acres, owned first by the bank and then a family trust from Minneapolis. He sold insurance for two years, then real estate. In 1990 he had bypass surgery. After that, he moved into a small apartment in town and began to sell cars and trucks. He was better at that.

Grace found work in a beauty shop in Sarasota while Sherry took classes to get her real estate license. In less than two years, she was managing over four hundred apartments. Grace quit the beauty business and joined Sherry to form what would become the largest property management company on the Gulf coast. They live together in a spacious townhouse overlooking the waterfront in downtown Sarasota, and hold hands while walking on the beach.

Miles' testimony cleared JoAnn, and the charges against her were dropped. She moved out of the apartment and in with her mother. In 1982, rising interest rates and the growing farm crisis depressed her business so much that she moved to Arizona, where she sells real estate and has not remarried.

Miles Richards was paroled after serving forty months of his sentence. Though eager to move back to Florida, the terms of his parole prevented him from doing so for two years, a period in which he worked as a bartender and telemarketer and lived with an older woman in Des Moines.

Frederick Heinold lives in a small trailer in the Florida Keys and works as a mechanic in a marina in Marathon. He still drinks, but no longer to rout his memories. The sky sometimes reminds him of the place he came from, so far away in miles and memory, up north where the big storms come from. Time has dimmed memories and regrets, and the sea reminds him that everything will change and be the same again.

THE END

ABOUT THE AUTHOR

Richard Schinnow began this story in 1982, his first attempt at a novel after trying his hand at writing film scripts. It's been revised numerous times and collected its share of rejection slips, so he's delighted to see it finally in print.

Like many writers, he's held numerous jobs—bartender, wrangler, commercial fisherman, diver, founder of the Iowa Independent Film Festival, and teaching college writing, among others.

Although he's lived in other parts of the country and traveled extensively, he's always been drawn back to Iowa by her people and her landscape. *Cast Away Stones* is set in northern Iowa, a place he knows well.

"Like every place, this part of the world possesses good stories and interesting characters. I hope I've done them justice."